Anthony Gilbert and The Murder Room

》》 This title is part of The Murder Room, our series dedicated to making available out-of-print or hard-to-find titles by classic crime writers.

Crime fiction has always held up a mirror to society. The Victorians were fascinated by sensational murder and the emerging science of detection; now we are obsessed with the forensic detail of violent death. And no other genre has so captivated and enthralled readers.

Vast troves of classic crime writing have for a long time been unavailable to all but the most dedicated frequenters of second-hand bookshops. The advent of digital publishing means that we are now able to bring you the backlists of a huge range of titles by classic and contemporary crime writers, some of which have been out of print for decades.

From the genteel amateur private eyes of the Golden Age and the femmes fatales of pulp fiction, to the morally ambiguous hard-boiled detectives of mid twentieth-century America and their descendants who walk our twenty-first century streets, The Murder Room has it all. 》》

The Murder Room
Where Criminal Minds Meet

themurderroom.com

Anthony Gilbert (1899–1973)

Anthony Gilbert was the pen name of Lucy Beatrice Malleson. Born in London, she spent all her life there, and her affection for the city is clear from the strong sense of character and place in evidence in her work. She published 69 crime novels, 51 of which featured her best known character, Arthur Crook, a vulgar London lawyer totally (and deliberately) unlike the aristocratic detectives, such as Lord Peter Wimsey, who dominated the mystery field at the time. She also wrote more than 25 radio plays, which were broadcast in Great Britain and overseas. Her thriller *The Woman in Red* (1941) was broadcast in the United States by CBS and made into a film in 1945 under the title *My Name is Julia Ross*. She was an early member of the British Detection Club, which, along with Dorothy L. Sayers, she prevented from disintegrating during World War II. Malleson published her autobiography, *Three-a-Penny*, in 1940, and wrote numerous short stories, which were published in several anthologies and in such periodicals as *Ellery Queen's Mystery Magazine* and *The Saint*. The short story 'You Can't Hang Twice' received a Queens award in 1946. She never married, and evidence of her feminism is elegantly expressed in much of her work.

By Anthony Gilbert

Scott Egerton series
Tragedy at Freyne (1927)
The Murder of Mrs
  Davenport (1928)
Death at Four Corners
  (1929)
The Mystery of the Open
  Window (1929)
The Night of the Fog (1930)
The Body on the Beam
  (1932)
The Long Shadow (1932)
The Musical Comedy
  Crime (1933)
An Old Lady Dies (1934)
The Man Who Was Too
  Clever (1935)

**Mr Crook Murder
  Mystery series**
Murder by Experts (1936)
The Man Who Wasn't
  There (1937)
Murder Has No Tongue
  (1937)
Treason in My Breast (1938)
The Bell of Death (1939)

Dear Dead Woman (1940)
  aka *Death Takes a
  Redhead*
The Vanishing Corpse (1941)
  aka *She Vanished in the
  Dawn*
The Woman in Red (1941)
  aka *The Mystery of the
  Woman in Red*
Death in the Blackout (1942)
  aka *The Case of the Tea-
  Cosy's Aunt*
Something Nasty in the
  Woodshed (1942)
  aka *Mystery in the
  Woodshed*
The Mouse Who Wouldn't
  Play Ball (1943)
  aka *30 Days to Live*
He Came by Night (1944)
  aka *Death at the Door*
The Scarlet Button (1944)
  aka *Murder Is Cheap*
A Spy for Mr Crook (1944)
The Black Stage (1945)
  aka *Murder Cheats the
  Bride*

Don't Open the Door (1945)
  aka *Death Lifts the Latch*
Lift Up the Lid (1945)
  aka *The Innocent Bottle*
The Spinster's Secret (1946)
  aka *By Hook or by Crook*
Death in the Wrong Room
  (1947)
Die in the Dark (1947)
  aka *The Missing Widow*
Death Knocks Three Times
  (1949)
Murder Comes Home (1950)
A Nice Cup of Tea (1950)
  aka *The Wrong Body*
Lady-Killer (1951)
Miss Pinnegar Disappears
  (1952)
  aka *A Case for Mr Crook*
Footsteps Behind Me (1953)
  aka *Black Death*
Snake in the Grass (1954)
  aka *Death Won't Wait*
Is She Dead Too? (1955)
  aka *A Question of Murder*
And Death Came Too (1956)
Riddle of a Lady (1956)
Give Death a Name (1957)

Death Against the Clock
  (1958)
Death Takes a Wife (1959)
  aka *Death Casts a Long
  Shadow*
Third Crime Lucky (1959)
  aka *Prelude to Murder*
Out for the Kill (1960)
She Shall Die (1961)
  aka *After the Verdict*
Uncertain Death (1961)
No Dust in the Attic (1962)
Ring for a Noose (1963)
The Fingerprint (1964)
Knock, Knock! Who's
  There? (1964)
  aka *The Voice*
Passenger to Nowhere (1965)
The Looking Glass Murder
  (1966)
The Visitor (1967)
Night Encounter (1968)
  aka *Murder Anonymous*
Missing from Her Home
  (1969)
Death Wears a Mask (1970)
  aka *Mr Crook Lifts the
  Mask*

Dear Dead Woman

Anthony Gilbert

An Orion book

Copyright © Lucy Beatrice Malleson 1940

The right of Lucy Beatrice Malleson to be identified as the author of this work has been asserted in accordance with the Copyright, Designs and Patents Act 1988.

This edition published by
The Orion Publishing Group Ltd
Orion House
5 Upper St Martin's Lane
London WC2H 9EA

An Hachette UK company
A CIP catalogue record for this book is available from the British Library

ISBN 978 1 4719 0966 5

www.orionbooks.co.uk

Contents

CHAPTER ONE

THE MAN IN THE DARK

THE fog, that had been deepening ever since midday, was, by dinner-time, so thick that pedestrians had to hug the railings to make any progress at all. The streets were a cataclysm of sound : cars hooted persistently, bicycle bells clanged, voices, sounding like the voices of ghosts, muttered eerily through the darkness. Dogs, who could see nothing, whined for lost owners ; cats, moving like eels in the gutter, tripped up the unwary. Pavements were invisible, and even the lights that many house-holders had turned on in halls and living-rooms as a possible guide were no more than a sickly glow in the fog's density. Now and again a lamp or a match showed, a minute flicker almost instantly extinguished. A few enterprising travellers had secured candles, and these they carried in one hand, feeling their way along the railings with the other. The shops that remained open as late as seven o'clock were packed with people, all putting off the inevitable plunge into the sickly darkness until the last moment. In Tube stations the crowds thronged the stairs, waiting for an opportunity to reach the platform ; workers would be hours late to-night ; they shifted their weight from one foot to another and waited with weary resignation. The omnibuses had stopped running some time ago, and no taxis plied for hire. An evil night, a fearful night, a night when anything could happen, and when those

1

safe in their houses sat recalling similar nights and their sometimes dreadful harvest.

In the cheerful ground-floor front of No. 12 Arbutus Avenue, S.W. 15, two women were waiting for the return of the bread-winner. Although the absent man was the father of one and the husband of the other, there was less than sixteen years between them. Nowadays few people mentioned the name of Jack Barton's first wife, the lovely destructive Beatrice Parish, who had gone to her sordid death more than nine years ago. His second bride, the homely home-making Jean, could not hold a candle to her predecessor for looks or charm or personal magnetism. Sometimes in the deeps of her simple mind she would wonder whether her husband ever compared her with that flashing creature, if he recalled with hunger the early days when the woman on his arm was the desired of every beholder. Beautiful, useless Beatrice ! She had been like a flame, destroying even where she illumined. Her last adventure, that had ended so tragically, had been one of a dozen. It seemed as if she couldn't let a man alone ; she fastened on him, she ravished him, she flung him away, she proceeded with the same enchanting vigour to her next conquest. Oh, no wonder that Jack had loved her so madly, forgiven her so often. No wonder, too, said his neighbours, that he had taken for his second wife a quiet woman, who burned like a lamp in his home.

His daughter, Margaret, had some of her mother's beauty and none of her cruelty. She was one of that great army of young women who go out to work in shops and offices six days out of seven, and contrive, amid a rush and anxiety that would debilitate a giant, to keep their complexions clear, their voices tranquil and their minds unclouded. One day Margaret would make some man a charming and lovely wife, but she would never set him on fire as Jack had been scorched and enhaloed by Beatrice ; she, like her stepmother, was a lamp, where Beatrice had been a torch flaming through the night.

It was a cheerful room, with plenty of plush and fancy china about it ; photographs in fancy frames stood on the overmantel, and there were rugs with fringe and curtains with tassels, and a bright red and blue Brussels carpet. It was the kind of room any man would like to come back to. It wasn't elegant, perhaps, but it was real ; and it was a perfect background for the woman who sat by the grate, darning her husband's socks. For some time silence had reigned ; the black marble clock on the mantelpiece, with its rearing horses on either side of the solemn white face, struck eight and, moved by some common impulse, both women looked up.

" He ought to be here any minute now," said Margaret.

Jean Barton's reply seemed irrelevant. " Meg," she asked thoughtfully, " do you ever remember your mother ? "

The question was so surprising that the girl put down her knitting and stared.

" My mother ? "

" Yes. Don't mind me asking, do you ? I don't seem to be able to get her out of my mind to-night. I suppose it's the fog."

" What on earth has the fog to do with her ? She was just the opposite."

" I dare say that's why. Not even a fog like this could have doused her. I remember them getting married. I thought if any woman in the world was

3

happy that morning it must be her, marrying Jack.
There was something about her—not happy, exactly,
now I come to think of it, but sort of victorious,
the way she went up the church, that I've never
been able to put out of mind. She must have made
him feel a prince for a bit."

Margaret's clear brow furrowed. Suddenly she
looked as she would look a quarter of a century
hence—haggard and embittered.

" If she did, it didn't last long."

" I sometimes wonder whether he'd have been
without it, all the same, his experience with her, I
mean. Living with her must have been like living
with half a dozen women. It wasn't just that she
was so lovely to look at, though she was that, all
right. It was something that goes beyond words,
as though you couldn't be cold when she was there.
And yet she must have been cold enough at the
last, drowning in the black water that awful night.
They say when you're drowning all your past life
rises up before you. I wonder if it's true. If so,
she must have seen a lot—a lot. I've never known
any one else like her."

" Why are you talking like this to-night ? "
demanded Margaret harshly. " You know I hate to
talk about her. You don't realise how she made
Father suffer, in his love and in his pride. He
worshipped her—you know that ; every one knew—
and look what she did with his love. She made
him a fool on all sides. All those years she took
in lodgers, the whole place knew what it meant.
When I was a kid at school the other girls used
to creep up and whisper things about her. Even
when I was too young to understand all they meant,
I knew it was something shameful. And all those
years Father was so wonderful ; he never said a

word. He forgave her and forgave her, until at last she went away with that man and they were both drowned in a fog."

" A fog ! " repeated Jean softly. " No, I didn't know it was a fog."

" There was a collision. That was what happened. The boat on which they were travelling went to the bottom almost at once. Father came back late —later than usual, I mean—and he got her letter telling him she was going for good, and the news of her death the next morning. It was awful for him. For a bit I thought he was going crazy. He used to sit about staring at the chair where she used to sit ; he wouldn't sleep in their bed any more. He got himself a little one. It wasn't safe to mention her name. I believe sometimes he thought he heard her voice ; he'd half get up and stare round, and then look at me to see if I'd noticed anything. I can't tell you how glad I was when he told me you were going to marry him. And he's been so happy since."

" Not the same kind of happiness," said Jean gently. " I couldn't give him that."

" He'd had enough and more than enough," retorted Margaret fiercely. " He deserved some happiness and peace."

" Well, he hasn't got either at the present moment," Jean told her.

" What on earth do you mean ? Of course he's happy."

Jean shook her sensible sandy head. " Not he. He's got something on his mind and it's driving him half-mad. He doesn't sleep, he doesn't notice things, he's forgotten how to laugh, and you know how merry he always is. That was one of the things I loved so about him : he was so gay. Nothing to look at, as he says himself, nothing special in any way, I suppose, really, but he seemed to bubble over, in spite of everything. And now something's gone wrong, and I don't know what it is."

" It couldn't be anything to do with his job, I suppose ? "

" Why not tell me ? I'm not a child. I'm a woman of thirty-nine, and I've been his wife for seven years in July. I've thought and thought. He hasn't said anything to you ? "

" Nothing."

" I wondered—couldn't it be some other woman and she was making trouble, but I believe he'd tell me about that. Besides, a man your father's age doesn't go with a woman without getting some fun on the way, and he's having no fun, poor soul."

" Perhaps it's one of those things you can't tell any one."

" And what kind of a thing could that be ? Aren't I the man's wife ? There's another thing, Meg : Why is he always out of an evening nowadays ? He says it's the firm, but he's been with the firm for more than twenty years, and they never started claiming his evenings before. And when he is here he's all of a dither. No, Margaret, the man's frightened, and I don't like it."

" He couldn't have done anything—wrong ? "

" He'd face up to it if he had. Your dad's not the kind to skulk in corners, and you don't need me to tell you that. One thing I've always said, though, and that is he's too good-natured for his own good. He'll do anything to oblige a neighbour and not think about the consequences till afterwards. All the same, I wish I knew. It's like—a sort of fog of the mind, groping the way I've been doing for this past month and afraid to go far in case I tread right on him and hurt him worse than he's hurt now."

Margaret rose uneasily and went to the window, where she stood pulling back the blind and pressing her forehead against the black glass.

" Like pitch outside," she said. " Must be awful to be blind."

" They say you sort of see with your mind," murmured Jean absently. " We won't wait more than another ten minutes, Margaret. He wouldn't want us to. And if it's as bad as this in town he will get something to eat there, as likely as not. Anyway, it'll be better to eat some of that steak before it's like a piece of shoe-leather than sit here worrying ourselves sick over a thing we don't understand and can't help."

She rose to her feet with characteristic energy. " I don't know why I should have been thinking about your mother to-night, I'm sure," she said half-apologetically. " Thinking about Dad, I suppose."

She had just reached the door when she heard a sound that brought her to an instant standstill. Margaret, who had heard it also, turned eagerly from the window.

" That'll be him," she said. " Did you hear the gate ? "

" Of course I heard the gate," returned Jean scornfully. " Do you know, I even hear that gate in my sleep when Jack swings it open. He ought to oil it, though, and that's a fact. You can hear it creak all down the road."

" He's a long time coming in," suggested Margaret. " Perhaps he can't find his keys in the fog. I'll open the door."

At that instant the electric bell pealed through the hall.

" Coming," called Margaret.

Jean's hand shot out and caught her shoulder. " Just a minute," she said. " Make quite sure it is Dad."

" Why, who else . . . ? "

" We don't know. We don't know anything, remember. We don't even know why he hasn't rattled the letter-box."

" Perhaps he's forgotten," Margaret was beginning when the flap of the letter-box began to agitate sharply. Rap, rap, rap. Margaret laughed with sheer relief.

" How he'll laugh at us when he hears. Well, it'll be a treat to hear him laugh again."

Behind her Jean's voice sounded, hoarse and urgent.

" Margaret, look. Only look ! "

" At what ? "

" That hand. It isn't your father, after all."

" What hand ? Jean, what are you saying ? "

Jean caught her fast by the shoulders. " I'm telling you to look at the hand, what you can see of it, and then tell me, if you dare, that it's your father outside that door."

Margaret felt the slow panic rising in her breast. Looking in the direction indicated, she saw, with a movement of horror, the tips of slim brown fingers lifting and letting fall the flap of the letter-box.

" Who—who could it be ? " she whispered.

" Someone who wants us to think it's Jack, so that we'll open to him. But we'll not, not if I stay in this hall the whole night."

The unknown gently rapped again. The women

8

stood there, fascinated, watching the flap rise and fall with the movements of the slender brown fingers. Suddenly Margaret shook herself free.

" We ought to be ashamed of ourselves," she announced. " Of course it isn't someone trying to make us think it's Dad. It's some poor fellow who's confused the houses in the fog and can't find his key and is probably wondering whether he's got to spend the night on the doorstep." And without heeding Jean's warning cry she ran forward a few steps and flung the door open.

The man on the step might have materialised out of the fog. Wisps of it hung limply round his soft, brown hat and his smooth, lively brown face, not the bronzed empirical brown of the pioneer of wide open spaces, but a shade more nearly resembling milk chocolate. He wore a brown raincoat, unbuttoned to reveal a brown suit, a brown and white tie, a fawn shirt, brown boots—altogether such a symphony in brown that Margaret caught herself wondering whether he were equally brown under his clothes, and barely repressed a giggle. The stranger did not seem at all disposed to laugh. Nor did he instantly apologise at the sight of Margaret, so it seemed as though he hadn't come to the wrong house after all.

Instead, he lifted a brown hand to remove the brown hat and said piercingly, " Mr. Barton ? Thank you."

There was a faint flavour of an accent in his voice, so that even if he hadn't had that foreign appearance you would not have supposed him to be English. That " Thank you " seemed the prelude to his entrance, and Margaret hurriedly half-closed the door.

" He isn't here," she said.

The foreigner did not seem distressed—merely unbelieving.

" If you tell him I am here you will, perhaps, I think, find that he is at home," he suggested.

Jean came forward and took a hand in the conversation. " What Miss Barton says is quite true," she told the stranger frigidly. " My husband is not at home."

" But you are expecting him ? "

" It will be quite impossible for him to see any one to-night."

" I have come a long way, please."

" I'm sorry, of course. It was a pity to come out on a night like this without making an appointment."

" There is no need for me to make appointments with Mr. Barton."

" You'd better write," Jean told him harshly. " In any case, he couldn't see a stranger at this time of night."

" Mr. Barton and I are not strangers."

" And he doesn't keep business appointments, either."

" I would not call this precisely a business appointment."

The stranger's self-possession filled Jean with an unnameable fear ; now she was assured that her secret panic had foundations in fact. Something sinister, something terrible, was afoot, something that threatened the husband she had loved for years, far back in the days when he was courting Beatrice Parish, and she was in a blackness as dense as the fog that pressed like a curtain against the windows.

She made an abrupt movement to shut the door, saying as she did so, " You must write, as I said.

You can't possibly see my husband to-night, even if he does decide to come back. Often in really bad weather he stops in town."

It wasn't true, of course, but there was only one thought in her mind : to get rid of this fellow before Jack came in. Then she might be able to persuade her husband to tell her the truth about what was worrying him, give her an opportunity to share his trouble, perhaps even show him how to solve it. But she had no sooner uttered the words than she regretted them. She had the usual prejudice of her class against foreigners, particularly when they were " coloured." In her own mind she thought of this visitor as a " nigger," although plenty of men and women would be returning from holiday coasts in the course of the next few weeks with browner skins than his. And now she had made him a present of the fact that she and Margaret might be alone to-night. She made a last effort to retrieve the situation.

" If you care to leave a name," she said. But the stranger only smiled, showing remarkably pointed teeth. Almost as though they'd been filed, she reflected.

" There is no need," he replied. " You will tell him that I came. He will understand."

And then he had disappeared. Just like that. One minute he was on the step showing her those regular pointed teeth, and the next he seemed to have immaterialised back into the fog. Maskelyne and Devant had nothing on him, Jean reflected.

" What do you suppose he really wanted ? " asked Margaret as the door closed and they stood listening, though for what neither could have told you. In such a fog, all footsteps would be muffled into the merest semblance of sound, and anyway he might have had rubbers on his shoes.

" He wanted your father," said Jean hardly. " What's more, he means to have him."

" But—what for ? "

" That's what I want to know. And I don't believe Jack will tell me."

Margaret looked at her critically. " You're as white as a sheet," she commented.

" I'm frightened," was Jean's simple reply. She turned and led the way back to the sitting-room. As she reached the fireplace she shot round, her eyes wide with terror. Margaret's involuntary cry was caught back in her throat.

" I've just realised what I've been listening for," Jean explained. " The click of the gate. *And it didn't click.* Do you realise what that means ? "

Margaret hesitated. " We might not hear in this fog," she suggested weakly.

" We heard it click when he came in," Jean reminded her. " No, it didn't click because he's still there—waiting."

" But why ? "

" He doesn't believe what I told him. He believes Jack will be back this evening, and he's going to wait."

" He can't do Dad any harm. I mean, people don't commit murder in your own front garden."

" A man like that might do anything. And, anyway, in your own garden, on a night like this, what could be safer ? Not that I think he is going to murder Jack. But he's going to wait and jump out on him. Oh, if only we could warn him ! "

" We don't know where he is."

" We couldn't get at him if we did."

" He won't do Dad any harm," Margaret protested. "After all, he came here for us to see him."

"And do you think you'd recognise him again, if they put up a dozen chocolate-coloured men in court ? Or any one would believe you if you did ? "

"What can he know about Dad that we don't ? "

"Perhaps Dad knows a bit too much about him. And a desperate man doesn't stick at anything."

"And you think he's out in the garden there, waiting for Dad ? I'm going out."

"Don't be a fool, Meg. What could you do ? "

"I'll go upstairs and see if the fog is quite so thick from that floor. If I could see him hiding in the garden I could get the police or something."

"I'd prefer the something. It doesn't look healthy to me, ordinary folk like ourselves getting the police in. Besides, you have to remember Dad. He mightn't want the police. And if you are going upstairs, I'll come with you."

Upstairs the fog pressed as densely against the pane as before. Nothing in the garden was visible. It might have been a waste expanse of water beneath them instead of a trim little lawn, a trim little shrubbery, tulips in a round bed and wall-flowers in the borders. But if the eyes were impotent, it was still possible to hear ; and after the window had been thrown up, letting the strong smoky odour of the fog into every corner of the room, a faint, faint sound was discernible in the darkness below them.

"Something's out there," whispered Jean tensely.

"Can you see *anything* ? "

"No. But I can hear. Listen ! "

They listened an instant in silence. Then Margaret said slowly, " Jean, I think it—he—is coming nearer. The sound's more that way now." And she pointed with her hand to their left.

" The kitchen window ! " exclaimed Jean. " Margaret, could he get in ? "

" It's shut, but not bolted."

" I've always told Jack that window was too easy to open from the outside. If he does mean that, he'll be in before we can get there."

" He can't move very fast on a night like this."

" These niggers are like cats. They can see everywhere."

Moving with self-conscious care, they came slipping down the stairs and along the narrow passage leading to the kitchen. It was Margaret who opened the door and put out her hand towards the switch of the electric light. The next moment she had uttered a scream and stepped back into Jean's arms.

" What is it ? Won't it go on ? Meg . . ."

Margaret was shivering from head to foot. " Jean, quiet. I—I touched something. I think it was a face."

" Margaret ! "

" Hush ! Don't you see "—the girl's voice had sunk to a mere thread of sound—" if it was a face, *he's in here, somewhere in the dark.*"

They clung together for a petrified instant. Then Jean said, " Your father would be ashamed if he could see us now, behaving like two mice, with not an ounce of spirit between us. Put on that light, girl, and let's see what it is we're up against."

Obediently Margaret reached a second time for the switch. But, although it clicked, no answering flood of light sprang up.

" The light's gone."

" There are some matches in the dining-room.
Get them, quick."

There was no gainsaying Jean when she spoke in
that tone. Even Margaret did not guess at the
storm of panic in the older woman's breast when
she found herself in the dark with something
unknown, moving she knew not whither, something
that might at any instant spring at her out of the
dark, drag her down. . . .

" If it is a criminal affair he'll not want Margaret
or me left to tell the story," she assured herself,
convinced that she heard laboured breathing not
many yards away. A gradual sifting of the acrid
odour of fog into the air made her realise that the
window must be open, a conclusion that admitted
of only one reply to her fears. She turned her eyes
to the place where she knew the window to be,
but on such a night it was impossible to trace its
outline in an unlighted room. Margaret, she thought,
was being an unconscionable time with the matches.
There was a sudden noise of creaking furniture.
Something—someone ?—had stumbled against a
chair. That sound enabled her to locate the intruder.
He could be barely five yards away. She forced
back a scream, and at that instant Margaret's voice
called from the passage, " I had to open a new
packet. But here . . ." Obeying a nameless
impulse, Jean stepped quickly aside ; as she did
so something moved ; she felt a rush of air strike
her face. Then at last Margaret struck her match ;
but before she could lift it high enough to pierce
the dark something—someone ?—blew it out. It
might have been a puff of wind—or it might have
been a human breath. Now the intruder was
making no attempt to conceal his presence. A
chair went over, Jean moved again, Margaret

ANTHONY GILBERT

kindled a second match, and a shadow vanished
through the open window. All in the same instant.
Another impulse sent Jean in the direction of the
window, and she slammed down the sash. It came
down easily enough, and too swiftly for whoever
was making his escape, for there was a violent jerk,
a ripping sound, and then feet in the little cobbled
path that connected the side door with the street.

" Well, he's gone, whoever he was," commented
Jean grimly, " but he's left something behind him.
Bring that light here, Meg."

Cautiously they pushed up the sash and Jean
extricated a scrap of material, probably torn from
a coat.

" He wore brown, didn't he ? I knew he hadn't
gone."

" We're not likely to trace him by that."

Jean was pondering deeply. " I'd like to understand what it's all about," she confessed. " Why
did he want to come in here to-night so badly
that he broke in ? Jack might have come back any
minute ; we might have got the police. What's
he after ? "

" I don't know," replied Margaret. " What was
wrong with the light ? " She had kindled a little
piece of candle, that she now lifted so that its ray
fell on the ceiling. " Why, there's nothing wrong.
Only the bulb's been taken away. Here it is on
the table here."

" Don't touch it," Jean cautioned her swiftly.
" Remember that case at Hanwell the other day ?
They got the man there through fingerprints on a
glass. Unless, of course, this chap had kept his
gloves on."

" I wonder how long he was in the house—that
is, if it was the same one ? "

" Why, how many of them do you think there were, you silly girl ? "

" I don't know," returned Margaret simply. " How should I ? But are we absolutely sure that the person who blew out the match is the same as the one who went out of the window ? "

" I hadn't thought of that," Jean confessed. " Well, it's no use taking any chances. We'd better search the house. No, don't touch that bulb. We'll lock the door and go through the place, room by room."

On such a night the most reassuring of houses may seem full of strange sounds, of ghostly footsteps, of voices haunting the stairs and dark corners. Every nightmare of childhood—Tommy Dodd, the man who lived in the dark cupboard and whose arms were so long that no matter where you crouched he could reach you—the Tiger on the Stairs, the Ghost in the Corner—all these returned to follow Margaret up the stairs and in and out of rooms rendered mysterious by fog. Even familiar objects seemed unfriendly to-night ; pictures assumed hostile meanings, furniture that one had dusted and polished light-heartedly for years seemed half-alive. Something brooded over the house, something alarming and beyond understanding. Once she paused to laugh abruptly at the thought that she and her stepmother, two calm, unimaginative women, were really checking up with stealthy footsteps on the movements of a man glimpsed for an instant on the doorstep. It was like a dream from which, surely, in another moment they must awake.

Meanwhile, here they were, snapping on lights, examining corners, peering under beds, opening the doors of cupboards, and at the same instant the

ANTHONY GILBERT

Brown Man might have stolen back down the
passage and be watching their progress from room
to room, eager to note their first slip and take
advantage of it. In Jean's mind, as, heart thudding,
hands shaking, she compelled herself to finish her
self-imposed task, was the thought, as they entered
each room, that perhaps another foot had just left
it an instant before. Once even she thought she
heard a door close, once she believed she discerned
a ghostly figure beside a window, but the light
dispelled the shadows, the door had blown shut in
a draught. Then the final shock smote them.
They were standing at the head of the staircase
when, without warning, the light in the hall went
out. Now, except for the scrap of candle, they were
in the dark again.

"He did get in," muttered Margaret. " Jean,
what are we going to do ? "

" Stop making a fool of yourself," retorted Jean
brutally. " Maybe it wasn't the man at all. Maybe
it was the fog. I've known electric currents to fail
in lesser fogs than this." She turned resolutely to
the window and stared out. " If there was a light
burning in yon window we'd see it ; and there's
none," she pronounced after a moment. " They're
all out ; and if you hold the candle that way, my
girl, that'll go out, too."

" If he's a man with a grudge against father, he
might think it would be a fine revenge to let him
come back and find—and find . . ."

Jean swung her arm and caught her stepdaughter
a resounding slap.

" And there's more where that came from," she
warned her. " Are you a woman or a jibbering
idiot ? It was the fog, I tell you. Margaret, *what
was that* ? "

18

" It was—perhaps it was the wind."

" If there was enough wind to make that noise, it would have blown the fog away. It was a voice, Meg, a human voice, and it was outside. I'm going down."

" It wasn't Dad. I know his voice. Take care, Jean, I believe it's a trap to get you outside."

" Why should any one take all this trouble ? "

" Suppose it isn't what we thought ? Suppose Dad knows something about this man, or has got something dangerous ? He may be a criminal and Dad's found him out ; then if he could get hold of you, he could dictate his own terms."

" This is Putney, not Chicago," Jean told her dryly. " Listen—there it is again. A cat. We're losing our wits as well as our heads. Come downstairs. There's no one in this house but our two selves, and the steak will be scorched to a cinder, and as for the pudding . . . Still, I'd give all the fried steak on earth for a cup of tea."

" I'm not as brave as you, Jean," Margaret confessed. " Are you sure those lights are just the fog ? "

" Try one of the upstairs rooms."

It was speedily shown that all the lights in the house were off ; but even that proved nothing. It was simple to cut off electricity at the main.

" Do we go down ? " Margaret questioned.

Jean said slowly, " If it is his work, and if this man's up against Dad, then I'm not so surprised he didn't come back to-night ? "

" Aren't you ? " observed Margaret dryly. " Ever known Dad to run away—and leave us ? "

" He wouldn't think the chap would come here."

" Looks to me as though Chocolate Face was pretty desperate." They were both silent a minute, remembering that merry little man they both loved who would never be kept away from home because of a fog, and so must be skulking somewhere, afraid to return.

" If only he'd tell me," Jean burst out.

" Perhaps it's one of the things you can't tell."

" But Dad's not like that. Dad's good."

" Terry says that often it's the good ones that get into the worst messes. Being bad is a sort of protection in itself, whereas the good seem to have a skin short. They don't know how to look after themselves in the same way."

It was midnight before Jean could be persuaded to go to bed.

" Dad won't come back now."

" It's funny he hasn't let us know. He's never done that before."

" Perhaps he's had to go off in a hurry on the firm's business. He once went to Halifax without any warning."

" What sort of a firm is it that's going to send a man out in a fog like this ? I know he has a bag packed at the office, but it doesn't make sense. Why, I don't suppose there are any trains running to Halifax to-night."

" Then perhaps he thought it was too bad to come back at all and he sent us a line—that's what he did the Halifax time, you remember—and it hasn't got delivered because of the fog."

" He might have made it a telegram."

" Perhaps he didn't think," countered Margaret weakly.

" I was wondering if we should ring up the hospitals. There are always accidents on a night like this."

" If he was able to tell them who he was they'd

have been in touch with us already; and if—if he wasn't, he'd have papers in his pocket. Either way, we'd have heard. And he won't thank us for making a fuss if nothing's wrong."

" There's something wrong, all right," said Jean grimly. " But most likely he wouldn't want us to start a scare. Maybe in the morning we'll hear something."

" After all," urged Margaret, " he has been kept late a lot by the firm these last few weeks."

" I know he's been late."

" You don't believe him when he says it's the office ? "

" Do you ? "

" Yes," replied Margaret calmly.

Jean did not pursue the point. Meg could be like that sometimes, like a locked box to which she herself kept the key. No telling what might lie concealed under the lid. Jean sighed and, stooping, raked out the fire.

" You're maybe thinking me a fool, and maybe you're right, but when you feel about a man the way I feel about Jack it makes you a bit silly."

" I know."

" How can you know, a girl like you ? "

" There's Terry."

" Wait till you've been married seven years. You'll laugh then at what you feel now."

" I'll never do that," returned Margaret soberly.

The electric current was still off, and they went to bed by candle-light. Margaret's was soon extinguished, but Jean allowed her candle to flicker down into a mess of wax before she put out a finger and thumb and pinched the wick to death.

A little while after this, when he felt the house had at length settled down for what remained of the night, the man who had been all this time concealed in the garden emerged, half-frozen, sick with the fumes of the fog, raging at his enforced vigil, and tiptoed softly round the house, trying all the windows and doors, without effect. A fly, he told himself savagely, could not get into a house so securely barred. Abandoning his hopes at last, he stole up and left an envelope propped against one of the uprights of the porch, and then crept noiselessly away. Only the treacherous gate betrayed him. Jean, waking from an uneasy doze, heard the tell-tale creak and, sitting up in bed, called her husband's name. It was some minutes before she recollected the position ; then, instantly wide awake, she put on a dressing-gown and went down to the hall. Once there, however, she hesitated. It might have been her imagination, in which case there could be no harm in opening the door and reassuring herself that she was simply the victim of her own nervous condition. But, on the other hand, it might be a trick of the stranger's to effect an entrance.

"It's queer how much more helpless you feel in a night-dress," she reminded herself.

Standing there, irresolute, she called, " Jack ! Jack ! " in a low voice. But there was no reply, and after a minute she stole back to bed, chiding herself for her folly.

At about the same instant the Man in Brown was fishing a latch-key out of his pocket and letting himself softly into the house where he had furnished rooms.

CHAPTER TWO

MYSTERIOUS BEHAVIOUR OF A HUSBAND

THE next morning everything had changed. A wind
had dispersed the fog, light shone bravely through
the windows, furniture and fittings assumed their
familiar guise, and last night's ordeal was no more
than a mirage of a disordered brain. Margaret,
coming in at seven o'clock with a cup of tea, looked
as fresh as a daisy ; only a certain solicitude in her
manner marked out this morning from hundreds of
others.

" No news, I suppose," said Jean, knowing herself
a fool to ask.

" Not yet. There'll probably be a letter by this
morning's post. I don't suppose there even was a
delivery last night."

" Has the paper come ? "

" It'll be here any minute. I believe that's the
boy now." She went down, to return an instant
later with the *Morning Sun* tucked under her arm.

" There was a lot of damage done last night,"
she announced. " Cars colliding, a bus ran into the
pavement at Hackney, four passengers in hospital,
a clergyman on a bicycle rode into the river, a
child——"

" Is there anything about Dad ? " demanded
Jean.

" No. Did you think there would be ? "

" Let me see the list of accidents."

But though two elderly men had been seriously
injured in various parts of London, the description

of neither tallied remotely with that of the missing Mr. Barton. The post arrived late that morning ; last night's collections had been thrown out of gear by the bad weather, trains had been delayed, letters had missed their customary deliveries. Jean sat reading the paper. Easy for Margaret to say, " I'm sure Dad's all right." But how could any one know ? They had a list of the accidents they'd discovered, but there might be others ; you couldn't tell. The curate need not be the only man who had missed his path and gone into the river and drowned there in the stifling dark, unheard by the slow-moving crowds on the parapets above. Jean, whose imagination was powerful where those she loved were concerned, thought of it and shuddered. In the bright morning light that lonely fate was too horrible for contemplation ; but she could not withdraw her mind from such a possibility. The other fear lurking in her brain she refused even to examine. It wasn't always an accident when a man walked into the river. Sometimes it had seemed the only way out. But no, no, she cried silently, clenching her hands on the paper she held. It could never be like that for Jack Barton, the merry, open-faced little man she loved and had married. In Beatrice's time, perhaps . . . A familiar pang stabbed her. In Beatrice's time that could never have happened. No matter how abominably that woman had treated him, she had possessed a quality of life that must make the bare thought of death insupportable.

The post came at last, and with it a letter in Jack's handwriting.

" I felt we were getting the jitters for nothing," said Margaret, barely attempting to conceal her relief. " Of course, he thought we should get it last night."

24

" Give it to me, instead of talking like a fool," demanded Jean tensely.

Margaret looked at her in surprise and handed over the white commercial envelope.

" It's what you said," Jean told her slowly, laying the sheet down. " The firm sent him off in a hurry yesterday afternoon. Northampton and round there. He'll be away two or three days."

" Does he give you an address ? "

" No. Says he'll be moving about ; and anyway he isn't sure about his hotel till he gets there. That's funny, Margaret."

" What's funny ? "

" Not to know his address, of course. He couldn't be going down there on a night like that without having some place to sleep."

" Probably go to the Railway Hotel for the night, and then move on."

" He says not to send on any letters. Well, if we haven't got an address we couldn't, of course. But keep them unopened till he comes back. He's never said that before. Laugh if you like, Margaret, but there's something wrong here, and I don't like it."

" He'll write again to-day," Margaret strove to console her. " He always does. There'll be some reasonable explanation, you see."

But though she said nothing more at the time, Jean was not satisfied. Margaret had to get off to work, so she busied herself with the breakfast and tidying the house. After the girl had gone she began to turn out cupboards and count stores, anything to take her mind off a situation that still appeared to her sinister. The place was always kept as neat as a new pin, and soon she again found herself unemployed,

" Might do a bit of work in the garden. The weeds come up overnight this weather," she told herself.

It was while she was sweeping the path that she found the envelope that had been left in the porch. The wind had caught it and blown it into some bushes, where Margaret had not seen it on her way out. Jean, espying a glimpse of white, stooped and stretched her arm through the twigs. It bore a sorry appearance now, soiled by dust and earth, but the address was unmistakable. The envelope was a thin one. By holding it up to the light it was easy to read the few words on the enclosed card.

" You still have three days," it said. And there was no signature.

.   .   .   .   .   .

It was one of Jack Barton's habits to send his wife a postcard every day that he was away. Other wives laughed at this ; some were jealous ; some whispered darkly in corners. It wasn't in man's nature to be so affectionate, they said. But, since every one liked him and because he was a plump, cheerful little man, adored by his wife and his daughter's best friend, nothing much was actually said. Just that Jean was a lucky woman, and they hoped it would last. On the day following her discovery of the letter she had no word from her husband. Margaret tried to make light of her fears. He was busy, she suggested ; he'd missed a mail ; there were a hundred reasons why no card should arrive. Jean said very little. There was one reason of which she wouldn't speak even to Margaret, and that was the mysterious visitor and the letter he had (she was convinced) left behind him. On the second day of Jack's absence she had another scare. She was returning from an afternoon expedition when she heard a rustling among the bushes, and though she saw no one, she was certain the stranger had paid a second visit to the house. Since the night of the fog she had been careful to bolt and bar all the windows, and leave the doors locked when she went out ; but a milk-bottle she had put on the back step had been removed, and there were scratches round the lock of the kitchen entrance. That evening she hardened her heart and went through all the papers that happy-go-lucky Jack Barton had left in his pockets. But there was nothing there to afford any clue to the mystery.

"That man wants something we've got in the house, and I've got to find out what it is," she told herself frantically. Of course, Jack might have taken it with him. But did even Jack realise his own danger ? Did he know that a time-limit had been set ? Her own ignorance and consequent powerlessness filled her with rage. What sense was there in loving a man like this if you could do nothing to help him in so dread an emergency ? It had been a Tuesday when the anonymous letter arrived ; this was Thursday. To-morrow was the last day. If he let that go past, what appalling danger lurked in the shape of a man in a brown suit with a face the colour of milk chocolate ? Jean had not the least idea.

That night she knew that all her fears were justified. There arrived for Jack a letter in a square white envelope, and stamped on the flap was the name of his firm, Moresby and Gregg.

"I knew there was something queer about that Northampton trip," she told Margaret. "They don't know he's gone. They wouldn't be writing here if they did."

" Perhaps he's due back to-night," urged Margaret, refusing to be stampeded into panic.

" And why hasn't he sent me a line these three days ? Why is he so mysterious ? Who is the man, and what hold has he got over Dad ? " She brooded. " I shall open this letter. Seeing it's from the firm, Jack couldn't mind."

The letter was signed Edward Gregg, and said that it was hoped Mr. Barton was now better and would be able to return to work at the beginning of the following week. If his absence was likely to be prolonged, the firm would appreciate a doctor's certificate.

" I told you from the first there was something strange," said Jean tonelessly. " What do we do now ? "

It was clear that whatever the trouble was, it had nothing to do with the firm for whom Jack had been working for upwards of twenty years. He was a valued employee, and they would be likely to give him rather more than a square deal. Margaret was out to-night, so she wrestled with her problem alone. Her instinctive reaction was a protective one. So long as she could prevent it, Moresby and Gregg should know nothing of their private troubles. She waited, hoping against hope, until the post arrived, thinking, " There may be something to-night." And even when the post had come and gone, leaving a letter for Margaret and an announcement of a mid-season sale, she sat on, waiting for the telephone to ring or a wire to arrive. At half-past ten she abandoned hope, and wrote a letter to his employers saying that Jack expected to be back on the following Monday. It was a few minutes to eleven when she set out for the pillar-box at the other side of the avenue. It was a clear night,

the air warm and scented by the flowers in the
little gardens all around her ; a girl was exercising
a dog ; a couple strolled past, their arms linked ;
dance-music poured through an open window ; a
great black cat sprang out of a laurel bush and
leaped on to a wall, where it crouched, spitting
softly at the eager dog that had dislodged it ;
somewhere a basement door slammed and lights
went out in an upstairs window. The scene was set
for absolute tranquillity ; such mysteries as a
disappearing husband and an unsigned letter were
no more than the ingredients of the cinema on such
a night. Feeling as though she had stumbled into
an unreal world, Jean posted her letter and came
back to the house. Some instinct warned her of
imminent danger before she lifted her eyes and
saw a long slender shape on the doorstep. It was
not Margaret, nor Margaret's young man ; it was
not one of the neighbours. Certainly it was not
Jack. She shut the gate and came softly up the
path. The visitor turned at the sound of that
familiar creak, and she saw it was the Man in
Brown.

He swept off his hat as she drew near. " Mrs.
Barton ? "

" What do you want ? "

" Mr. Barton is perhaps at home, please ? "

" Mr. Barton's out of London. I couldn't say
when he will be back."

" I think, if Mr. Barton is wise, he will decide to
be in London to-night, Mrs. Barton."

" It isn't a question of wisdom. He's away for
his firm."

" You could perhaps tell me where I could find
him. Yes ? "

" Certainly not."

" But they would know—his firm, I mean. And it is most urgent."

Jean hesitated. The last thing she desired was to have any one making trouble with Moresby and Gregg. The stranger, perceiving her indecision, suggested in suave tones, " Perhaps if I were to come in for a moment, Mr. Barton might return."

" Of course you can't come in at this hour. It's ridiculous. We're all just going to bed—Miss Barton and myself, I mean. As for my husband, I couldn't tell you when he'll be back. I don't know myself."

She would have opened the door and pushed past him into the house, but the Brown Man stopped her. " You have perhaps told him of my visit on the night of the fog ? "

" I told you I haven't seen him since that night."

" And—who has seen him ? "

" The men he's been doing business with, of course. What did you mean by that ? "

" Sometimes a man gets into bad trouble and he goes away and—he does not come home again—ever. It would be sad if that had happened."

" Look here ! " Jean faced squarely round to him. " What are you driving at ? Are you suggesting—blackmail ? Because, if you are, it's the worst crime in the English language, and gets the most heavily punished."

The stranger leaned down to her level ; his lips parted, those pointed white teeth flashed. When he spoke his voice was lower than before.

" Not the most heavily," he reminded her. " Not, for instance, so heavily as—murder."

He did not wait to watch her reaction to that, paid no attention to her involuntary cry, " What does that mean ? " He turned towards the gate, and the atmosphere seemed to swallow him up as it had done before. It was ridiculous, of course ; he was just one human being like a million others ; he couldn't appear and vanish at will. Yet the fact remained. One instant he was there and the next the gate had clanged and, like Wells' *Invisible Man*, there was no trace of him. Of course, she found herself thinking mechanically, it's dark now, and those trees shut off the road.

She pulled off her hat and called, " Margaret ! " But instead of her stepdaughter's voice she heard another that sent the blood pounding to her heart. Her husband's voice from the kitchen called, " Jean, is that you, Jean ? "

She ran along the corridor right into his arms. She was bigger than he, but she felt like a woman without any strength at all as she felt his firm warm arms close round her, heard his voice muttering consolation. " It's all right, old girl. What's got you ? Did you think I was a ghost ? "

" Where have you been, Jack ? I've been terrified."

" I told you. I wrote . . ."

" You can stop that. There was a letter from the firm this morning, wanting to know when you'd be well enough to be back at work."

" Did you do anything about it ? "

" I wrote to say you expected to be back on Monday. Where have you been ? "

" Away. Was that someone with you on the step ? "

" Yes. He wanted you. That's the second time he's called."

She saw a change come over her husband's face ; it seemed to go rigid, as though at all costs he must defend himself against her too-curious gaze.

31

" Who was he ? "

" He said you'd know."

" What was he like ? "

" Brown—sort of nigger-brown. Do you know who he is ? "

Jack Barton paid no heed to her questions. " What did he say ? "

" That if you knew he was there you might be at home after all. Oh, and something about murder."

" Ah ! " The man's fingers drummed a rapid and maddening tattoo on the table. " What about murder ? "

" Only that it was a worse crime than blackmail. Jack, if you don't tell me at once what he meant by that, I'll scream."

Mechanically he put out a hand to soothe her. " Don't do that, Jenny. It wouldn't help."

" And he tried to get in, too."

" He didn't, though." Instant fear showed itself on the man's face.

" No. We kept things bolted and barred after that first night. What's it all about, Jack ? What does he know that can make you afraid of him ? "

" It's about Bee," said Jack slowly.

" Bee ? " Jean sounded incredulous. " But she's dead. She was drowned . . ."

" No, she wasn't. That's what this fellow knows. He knows she died here, in this house, of strangulation. Now do you understand why I'm afraid ? "

CHAPTER THREE

THE SECRET OF THE CELLAR

THERE are some truths so appalling that the mind cannot at once accept them. Jean Barton's reaction to her husband's admission was neither horror nor shock, but blank incredulity. The words resounded in her intelligence, but she could not accept them, and her first mutter was neither violent accusation nor blind panic, but the instinctive question, put like a child, " But why didn't she go ? "

Jack moved his head in a queer gesture, as though he were a beast in intolerable pain.

" How could she ? "

" You mean *he* killed her ? "

" I don't know. It's queer, seeing she was my wife for sixteen years, how little I did know about her. Only I can tell you this : She wasn't an ordinary woman ; you couldn't expect her to be like the wives of other men I knew. I've often wondered why she ever married me. I dare say she often wondered herself."

Jenny's anger burned up against the dead. " She hadn't the right."

" It's no use, Jenny. You can't talk of rights where people like Bee are concerned. It's as if they didn't live in quite your world and mine. They see things differently."

" You always made excuses for her, didn't you ? " There was a wondering note in her sad voice. " And yet she never gave you a thing."

At that he turned on her, a kind of blazing excitement in his face.

" Why, she gave me everything I ever had," he exclaimed. " You've never understood about her—never. No one ever did. I suppose she thought I was a different kind of chap."

" Weren't you good enough for her ? "

" Oh, she didn't specially want any one to be good. But—the truth is, I wasn't enough for her ; no man was. She was like six women rolled into one. You might please one of them, but sooner or later one of the others would get tired of you. And she did get tired—often and often—I always knew the signs. But, up till then, she'd always come back in the end."

" Did you know she was going away with this fellow ? "

" Not till that night, when I found her letter telling me."

The way in which he said that, not even now accusing her of breaking up his home, making him a laughing-stock to the neighbours, killing all his happiness, frightened her. It confirmed what in her own heart she had always known : that although he was fond of her and grateful for the home she had made for him, she would never be anything but second-best, and that if he did not compare her with the dead woman, it was because any such comparison would be absurd. It wouldn't simply occur to him to make it.

" Then—oh, what happened, Jack ? "

" I don't know. Only she didn't go with this fellow, because she couldn't."

She said, in a voice quiet with despair, " You're not being fair to me. You know there's nothing I want to do except help you if I can, and you're

34

simply shutting me out, as if I wasn't any one at all.
I am your wife and I love you. I've loved you for
more than twenty years, before Beatrice even
realised you were alive ; and everything that's
happened to you all that time has mattered to me.
All these years there was never an occasion when
things were wrong for you that they weren't as
wrong for me. Even if I didn't see you I knew in
my bones when you weren't happy, just as I've
known all this last month you haven't had a
minute's peace, even though you've never said a
word."

" How could I, Jean ? A thing like this ! Making
you an accessory after the fact."

A cold finger touched her heart. " What are you
trying to say ? Jack, you didn't kill her ? "

" If—when—the truth comes out, you'll be about
the only person living who doesn't believe it, you
and Margaret."

" Aren't you going to tell me ? "

" I can't tell you who killed her, because I don't
know. What I do know is bad enough."

A new thought struck her, causing her to stammer
as she spoke.

" Jack, where is she buried ? "

He lifted his head. His eyes were like dark hollows
with no light in them. " In the cellar."

" In this house ? " All Jean's self-control could
not keep back that cry.

Her husband nodded. He also seemed beyond
speech.

" You mean she's been here all these years ? "

" Yes."

" So that's why—why . . ." But here her
tongue failed her. A dozen tiny mysteries were
instantly made clear. Jack never allowed her or

Margaret to go down to the cellar. He had kept the key all these years, saying the place wasn't safe, that he had once had a serious accident there, slipping on the steps, that they had a perfectly good shed in the garden for coal, instead of having to bring it up the steps, too hard a job for a woman, he said. By this time it would not have occurred to either woman that there was anything strange in his attitude or in the fact that the door was locked and they had never seen the key. The situation had become as natural as all familiar things.

She remembered, too, another incident that, though it had struck her as odd at the time, had become just a casual incident to which nowadays she gave no thought at all. She had been married about two years when one day she returned unexpectedly early from some excursion. At first she had thought the house was empty, but after a few minutes she heard sounds coming from the cellar. To her surprise, the door had been open an inch or two and, pushing it wider, she heard distinct sounds coming from the darkness. Now she was certain that somebody was there. She called her husband's name :

" Jack ! Jack ! "

Instantly the sounds ceased. She called again, but received no reply. Then it occurred to her that the person concealed in the dark was not her husband, but some tramp or casual thief who had broken into the house during their absence. At about this time the neighbourhood had been alarmed by tales of some maniac concealing himself in dark doorways and alleys, and assaulting women and children, and immediately she thought, " Perhaps this is the man." She had not stopped to wonder how he had opened the door ; a form of panic swamped her common sense. She, therefore, slammed the door, turning the key that stood in the lock, and went to summon the police. As she reached the front hall she heard, like some faint echo, a voice shouting her name :

" Jean ! Jean ! "

" It must be Jack, after all," she told herself, and called out, " Where are you ? "

The faint voice answered, " I'm in the cellar. You've locked me in."

A cautious woman, she hesitated before releasing her prisoner. This might be only a ruse ; then she remembered that a tramp would hardly know her name. While she paused the voice, stronger now and undeniably that of her husband, said, " Jenny ! " and she came hurrying back to set him free. His panic, that was greater than her own, startled her.

" Was that meant for a joke ? "

" I didn't know it was you," she defended herself. " I called out . . ."

" I answered you."

That surprised her. " I didn't hear."

" I said I was coming. I thought I heard a queer noise down there, as if a cat had got in ; though how it could, with the cellar door locked, I couldn't imagine. However, I went down, and there was nothing there. I was just coming up when you appeared. What on earth were you going to do ? "

" I thought you were a burglar. I was going to get the police." She began to laugh, but his face sobered her.

" It isn't funny."

" Isn't it ? I was just thinking what Sergeant Medlock would say if I called him in to arrest my husband for house-breaking. Probably he'd have thought you were trying to murder me."

At that fatal word every atom of colour had drained out of his cheeks. She had seen that, and her heart had leaped for pleasure. It was as though the bare idea of losing her filled him with dread. To-night, sitting beside him, she understood more clearly. It hadn't been she who filled his thoughts, but Beatrice who, dying, still had more power to shape his life than she, warm and breathing at his side.

" So you were down there that night when I locked you in, because of her ? " She voiced her thoughts with an artless simplicity.

" I was always afraid that somehow she would get out. It didn't seem possible that anything could keep her down there in the dark."

" But you knew she was dead."

" I suppose so."

" Hadn't you better tell me what happened ? After all, she's not the only one in the dark."

Jack drew a breath so deep it was almost a groan. " It won't take long. I came back one Saturday afternoon rather late—a Saturday before the Easter Bank Holiday, it was ; I'd been to the pictures after the football match—and there was a letter in the box from her, saying she was going away and this time she wouldn't be coming back. If you've never had that sort of letter you wouldn't know how I felt. She told me the man's name and the boat on which they would be travelling ; they were going out of England, she said. I read it through, and I knew what it meant, but I didn't believe it. I couldn't. I'd known she was going about with this fellow, but it wasn't the first time that had happened, and she'd always come back to me, whatever happened in between. At first, of course, when it first happened, that is, I'd thought I couldn't bear it, but presently I began to see that if I was to keep her at all it would have to be on her own terms. We never said anything after that first time ; but she must have known I knew. I used to tell myself they were like illnesses, these men she had, and when she was over them she was all right again—to me, I mean. My mates thought it poor-spirited of me, and perhaps they were right ; a lot of people would have agreed with them. But they hadn't been married to Bee—so how could they tell ? "

" No," agreed Jean, in a voice like a warning of death. " They couldn't tell."

" When I got this letter it was as if I'd been told I only had a few weeks or a few days to live. I couldn't see anything straight. I felt rather as though I had received sentence of death. I remember I began walking all over the house, into this room and out of that, staring through the windows, seeing people in the streets and thinking how funny it was that the world outside should look just the same. You'd have thought everybody must know, but of course they didn't. It was a little thing to them, just something that happens every day of the week to somebody, but not little to me ; all my life, Jean, to me. I remember pulling open her drawers and picking up her clothes and holding them, as if they were still a bit of her left behind. She hadn't taken much, I thought ; but perhaps this chap wanted her to have nothing that could remind her of me. I knew that was the way I'd feel in his place. I went downstairs and read her letter over again, but I didn't need to. I had it by heart. I have it by heart still. I can see the very words as they were written, the place where she'd left one out and scribbled it in, very small,

over the top. I stared longest at her signature ;
she wouldn't put Beatrice Barton—just Beatrice.
She didn't ask for a divorce or anything ; but that
was like her. There's no sense in women like Bee
being married. I mean, it doesn't make any difference. They'd stay with a man without a ring if
he was the man they wanted ; and if he wasn't,
no ring would bind them. I knew she hadn't stayed
with me because of some words said over her in a
church, but because, in spite of all these other men,
there was some feeling in her ; she spoke of it
sometimes. ' You're like my backbone, Jack,' she
said. ' If that broke I'd be a cripple, a dying
woman.' ' Don't say such things,' I told her. Just
the thought of her dying was enough to make me
feel half-dead myself. I used to remember that
sometimes, when she was out with other men. It's
not easy to explain. I don't think she ever really
needed any man, not in the way, for instance, that
I needed her. Unless it was this last one. I don't
know. But they—they couldn't leave her alone.
I couldn't leave her alone. I was at her and at her
to marry me. ' You may be sorry,' she told me.
' I'm warning you.' Why, once she even suggested
I'd be better to marry you. Why, what's the matter,
Jenny ? " for Jean had writhed back with a mutter
of intolerable pain.

" Nothing, Jack. Go on. Is that why you
did ? "

" Marry you ? No, of course it isn't. I wanted
peace and security, and you were the one woman
I knew who might give them to me. You've been
good to me, Jean, better, a lot, I suppose, than
I've ever deserved."

" Oh, deserving ! " She dismissed that con-
temptuously. " What's deserving got to do with

love ? You know that. Why, you love Beatrice still. And what did she do to win it ? ''

He looked at her strangely. " I haven't made you see. I'm not much of a hand with words. You don't blame the sun because it goes in sometimes, do you ? You just remember what it's like when it's out, how it lights and warms the world, makes things grow, makes you see all manner of things you don't even notice when there's no sun there to give them life. And suppose suddenly you heard that the sun had gone in and would never come back. Think of it, Jean. Never come back."

" Perhaps she would," said his wife very quietly. " Perhaps she'd have tired of this one, as she tired of all the rest."

" No," said Jack Barton, very low. " I've never let myself think of that." He was silent a moment, then continued vehemently :

" Margaret's not to know. I'll not have her life clouded. I used to think sometimes that Beatrice stayed with me on the child's account."

" Was she so fond of Margaret ? "

" She said something about it in her letter. ' This isn't the right place for me,' she said. ' Everything will be much tidier without me. I can't really grow well in a nice, neat little border. I did warn you. Margaret's old enough to keep your house now.' Meg had just begun work," he added. " She's more like me than her mother : settles to a job and stays there. But—she's all that's left me of Bee, and sometimes I see a bit of Bee in her."

He dropped his head into his hands and stayed perfectly still for a minute, as though even the energy of speech was more than he could contrive.

" I burnt the letter," he went on presently. " I

didn't want to keep that. I knew it, anyway, and you can never tell. I might have an accident, or be ill, or in some way it might fall into other hands, hands of people who wouldn't understand. Then I went upstairs and began to collect some things for the night. I couldn't sleep in that room—our room. There was another we didn't use, really, except for boxes. I remembered there was a camp-bed in there, and I thought I'd manage a shake-down. Meg was away, staying with her granny, and wasn't coming back till the Tuesday. I thought I'd have everything shipshape by the time she came back. I didn't know what I'd tell her. Probably Bee was right, and the truth would be best. She'd be bound to find out sooner or later. I went along to the boxroom and fished down the bed and opened it and put on a blanket or two, but it was much too early for sleep, and I couldn't stay in the house, so I went out again. It must have been about nine o'clock. I hadn't had anything to eat, but I forgot about that. The woman next door—Mrs. Lewis, that is—called out that someone had called with a watch for Bee. I didn't know what she was talking about, but I said she'd had to go away for a few days and I'd collect the watch. I went to the Ring O' Bells—I couldn't stand the Bird In Hand that night ; there'd be too many chaps there I knew—and had something, and stayed there till closing time. Then I came back and got into my bed and tried to sleep. But it was no good. There was no blind and no curtain to that room, and the moon made queer shadows everywhere. More than once I thought I heard someone move ; but, of course, it was only imagination. And once, when I had dozed off, I awoke hearing Bee's voice, and called out, ' I'm coming, I'm coming.' But that was imagination, too. It was a Sunday morning, and there was nothing to get up for, so I just lay there, feeling I'd lie for ever. I thought I wouldn't stay in the house. I'd get some rooms for Margaret and me. Someone rang the bell presently, but I let them ring until they got tired and went away. I wondered what I'd do with all her things. I didn't want to keep them, and I was sure she wouldn't send for them. I thought of burning them, but everything she touched seemed a part of her, so at last I decided I'd send them away to some charity, to people who'd never known her. I got up quickly after I'd thought of that, and decided to get them packed during the day. When I went to get the milk I found a parcel on the top, and it was Bee's watch. I thought perhaps I'd keep that, if she didn't ask for it. It's odd, Jean, but I never thought about the man at all. He didn't seem to matter. I planned everything out in the sitting-room. It was the one room she never liked much. ' Too cosy,' she said. ' Well, and aren't we cosy ? ' I'd ask ; and she'd look at me and laugh in a way I didn't quite understand. ' You shouldn't have married me if you wanted a cosy woman,' she'd say.''

Jean said nothing. What was the use ? She knew what love's like : unreasonable, no sense in it. Women loved men who beat them, humiliated them, betrayed them. And men loved women when they weren't faithful, weren't even kind.

'' After a bit, though, I found it was more than I could stand. I'd stacked some of her clothes ; but I couldn't go on, so as soon as the bar opened I went down to the Bird In Hand. There were a lot of chaps I knew there. I felt better just to be with them. I thought, ' Well, they're still there.'

43

It sort of made me feel I was still alive. I can't explain."

He fell silent for a minute.

" It was after I'd been there about a quarter of an hour that some fellow called out, ' Seen about this Channel boat going down ? That's a piece of rotten luck.' ' What boat's that ? ' I asked, but not really thinking what he was saying. ' The *Empress of Araby*,' he read out. ' Head-on collision in a fog.' There was more to it than that, with the other chaps joining in, but I couldn't think any more. It was as if the fog had come into the pub and blinded me. Then someone said, ' Hallo, look at Jack. What's the matter with you ? ' I said, ' Look here, you chaps, my wife was on that boat.'

" I've never heard anything like the silence after that. They just sat and stared. It's queer, Jenny, that it's nearly ten years ago, and it's as though I'd just come back. They didn't ask questions ; didn't need to. Well, they know that our kind of people don't go away from one another on Channel boats, not if there isn't something pretty wrong. And naturally they'd heard the talk about Bee ; joined in it, probably, when I wasn't there. I said, ' Give me that paper.' I hadn't looked at my own. Someone gave it to me. It was just as Bill Harvey had said. Every one had gone down, so far as they knew. There had been a high sea running, and in the fog . . . Besides, the collision took place at night, and it was pitch dark. I couldn't believe it at first. . . . There wasn't any passenger list, of course, though the next day names began to be printed. I suppose the relations supplied them. At first," he repeated like a child, " I couldn't believe it. Even now it sometimes seems difficult to think of her as dead. But not a soul was picked up alive—not a single soul. She'd never liked the dark. We used to have a night light going always. After the official announcement that it was no good hoping for better news—on the wireless that night, that was—I made myself believe it. Up till then I'd told myself that, whatever happened to any one else, she'd be all right. I suppose you know who the man was, Jean ? "

" Paul Fryer ? "

" Did everybody know ? "

" I don't think so. I don't see why they should."

" But if you knew . . ."

" Because it mattered so to you."

" Anyway, if they didn't know his name, they knew she hadn't gone by herself. I could see that much in their faces that day at the Bird In Hand. Perhaps all men whose wives leave them feel the same, but it seemed to me as if nobody could ever have felt quite like this. I don't know why it should be supposed to be so comic when a man's deserted, but it's a thing I've heard fellows laugh at over and over again. Bill Harvey made me go back and eat some dinner with them. They were tactful enough, but you could see Mrs. Harvey was bursting with curiosity. But we didn't say a word. And presently I cleared out and came back here. I'd no idea Bee had so many things ; every cupboard seemed bursting with them. I stacked them on the bed and sorted them as well as I could, and decided to start the actual packing the next day. That would give me the whole of the Bank Holiday, when there wouldn't be any interruption, to tidy the place up before Meg came back.

" I slept in the boxroom again that night, and next morning, when I cleaned the place up a bit, I got to work. I was going to send everything to

ANTHONY GILBERT

some charity that wanted women's clothes. It was
a dampish sort of day, very misty, and the room
smelt close. The boxroom, I mean. I opened the
window and began to pull out the trunks. There
was a big domed affair Bee had brought with her,
that had belonged to her mother, and a long sort
of wicker basket—it must have been six feet long—
that had belonged to my side of the family, and
was called Brown Miggs. When we were kids my
mother used to stuff everything into it. I thought
I'd put the dresses and coats and things in the
trunk, and the other things in the hamper. As I
say, Bee hadn't taken much, not even the fur coat
I'd bought her. Perhaps he wouldn't let her. I
don't know. I stuffed everything in and strapped
the trunk down, and then I dragged out Miggs. She
was under a folding tent and some rugs and old
cushions, and she seemed awfully heavy. I couldn't
imagine what Bee could have packed in her. I had
the light on because it was so dark, and I pulled
Miggs into the middle of the floor and unfastened
the straps. Then I threw up the lid—and I knew
why it had been so heavy, and why Bee hadn't
taken the fur coat or any of her special things that
I'd found in the dressing-table drawers."

CHAPTER FOUR

THE GHOST STIRS

FOR a moment there was a silence in that room as deep as death. Only Jack Barton's breath, whistling through the cold night air, only a faint movement of Jean's hand stretched out to touch his, that lay ice-cold at his side. Nothing more.

At last the woman spoke. " You mean, she—she—— ? "

" When I threw up the lid, Jean, there she was, as I had never expected to see her in all my life. Her face dark and dead, her hair sprawling, her eyes empty. And for two nights, Jean, I'd slept beside her, beside my wife, as a husband should. Two nights, and I'd never guessed."

Her grip on his hand tightened. " Jack, don't. You don't want to go mad."

" Sometimes I think I am mad. I think perhaps it isn't only she who lies in the cellar, but . . ."

" Be quiet. You've stayed sane for nine years. You're not going to lose your reason now." She remembered those ominous words he had spoken when she came in to-night. " She wasn't drowned, and he knows it. She died of strangulation under this roof. Now do you see why I'm afraid ? "

As these words repeated themselves in her brain she was fiercely aware of his peril, of the peril that had surrounded him ever since she had been his wife, but had never been so acute as now. Here in this still room horror seemed piled on horror ; the ghost of the dead woman was stirring, dragging

47

him back from her, into the grave where she had lain for so long. Jean's face seemed suddenly to come alive ; the white mask was informed by a brilliant vitality.

" Jack, you've got to tell me the rest—quickly. You mean, you saw her and you knew she'd been murdered ? But what did you do ? Didn't you call the police ? "

" To be told I'd done it and thought up a clever story to account for her disappearance ? I'd destroyed the letter ; I had no proof at all. I tell you, I was afraid. And I thought nobody must see her like this. I shut down the lid and fastened it and wondered where I could put her where she wouldn't be seen again. Every one would think I had done it and told the story about the *Empress of Araby* to put them off the scent. If I'd told the story before we knew the boat had gone down, that would have been different. But I hadn't."

" Still, the police might have argued that going to them was the act of an innocent man."

" Or the way I'd argue an innocent man would act. Besides, they know that in every murder the difficulty is to get rid of the body. And this would be a chance of accounting for it. For, naturally, I couldn't leave her in the boxroom for ever ; it would be too dangerous. And if I moved away from the house I couldn't take her with me, and equally I couldn't leave her behind. I couldn't sell the trunk and I couldn't leave it at a Left Luggage Office, because sooner or later it would be opened, and most likely I'd be traced. Besides, a hamper like Brown Miggs is conspicuous. You'll laugh, perhaps, but I felt I'd give anything if I could come and tell you what had happened, ask you what you thought I'd better do. If I could ask Jean, I thought, she'd advise me. I felt so helpless; I couldn't think properly. I remember I bent down and put my arm under her shoulders and lifted her a little, as if she weren't dead. But, of course, she was. She was dead when she was put in that box. And I couldn't stop myself wondering what she'd think if she could see herself now, or what any one else would think if they could see me holding a dead woman in my arms. I suppose actually I wasn't sane just then. I laid her back in the box at last and strapped it down and dragged it down to the cellar. I thought if I could be alone I might be able to think clearly. But I've never been absolutely alone, absolutely free of her, since then—never Jean. Before I married you I'd sit in this house night after night remembering her, as she had been and as she was now. I'd feel her calling me."

" And you'd go down ? You do go sometimes, don't you, Jack ? "

" I have to." He made the confession in a rapid whisper. Outside the wind had risen, and now came tapping insistently on the pane. The man looked up, his face sharp with apprehension.

" She used to do that," he said.

" Do what ? "

" Tap on the window. She had a key, of course, but half the time she'd leave it at home. It was as though she couldn't be bothered with little things like keys."

" But you might not have been here. She might be locked out."

" She wouldn't trouble over that. Or perhaps she knew there would always be someone waiting for her, if it was only to destroy her." There was such a wealth of anguish in that bitter word, " destroy," that Jean looked away at the dark windows, feeling as though she sat with a stranger instead of the man to whom she had been married for more than seven years. That insistent tapping at the window continued, like demoniac fingers summoning them both out—to what ? Jean's terror grew with a slow ferocity that compelled her to realise with ever-increasing clearness exactly how near the gallows her husband stood.

" Why do you go there ? " she forced her ashen lips to ask.

" Because she's there."

" No, no."

" I feel her there, all the same, though I know that what actually is in Brown Miggs is something she'd be the first to shrink from. Because she hated death. Nothing else frightened her—not being poor or unsafe or losing a lover, but death. I've seen her turn white when any one spoke the word. I wonder sometimes if she knew it was coming to her. Would you know, do you think ? "

To Jean it was as though, during the past hour, the whole world had turned turtle. Nothing made sense any more. It was like a child's crazy scribblings or writing reflected in a mirror.

" Don't think about it," she whispered with an urgency that pierced even her husband's absorbed mood. He took her hands gently in his.

" I oughtn't to have done it, Jean—married you, I mean. But I felt I was going mad, and you were my one hope of sanity. Before you came I'd go down there night after night ; I couldn't prevent myself. I'd creep down like a ghost for fear of disturbing Meg, and come down those dark stairs. I never took a light. I'd pass my hands all over the trunk, feel the buckle of the strap. It's rusty now, that buckle is. It's damp in the cellar. I never opened the box, though sometimes I'd stumble against it in the dark and think, ' It's lighter than it used to be,' and I'd remember that of course it would be lighter as time went on."

" And this man—Copper Face—what does he know ? "

" Only that she wasn't drowned."

" How does he know ? "

" I don't know, except that he knows it."

" Did he know her ? "

" I don't even know that. I don't understand how he can know."

" Perhaps it was a shot in the dark."

" A pretty dangerous shot, going up to a stranger and suggesting that he murdered his wife nine years ago."

" Why should he want to harm you ? "

" He wouldn't, if I'd agree to his suggestions."

" Blackmail ? "

" You could call it that."

" No, Jack, never. Once you start that you're never free."

" I know. All the same, he's not going to let me off so easily."

" What can he do ? "

" Inform the police."

" But it's no concern of his."

" We don't know. We don't know anything. We're as much in the dark as she is."

" But who is he ? Do you even know that ? "

" He's a chap with a bad record, a chap who wants a job and can't get it and thinks I can get it for him. It 'ud be jam for him if I did. Always on the spot, always turning the screw a little tighter. No, no, I'd face anything rather than that. That's why I've been away these three days. I didn't want to weaken so that, just to gain time, I agreed to his offer ; and I couldn't stay here and do nothing. He dogged me at the office. I didn't think of his coming here."

There was a sound in the hall, the click of a key, and Meg came in. It seemed to Jean typical of their respective outlooks that the girl's reaction to her father's presence was a tranquil and reassuring one.

" Hallo, Dad. So you're back. Jean was getting all worked up about you."

Her face was rosy and fresh, her eyes full of secrets. Jean saw that neither of them really mattered to her ; she was obsessed by her own life, her own hopes. She knew why Jack had taken such tremendous risks to preserve her from learning the truth.

Jack played up, as you might have expected. " I've been telling her the tale," he said, and winked at his daughter.

" I bet you have. You do fancy yourself as a gay deceiver, don't you, Dad, whereas anybody could look right through you."

" No bamboozling the young, is there, Jenny ? "

How could he do it ? Wear that casual grin, seem to laugh with eyes as well as lips.

She tried to do her bit. " Have a good time ? Where did you go ? "

" New picture at the Regal. Charles Laughton. Grand." She pulled off her hat and unbuttoned her jacket. " Made a fortune while you've been away, Dad ? By the way, did you tell him about the Brown Man ? "

" Nobody he knows," said Jean, marvelling at her own calm.

" Well, he seemed to know Dad. Sure, Dad ? "

Jack stiffened a little. "Matter of fact, I didn't want to alarm you, but he's a fellow we've had a bit of trouble with at the office. Thinks I did him out of a job. Haunting around ; it doesn't mean anything."

"He looked as if he might have meant a whole lot. You should look out, Dad. I was telling Terry about it. After all, he's in the police and he ought to know, and he says there are a lot of queer people going round, and if you're wise you won't let any one in after dark. There's a gang been working the houses here. He says if you have any more trouble, you just send for the police."

It was as though a burning wind had touched the man, shrivelling and scorching him. Only Jean saw his involuntary flinching from the word that might now spell disaster to him. The police ! In that house !

"Well, why not ? " demanded Meg. "What are you looking so queer about ? "

"Think I can't look after my own house ? I've been keeping it safe for years, haven't I ? "

"This man hasn't been crawling round before." That was true. That got home.

"What does he think he can do, anyhow ? "

"Nothing," said Jack steadily. "Nothing. But you know how it is with these fellows."

"Well, you take a policeman's advice and get someone to search the place from attic to cellar. You've a right to something out of the rates." Margaret's voice was like a bell. On such a night she could not conceive of the existence of fear. She didn't see the effect of her casual speech on her audience, for, catching up her hat, she whistled her way out of the room.

"Better lock up," said Jack. "We can't do any

good standing here." He snapped the catch of the kitchen window and they came into the front room. The man went to stand by the glass for an instant, watching the wild, triumphant sweep of the branches against the night sky, hearing those mysterious sounds of grass and stone that are only discernible to the attentive ear after dark has fallen.

As he stood there, there arose from the darkness a shadow in human shape, who approached the window and whose voice, soft as a wailing wind, drifted in through the open bar of the sash.

"Mister Barton! Mister Barton!" said the voice, with its faint, husky foreign inflection.

Jack Barton turned corpse-white. He had forgotten that he might be visible. For an instant he appeared riveted to the window by that apparition ; then, with a mutter, he slammed the shutters and lurched into the hall.

CHAPTER FIVE

THE GHOST WALKS

SERGEANT TERRY LANE turned into the Bird In Hand for a friendly drink and a shy at the darts board. The saloon bar was crowded, as was customary. He saw a number of familiar faces. His prospective father-in-law was there, looking as though he were recovering from some deathly illness ; old Dan Peters, who threw as pretty a dart as any of the younger men ; Andrews, who fancied himself as a psychologist and was always prepared to explain other men's difficulties to them ; Mullins, the jeweller on the hill, a big middle-aged man, and possibly the best darts player of them all. Terry knew them well enough ; it was odd to reflect how much he did know about them. Peters, with his wife in the asylum ; Mullins, with his woman over at Vale End and his mousy hypochondriac wife in Prior's Lane ; young Andrews, who might amount to something if he could keep away from girls ; Roberts, who'd been chucked by his girl last year and now spent all his time at the Bird In Hand. It was queer how women came in everywhere. He wondered suddenly what he'd feel like if Meg discovered she had no use for him.

Altogether it looked like a good evening. Terry was a convivial soul and popular with the locals. He was a big dark fellow, with a strong dash of Irish blood and great hands that, once they held, would never let go. The first of the Irish bulldogs, Mullins had once called him.

His thoughts came back to Jack Barton. The man was looking really ill ; other people had commented on his appearance. Terry couldn't remember ever seeing Jack like this before. Of course, when he lost his wife he had been desperate, but that was understandable. This was different. Terry had met Jean, too, that afternoon, and it had seemed to him that she also had something on her mind. She had greeted him self-consciously and hurried past. Surely there couldn't be trouble there. They were supposed to be an ideal couple, very different from Jack and Jack's ill-fated first, who was always making local history. Still, you never could tell. The quietest stream has been known suddenly to leave its bed and rush wildly over the landscape. It was a standing joke at the Bird In Hand that when Moresby and Gregg hadn't any further use for Jack Barton he'd be able to get a job as an advertisement for somebody's breakfast food. Are You Fit and Forty-five ?—something like that. He wondered whether it would be wise to question Margaret ; but even she hadn't seemed quite her normal self these last few days. She would have moments when she seemed miles removed from him, which was odd, for as a rule the Bartons, all three of them, were as transparent as glass.

He put his hand on Jack's arm, and Jack started violently. " What the hell . . . ? " he began. Then he saw who it was and laughed in a forced sort of way.

" Thought you were after my pocket-book," he exclaimed.

" It 'ud be a smart chap who got that," returned Terry with a grin, it being considered humorous in his circle to twit with miserliness a man who was notoriously open-handed. " How about a turn ? "

Jack hesitated. It was Mullins who encouraged him : " Come on, old chap. What's up ? "

Jack muttered something about having to get home.

" Not getting henpecked after all this time ? " called one of the younger men hilariously.

" It's a chap I have to see."

" If you ask me, Jack doesn't like being so close to a copper." That was another local wit.

Jack unexpectedly didn't join in the general laugh. Old Dan Peters, who thought Andrews an unlicked cub, growled, " Wait till you're man enough to get a woman of your own," and the laughter increased, this time at the young man's expense.

" Dick gets 'em, but he don't seem able to keep 'em."

" Tell us something about the psychology of women, Dick."

It was Mullins again who put an end to things by catching Jack by the arm and leading him away towards the darts board. Jack took the dart between his fingers and poised himself to throw.

But it was not his night. Probably he had never made so poor a score and Terry, who came after him, pointed the contrast by as neat a display as the Bird In Hand had ever seen. It was a pleasure to watch him. He had a neat little trick with his fingers—no one could describe it—but he seemed to give a little derisive flick, and the next instant the dart was quivering on that spot where every man desired to see his own. Mullins came after him, and he, too, was on his game, beating Terry by five points. Jack didn't wait any longer ; with a muttered good-night he shoved his way out of the crowd. As he pulled open the door a man came in from the street, a tall man with a face the colour of milk chocolate.

The new-comer said something that passed for an apology, but Jack waited for nothing. His head lowered, he seemed to barge his way out of the place, and left the door swinging violently behind him. Mullins turned and looked at him in perplexity. Terry felt his unease grow.

" Jack's off his feed," said someone.

Young Andrews took up his position in front of the darts board.

" Can't have got the sack or anything," suggested another voice, still referring to the man who had just gone out.

" Not him," said Peters scornfully ; but there was not as much conviction in his tone as he would have liked. In these days anything was possible. You only had to remember happenings in their circle during the past six months. There was Thompson, for instance, Bob Thompson who had driven for the Vanguard Foodstuffs for eighteen years and was suddenly handed his card ; the only palliative they offered was to take on his son in his place. They could get him for twenty-eight shillings a week, where Thompson drew fifty-four. But it wasn't much of a consolation to the older man. Nobody wanted men of nearly fifty. It meant the dole for him so long as it lasted. With first-class luck he might get a night-watchman's job ; but the waiting list for these was as long as your arm.

The chocolate-coloured man moved towards them. He was a stranger to them all, and although they did not precisely offer him the cold shoulder, neither did they extend any particular welcome. He found himself standing between Terry and Peters, and he turned to them, first one and then the other, saying in urgent tones: " Who was that, please, that man who went out just now ? "

They looked at him in surprise. " He means old Jack."

" Please ? "

" That was Jack Barton. Why ? Did you think it was Neville Chamberlain ? "

The Eurasian looked puzzled. " Please ? That was Mr. Barton ? "

" We told you so, didn't we ? "

" Ah, yes. That is what I thought."

They waited for him to continue, but he remained silent. " Well, go on, Sobersides," young Andrews encouraged him. " What's the big story ? Doesn't owe you anything, does he ? "

The stranger's manner had aroused their curiosity. Even now his gravity remained untouched by the most punctilious of smiles. His expression was troubled ; and this sudden encounter, coming on top of Barton's unusual behaviour, intrigued them.

" He had a wife ? " the Eurasian continued.

They noted the use of the past tense. " He's got a wife now," growled old Peters.

The new-comer seemed surprised. " Ah ! Tall and with red hair ? A dangerous woman ? "

" Look here," said Terry, " what do you think you're driving at ? "

" Crummy, he means old Jack's first ! " ejaculated someone else.

The brown man's quick ear caught the words. " His first ? Then—something did happen ? "

No one pretended to be interested in darts any longer. " What do you mean—something happened ? "

" It was written in her hand," said the stranger simply.

Even Mullins turned at that. " What was written in her hand ? "

The other seemed unaware of the stir he had created. " Sudden death," he replied.

There was a sharp intake of breath, then several voices spoke at once.

" What are you talking about ? "

" Where did you meet her ? "

" When was all this ? "

" It would be about ten years ago, perhaps a little less. I remember her well. She was a woman it would be difficult to forget. And he—he has not changed much. But—what happened ? "

" She was drowned," said Mullins shortly. " A Channel boat went down in the fog."

The stranger's denial burst from him as though nothing could stay it.

" Drowned ? No, that is impossible."

" Impossible ? How do you mean ? She was drowned. Barton told us so himself."

The coloured man shook his head. " Of that I know nothing. But, I tell you, that woman was not drowned. It was not written in her hand that she should die by water."

A laugh, part impatient, part amused, went up from the group. Andrews, who saw in almost every occasion an opportunity for wit, pushed his way forward, his hand extended, palm upwards.

" So that's your line, is it ? Cross my palm with silver, pretty gentleman . . ."

The stranger stiffened. Into his face, thin, cunning, lined with experience, came a new look, one of bitter anger and pride.

" It is a science," he said. " Knowledge is not to be bought with money. But I tell you," he repeated, his face so haughty with rage that even the ribald young man was impressed, " that woman did not die by water. Violent death I saw there, but not that she should drown."

Several of his audience appeared shaken by this earnest persistence. Only Mullins and old Peters exchanged a glance, and the former said, " Look here, I don't know what you think you know, but Mrs. Barton was drowned in a Channel steamer that went down with every soul on board. And if you take my advice, if you should happen to meet her husband, I wouldn't remind him that you ever met before. It's best not to remember he was married before he married the second Mrs. Barton."

The Eurasian's brows twisted. He stared straight ahead of him. Then he shrugged his angular shoulders.

" It is nothing to me," he agreed. " But what I say is true. If he saw her on board, then she left again later. She is dead—yes, I believe that, for her fate was close upon her—but not like that—no, not like that."

" Look here," exclaimed Terry, losing patience. " What the hell do to think happened to her ? "

" How should I know ? But she did not die as you say. Since you are so sure—who saw the body ? "

" No one actually saw the body," acknowledged Peter sulkily. " Well, how could they ? You can't go down to the ocean bed for bodies. They didn't get more than two or three out of the whole crowd aboard, and they were picked up by the boat that ran them down."

" They said she was on board ? "

" They didn't say anything. They couldn't."

" They were drowned ? "

" Yes. Pity you hadn't read their hands just before."

But for all this vehement denial, a sense of deepening unease had settled on the company. Mullins did what he could to break it by turning back to the darts board.

" The chap's daffy," he said, in a half-audible aside. But if the Indian heard him, he didn't seem to mind.

The presence of this stranger was proving irksome. Mullins turned back to say, " If you take my tip, Mr. Whoever-You-Are, you won't start talking about the first Mrs. Barton—not around here, anyway. Jack Barton's a nice chap, but every one has his tender spot."

" I understand," replied the stranger, and there was such a wealth of significance in his voice that the least sensitive was startled. He remained an instant or so longer, then, turning, without giving any order to the man behind the bar, he went out.

There was an instant's silence, then the men turned, half-guiltily, to look at one another.

" That was damned queer," said one.

" These Indians are all alike, full of magic and crystal-gazing. You can't trust 'em as far as you can throw 'em," returned Mullins. " Probably touting for a free drink."

There was a sudden chuckle of relief. " Well, he didn't pull it off."

They turned back to the darts board. Until closing time no one spoke of the first Mrs. Barton. But the younger ones were more sceptical, or else more easily enticed by the possibility of mystery. After all, they reminded one another, old Jack had looked as though he'd seen a ghost when he ran into that fellow on the step. It was clear that something was up.

" Your number, if Jack hears you," observed

Terry, coming upon a group murmuring and hazarding under the street-lamp at the corner. " Of course she was drowned—and a good thing, too, if you ask me."

" Of course, if you say so, sergeant," agreed one of the group with mock humility.

" What do you think Jack Barton did with his wife if she wasn't drowned ? " Terry continued. " She wasn't the sort of woman to vanish like a puff of smoke. Cut her up and put her in the cellar ? "

" She wouldn't be the first," said Andrews truculently.

" Anyhow, it's his trouble," remarked a more peaceable member of the party.

That seemed to be the general opinion. Anyway, what did it matter to them ?

" Perhaps the darkie's right and she isn't dead," was Andrews' parting shot. " P'raps she just oiled off and now she's married to someone else."

" P'raps you're the Duke of Windsor," suggested Terry. " You take care what you're saying. There's such a thing as defamation of character. And as for this chap, he's loopy. Probably one of the asylums is looking for him at this instant."

But after they had dispersed he walked home himself in a very thoughtful frame of mind. At the corner stood the old man who for nearly thirty years had peddled tracts and penny books of the New Testament. As usual, he was hung about with sandwich boards and awful Biblical warnings in red letters.

" There is nothing hid that shall not be revealed," read Terry, and for some reason he shivered.

As soon as her husband entered the house Jean

Barton was aware that a fresh development in this appalling affair had occurred. Jack might put on an air of nonchalance, ask with unusual interest about her own movements during the day, fiddle with the wireless and wonder aloud why it was that those responsible for programmes assumed that after 10.30 p.m. all their listeners were of a like mind; but Jean was not for an instant deceived. After fifteen intolerable minutes of hedging she was goaded into saying violently, " A lot you care whether I saw Daisy Garrett or Hilda Webb. What you want to know, really, is whether I've seen the brown man again. Well, I haven't; and, what's more, I don't want to."

Jack drew a long breath, part relief, part undisguised misery. " No ? " he said. " Well, I have. And so have half the chaps at the Bird In Hand."

Jean looked up her face full of instant alarm. " He didn't say anything ? "

" I don't know what he may have said. I was going out. I don't know how long he stayed. But he may have said anything."

" I don't see what he could say."

" Don't imagine this is going to stop here. That chap hates me, because I wouldn't do what he wanted. He won't stop short of anything to pay me out. And he's the revengeful kind. Nobody can stop him . . ."

" There's the police."

A look of horror leaped into her husband's eye. " The police ? That's the last thing we want. Suppose he gets them to start making inquiries ? "

" He couldn't do that, could he ? "

" Why not ? "

" But nobody except the King of England can go to a station and say, ' There was a murder done here ten years ago, and I want to have So-and-So's house searched.' Can they ? "

" Matter of fact, I believe they can. Anybody can bring a murder charge. Only thing is, he's not quite sure of his facts. How he knows anything about it I can't tell you, but I'm jolly sure he does. Anyway, he won't need to go to the police. He's only got to drop hints at the Bird In Hand and the Ring o' Bells, and people will start wondering and talking and asking questions. I don't mean of me, but of one another. And presently Mullins or Terry or old Andrews will say, ' I think you ought to know what this fellow's saying about you and your wife. Of course, we know it's all rot, but this kind of thing doesn't do a man any good, and how about shutting his mouth ? ' Well, what can I say ? Invite them to examine the cellar ? You know I can't do that. Say it's beneath my con-tempt ? That would be just as bad. No, if I can't shut his mouth somehow I'm done for, and you know it."

" You can't shut his mouth, can you ? " asked Jean uncertainly.

" There are ways ; but I don't want to take 'em if I can help it. I'm not sure I wouldn't sooner swing. You see, a jury would think what I've confessed I've done is pretty nearly as bad as murder . . ."

" You can't give in to blackmail ! Promise me, Jack."

" Oh, blackmail ! " He dismissed that with a snap of his fingers.

So then she knew that what he was considering was something worse, and she lay awake all night filled with a terror she dared not put into words.

CHAPTER SIX

A VOICE CRIED " MURDER ! "

IT was two weeks before the anonymous letters began. During that time even a stranger must have noticed the difference in Barton. From being a rotund, comfortable little man, with a jaunty manner and a chuckle in every paragraph, he seemed to shrink, not only physically—his clothes had already begun to hang on him—but mentally. He developed the habit of looking out of the window before opening the front door, of hanging about at the office until some other member of the staff was leaving and coming out in his company. He even made a serious mistake in his work that caused Gregg to send for him and say, sharply, yet with genuine interest, " What's the matter with you, Barton ? You're not doing yourself justice these days. That illness must have taken more out of you than you realised. Seen your doctor again ? " To which the haggard victim replied, " Not sleeping too well, sir, at the moment. Nothing to worry about, though."

Gregg sent him a searching glance. " No private troubles ? " he inquired, on a more human note. Jack was a popular as well as a valued employee, and Gregg remembered the time when he lost his first wife, and for some months had looked like this.

" No, sir. Thank you. Nothing."

" Money worries ? Sure ? You know you can talk to me, man to man."

" Nothing, sir, thank you very much. No, really, it's nothing at all. Very sorry about this,

sir. Shan't occur again." And he bundled himself
out of the partner's presence.

Gregg had to let him go, but he confessed himself
dissatisfied.

" There's something I don't understand there,"
he told his partner, George Martin. (There hadn't
been a Moresby in the firm for five-and-twenty
years.) " And what I don't understand I don't
like. That chap's in a bad way. He says it isn't
money and it isn't his wife. Then the odds are it's
someone else's wife."

" You've checked his accounts ? " suggested his
partner.

Gregg looked genuinely shocked. " I'd as soon
suspect myself," he said.

During those two weeks Jean also was infected
with fear. She began to see the chocolate man in
her dreams, and once she awoke with the conviction
that a stranger was in the room. But she was too
much afraid to move, and presently she dropped
back into a troubled sleep, and by morning she
could not be sure whether she had been dreaming
or waking at the time.

Then, after those two weeks of silence, the terror
began.

It opened with a series of postcards sent to various
local citizens. Mullins was one of the first to receive
one. It said *tout court*, " How did Mrs. Barton
die ? Ask him."

Mullins put the card into a drawer, but he did
nothing about it. This fellow was clearly a mono-
maniac, and the less notice you took of chaps like
that the better.

The Vicar of St. Sepulchre's got one that said :
" How did Mrs. Barton really die ? " and threw it
across the table to his wife.

" These publishers are up to everything these days," he remarked.

" Publishers, dear ? " Mrs. Price was wondering which is the more economical, shoulder or best end of neck of lamb (New Zealand, of course).

" Can't you read between the lines ? Obviously some publishing house is bringing out a book in which a character called Mrs. Barton dies mysteriously. This is a sort of advance notice. Next week there'll be another, to stimulate curiosity."

And next week, sure enough, the second card arrived :

" The Barton Mystery. What became of Mrs. Barton ? What does her husband know ? "

" It would be a bit more useful if they told me the name of the book and the man who wrote it," the Rev. Edward Price agreed. " Still, it keeps me wondering, and that's what we're all out for these days. I often think that if only the Church could arouse the curiosity of man. . . . The trouble is that people always want something new, and we can't offer them a new dogma, which is the only thing that would be likely to hold their attention."

" Mince or hash, dear ? " asked a preoccupied Mrs. Price. He reflected, without bitterness, that a dozen new dogmas would not hold Edna's interest or stimulate her curiosity.

But others besides Mullins and the vicar were receiving these anonymous communications. Miss Povey, who kept Putney's most select boarding establishment, received one, thought it was a joke, and stuck it up in the hall for every one to see. (Neither she nor her client ever went inside a public house and knew nothing of Jack Barton or his domestic affairs.) Two or three of her younger boarders took up the phrase like a catch-word. They formed a foolish habit of winding up their casual conversations with the words thrown over their shoulders :

" Good-night, old thing. And—I say—how did Mrs. Barton die ? "

And that set the ball rolling at a fine gathering pace.

It was not, however, until Margaret herself received a letter that matters became public property, and the long train of events opened that was to lead to a solution of the years-old mystery. Margaret's letter said :

" Ask your father to tell you, if he dare, how your mother died."

Margaret stood staring at the slip of cheap paper, the obviously disguised handwriting, the incredible message. " Ask your father . . ." She found that she was speaking the words softly under her breath. She took the letter, not to Jack, but to her stepmother. When Jean had read the message she turned as white as death.

" When did that come ? "

" This morning. I couldn't speak of it with Father here. Jean, what does it mean ? "

" It just means that someone wants to make trouble for Jack."

" But how can he ? We all know how my mother died. She was drowned."

" I suppose the idea is that you might think he drove her to go away."

" As if any one could think that. He was an angel to her. Who do you suppose wrote this ? Some other man who wanted her ? There were always dozens."

" You haven't said anything to your father ? "

" What do you think ? I never speak of her to him. I couldn't."

" That's best. He's had enough."

" You might think they'd let her lie in her bed after all this time." She paused. " Jean, you know you said yourself how worried he was. Do you think he's been getting letters, too ? "

" Why should it happen after all these years ? " cried Jean, half-distracted.

" Did he ever hear any more about that man that called on the night of the fog ? You don't think he . . . ? "

" I don't know," lied Jean desperately. " I don't know anything, Meg, except that something's wrong, and there's nothing I can do."

Margaret slept on her decision to discuss the matter with Terry Lane. If anything was wrong it would be unfair to him, in his official capacity, to involve him. But what on earth could be wrong ? Beatrice was dead—had been dead for nine years. Every one knew the manner of her death, as so many had known the manner of her life. It was absurd to suggest that Jack Barton had in any way contributed to that tragedy. Yet obscure fears were stirring in her, fears more for her father than for herself. The following evening she met Terry after he came off duty and put the letter into his hand.

He said sharply, " How many people have seen this ? "

" I showed it to Jean. That's all."

" Did she handle it ? "

" Handle it ? I—I suppose she held it, if that's what you mean."

" I was thinking of fingerprints," Terry explained.

" I don't know who this chap is, but he's dangerous. I dare say you're not the only person who's getting this sort of letter. In fact, I know you're not. And it's got to stop."

" What could it mean, Terry ? "

" I can only tell you this : A chap, a sort of nigger, came into the bar two or three weeks ago and recognised your father. Said he'd seen him with your mother some time before she died, and he'd read her hand."

" That's ridiculous. She didn't believe in that sort of thing. I remember being smacked once when I was about ten because I tried to tell fortunes by cards."

" Well, this fellow had it all very pat. . . ."

" Did you say—a sort of nigger ? "

" Yes. Copper-coloured."

" That must be the same one."

" Same as what ? "

" As the man who got into the house on the night of the fog."

" You didn't tell me anything about this." His voice was sharp.

" I didn't think it was any one's affair but ours."

" What did he want ? "

" We don't know. He asked for Father, wouldn't believe he wasn't in the house."

" Did he come back ? "

" I never saw him again, and if Jean did, she didn't tell me. Father's never spoken of him, either, but there's no question about it, he's looking awfully ill. Something's wrong."

" Any one could see that," agreed Terry absently. " Look here, give me this. I'll have it tested for fingerprints."

" Did you say there had been others ? "

" The vicar's had one or two rather odd cards that he thought were an advertisement of a detective story. I'm not so sure. He hasn't put two and two together yet, and probably won't, but he did tell me it was a bit strange. He showed them to me when I asked, and the handwriting's similar. Don't get too scared, Meg. The chap's probably a maniac ; only, if so, he's better under restraint."

And so, at last, the affair got into the hands of the police.

At first they were only concerned officially. Terry reported the matter to his superior officer, admitting that he had not been asked, in a professional capacity, to lend a hand.

" But the thing's getting beyond a joke," he added. " All sorts of people seem to have had these cards."

" And you think they refer to this particular Barton ? "

" Surely the one to Miss Barton proves that. Somebody knows something, or thinks he does, and is out for trouble."

" Why doesn't he come to us direct, if he thinks there was any funny business ? " speculated Madden, the police officer in question. " Seen Barton himself ? "

" He hasn't said a word, but he knows something. Only—he doesn't want to talk."

" That looks bad. All the same, if he isn't asking for an inquiry, we shan't be thanked for butting in."

" Quite so, sir. But we might be on the watch, and if anybody else gets one of these cards . . ."

" We can't do anything until we're approached direct. But I expect it's some lunatic, actually. Mostly it is."

A few days later Jean was setting the table for tea when the front doorbell rang, and when she went out she found Terry on the step.

" If it's Margaret you want, she's not back yet," she said.

" It's not Margaret, not to-night. I wanted a word with you."

" You haven't been having trouble with Meg, surely ? "

" No, no, it's nothing to do with Meg. Mrs. Barton. It's—look here, funny things are going on round here, and it's time they were stopped."

She knew at once to what he referred, though she only said, " What sort of things ? "

" About Jack. Haven't you had any of the letters ? "

" Letters ? What letters do you mean ? No, none have come here."

" Like that letter that came for Meg. She showed you that ? "

" That ? Yes. I thought it was the work of a madman or perhaps someone who had been jealous of her—of Beatrice, I mean."

" Nine years is a long time. Has Jack had nothing ? "

She shook her head. " We didn't show him the letter. He's got enough to bother him as it is. We—there's nothing we can do. We don't know who wrote them."

" The police might find out. It's not a joke, you know. Too many people have had these letters. They're beginning to talk."

" About Jack ? "

" Yes."

" But what can they say ? Every one knows what he felt about her."

73

Terry said slowly, " No one saw her go on board, did they ? And, of course, the body was never found. So the evidence for her death rests on Jack's word."

" What other proof could there be ? "

" I wonder why this fellow's got the idea that she wasn't drowned."

" Because he's mad, like I told you."

" You're sure you don't know who the coloured fellow is that tried to butt his way in here and gave you and Margaret fits ? "

" I'd never seen him before."

" He sounds like the one who came into the pub the other night talking about Mrs. Barton. Now, what does he know or think he knows ? Or what's he going to gain from it ? "

" Money, of course. He's like all these black-mailers . . ."

" But he can't blackmail without something to go on."

" I told you he was mad."

" I'm wondering whether Jack wouldn't like us to take this affair up, for the sake of others, if not for himself. These poison-pen fiends are worse than murderers, in my opinion."

" No, you can't do that. Didn't he have enough trouble with her when she was alive ? "

" They have had letters," Terry told Margaret, whom he met later that evening. " I don't mean that Mrs. Barton admits it, but she's plainly terrified. There's something underground going on, and sooner or later it's bound to come to the surface."

The next morning, for the first time, an anonymous letter was addressed to the police.

" Mrs. Barton never left Arbutus Avenue alive," it read. And added a Biblical context : Matthew 7.7.

74

" This chap likes to give us a run for our money, doesn't he ? " grumbled Madden. " I've sent for a Bible. Hallo, look at this. ' Seek and ye shall find.' That's queer. Why the devil doesn't the chap come to us direct and ask us to investigate ? "

" Doesn't care to push a charge, perhaps. Dare say his hands weren't always clean. Matter of fact, I wonder if we have a record of his fingerprints. Might be worth trying. I've got four clear specimens from various letters that have been handed in."

" What's the postmark ? "

" Putney in each case."

" That doesn't necessarily imply anything. Still, it might be worth while getting them to search the records. Has any one seen anything of this copper-coloured chap lately ? "

" He seems to be lying low."

" Of course, it may not be anything to do with him. Right. You get ahead with those inquiries and see where that leads us. Into a blind alley, as like as not."

By nightfall the fingerprints had been identified as those of an Eurasian calling himself William Jones, who had served a sentence for embezzlement almost ten years previously.

It was Terry who checked up on dates. The *Empress of Araby* had gone down on the 28th April. William Jones had been arrested on the 30th, and had received a sentence of ten years. Good behaviour had reduced the term of imprisonment to eight, which meant that he must have been released about twelve months ago.

" Wonder how long this has been going on," Madden reflected. " I dare say he tried to square Barton before he began spending money on stamps. Next thing to do is to discover his whereabouts."

75

This next step was accomplished through the vigilance of a local postman, who recalled collecting one of the cards in a certain pillar-box in Athelstan Road. The card had slipped to the pavement and the name Barton had caught his eye. He had heard no rumours of any persecution of Barton, and had merely thought it some game that didn't particularly interest him. Terry was, therefore, stationed in plain clothes (since his uniform might act as a deterrent) near this box, and kept patient watch. The anonymous letters had always been posted on the night mail, and it was assumed that the stranger preferred to take no risks of being recognised in daylight. Athelstan Road was a small side-turning where few people walked after dark, and a man might drop in a card and turn back into the highroad, or dive within a couple of minutes into the Underground without exciting any attention or provoking any encounter. On the second day of his watch he saw a man enter the street from the highroad and approach the pillar-box. He seemed to hesitate for an instant when he saw a stranger near the box, but the fellow had his back turned and was lighting a pipe. Only as he extended his arm to post the letter he held, the figure whirled round and caught him by the shoulder.

" Thanks very much," said the voice of Terry Lane. " What's that in your hand ? "

The man wriggled furiously. " That is my affair. You have no right——"

" Haven't I, though ? Looks to me as though this might be the affair of the whole borough. Let's see." He jerked the letter unceremoniously out of the long brown hand. " What's your name ? "

" This is all most improper ! " gasped his captive. " You say you have fair play here . . ."

" So we have, but you've got to do your share.
What's your name ? "

" I am William Jones."

" I thought as much. Why haven't you reported
your whereabouts to the police for the last six
months ? Don't you know a ticket-of-leave man
can be taken back to finish his sentence if he doesn't
comply with that order ? "

" I don't know what you are saying. I have only
been here for a few months . . ."

" Only been out a few months, you mean. We've
got your prints on the register all right. You
come and tell the inspector about it."

Still protesting violently, the stranger was lugged
along to the police station, where his letter was
handed over to the authorities. It was addressed
once again to the vicar, and was in a sealed envelope.
The message ran :

" Tell the police to ask Mr. Barton what he
did to his wife."

" Well," said Madden dryly, " what did he do ? "

The Eurasian flung up his hands. " He tells
every one she was drowned. She was drowned in
the *Empress of Araby*. And every one believes him.
But I—only I and he—know it was not so."

" Yes, yes," agreed Madden. " You saw it in her
hand. You told us before."

" I did not see it in her hand. I am not a magician.
I know it because I saw her—afterwards."

Terry Lane barely repressed a start. Madden
looked like a stone image.

" When was this ? "

" Two days after she was drowned."

" And where was she then ? "

77

" In *his* house, where she had been all along."

" In Barton's house ? "

The brown man nodded his head up and down, up and down, like a child's mandarin that for some reason has gone wrong and cannot stop.

" What were you doing in Barton's house ? "

" I was not in his house."

" Where were you then ? Looking through the window ? "

" Yes."

Even Madden was a little startled by the sulky conclusiveness of that.

" How did you manage ? "

" I will explain. I was in a house at the corner, a strange house, where I had a room. There had been some trouble . . ."

He hesitated and Madden said woodenly, " We know about that. The police were after you."

" Yes. As you say. I had no friends, I did not know where to go. Only I knew that soon they would come. I did not wish to be caught, and I opened the window of my room to look out. I was on the second floor at the back, and I thought perhaps I could leave the house that way. First of all I had to see there was no one watching. This is a very interfering country," he commented resentfully. " They might ask questions if they saw me coming through a window. It was morning, but dark and rainy. I had not put on my light, but in a house close by I could see a man standing at his window, and in this room the light was burning. I was quite near, you understand, for my house was at right angles to his. He was in the corner house, and the window was open. So I looked right across and saw him most clearly. I waited for him to go so that I could escape, and after a moment he went back into the room. But he did not go away, and he kept his light burning. I was watching him to see if it would be safe to take a chance, and I saw him stoop over a trunk and open the lid. And I saw—I tell you, I saw that there was a woman in the box. He seemed as though he were trying to take her out. He raised her a little, and I saw red hair, much red hair, which had fallen around her face. Her face I could not see. I stood there watching, forgetting my own affairs for the surprise. Well, it is not every day that you see such a sight."

" Not even we do that," Madden agreed. " What happened ? "

" Suddenly he pushed down the lid and fastened it, and then I saw the box begin to move. I knew he was taking it away—I did not know where. Then I remembered myself and how I must escape. After all, the woman was no concern of mine, I said. But it was too late. As I placed one foot on the sill I heard feet at the door. They are poor houses there." He spoke with a vast contempt. " The lock held no more than a few instants. And, anyway, where was the use ? There were men everywhere. I waited for them to come in, and they came."

" I see," said Madden. " You seem very sure of your story. Are you prepared to swear that the man you saw was Barton ? "

" I know it was he. Listen. While I was in prison I did not think much about him, not after the first. I had to think for myself. Then I came out and I must work. They found work for me, but I did not like it, no, I did not like it. It was not to be expected that I should. For one thing, they knew about me. I could feel their eyes following me. Oh, I could not remain. Then there was some trouble, and everybody, of course, blamed the man who had been unfortunate. After that I saw an advertisement in a newspaper. I went to apply for this position, and so did a great many others. While we were waiting a man came through the room. I tell you, I knew him at once."

" After nearly ten years ? A man you'd caught a glimpse of through a window on a dark morning ? "

" I tell you he stood at the window with the light behind him. I saw him standing there, and I saw him turn. No, he had not changed. Besides, the faces I had seen since then were different—not free faces. But you do not understand." He drew a long breath and looked round him as though he could draw strength from the walls or the ceiling. Neither of his listeners helped him in the least. He had the sense that they didn't believe a word he said. " Well, I did not get the position. I could bring no references, you see. I said I had only been in England a few weeks. It was no use. Everywhere it was the same. There was no work for me. The people for whom I had worked since I came out would do nothing. They believed me guilty again. Besides, I did not wish my story to follow me for ever. So I thought about this man. He— he, the murderer, was free and secure, he had employment, he was everywhere trusted, while I—I was an outcast, who might soon have to beg my bread. I waited about near his office, and one day I followed him home. He was living in the same house still. I wondered where *she* might be. I found a room not far away, and I began to ask questions—oh, very discreetly, one here, one there. I learned that this man's wife had died by drowning nine years before. There were even those who remembered the date ; it had been a holiday, you see. ' She had red hair ? ' I asked. And they told me, ' Yes.' So then I went one day to visit him. I waited until he had left his office, and I crossed the street to speak to him.

" ' Mr. Barton ? ' I said. And he told me, ' Yes.' " I said, ' I saw you the other day when I came to your office about an appointment.'

" He said, ' I do not remember.'

" I told him that he had come through the room. But no, he was not interested. Then I said, ' But I was not fortunate.' "

" Meaning you hadn't got the job ? " interposed Madden.

" But yes. To have work and the wherewithal to buy bread—what better fortune is there for any man ? "

" You can cut out that platform stuff," the sergeant told him. " Get on with it."

The Eurasian's face burned with a swiftly suppressed anger. " He said he was sorry, it was not in his hands. Then I told him that I had met him before. He said, ' Are you sure ? ' And I said, ' I could not forget. It was on the 30th April,' I said, ' nine years ago. Bank Holiday Monday. But perhaps you forget.' But he had not forgotten. A blind man could have told you that. It was almost as though he had died while I spoke. ' I do not understand,' he said. ' I do not ask to understand,' I told him. ' It would be better for you that I do not. But there is this for you to understand : I am a desperate man. I have no work, no money.' "

" Blackmail, in short," commented Madden in a grim voice.

" It was not very much that I desired in exchange. I offered him a bargain. He should find me work, any work, and I would forget what I had seen."

81

" For how long ? " Madden inquired.

The Eurasian showed his teeth. " That is what he said. Oh, he was so righteous. He learned, I do not know how, that I had been in prison. ' It would be impossible,' he told me. ' I was a thief.' ' And is murder so much less ? ' I asked him. But he would not listen to reason, although both of us desired the same things : just a chance for others to forget. I thought then "—here the lips curled back in a blank grin of rage—" ' he is such an honest man. Then he, too, shall pay.' Oh, yes. I promised myself that."

" Why not come forward in the open, instead of all this backstairs work ? "

The man he was examining threw back his head. There was such bitterness in the lines of the mouth that Madden felt an involuntary stab of admiration for Barton, who had dared to resist such a man.

" Because all you here see to it that a man shall pay and pay all his life if he makes a mistake. Who would listen to me, a man on ticket-of-leave ? "

" More likely to listen to you than to an anonymous correspondent."

" But now," cried the brown man, his face stiffening with relentless vengeance, " now he shall pay. For I accuse him of the murder of his wife, and I demand that you shall prosecute inquiries."

CHAPTER SEVEN

" HE's within his rights," said Madden. " Golly, what a story. Y'know, whichever way it goes, I'm sorry for Barton. You'd expect even a woman like the late Mrs. B. to stay dead after nine years."

" We haven't found anything incriminating on the premises yet," Terry reminded him, dry-lipped and pale. " If we don't, what is there to support such a cock-and-bull story ? "

" He's thought it out very neatly, if it isn't true. Besides, unless he's a maniac, what does he expect to gain from it ? We'd better get Barton down here and put it to him."

That same evening Jean, after much consideration, said to her husband, " Jack, have you had any of these letters ? "

" Letters ! From . . . ? "

" You know what I mean. People are getting them all round here, saying that Bee wasn't drowned, after all. Margaret's had one."

" You didn't tell me."

" It only came yesterday, and Terry Lane came up to see me last night—no, the night before."

" Ah ! " Jack's voice was very soft. " So it's come to that."

" It was quite unofficial."

" The next one won't be. Why, it might be this evening, the gate may swing any minute."

83

" That's what I thought. Jack, what are we going to do ? "

" There's nothing we can do. If they insist on going over the house, we can't stop them."

" We might do something before they come."

" What do you mean ? "

" About—her ! "

" What do you think we can do ? We can't leave the house. They'd find her just the same, and they'd get us, too."

" Can't we put her somewhere where they won't find her ? "

" There isn't any place."

The horror in his face was now so intensified, she thought he was about to faint.

" There's the garden. You often work there of an evening. You could be digging, and later on, when it's dark . . ."

" They'd find her there, too."

" Most likely they wouldn't look. After all, nobody really believes this story. If they go over the house, it's the most they'll do."

" The neighbours would see us."

" Not if we waited till it was dark. Jack, we can't lose any more time. And it's such a good evening. Meg won't be coming back to-night. She's gone to a dance with that girl friend of hers, in London, and she said she might as well put up at her flat, as it would be so late. It's our only chance."

He sat at the table, his chin cupped in his hands, considering the odds. They were so tremendous, it hardly seemed worth the fantastic effort involved.

" I ought to have told the truth at the start," he confessed in desperation. " They mightn't have believed me—most likely they wouldn't—but at least it would have been a chance. Now I haven't a hope. Once they find her there'll be no pause till the judge says, ' And may the Lord have mercy on your soul.' "

" It's too late to think about what you ought to have done nine years ago. And if you're not quick, it'll be too late to do anything now. There's the rockery. You're still making that. It's a chance. And if you come to think of it, after so long there can't be so much . . ." But here even Jean's courage faltered, and she turned her face away.

By sheer force of will she drove him into the garden ; by force of will she compelled herself to stand with him, making commonplace conversation with Mr. Burman from next door. She went inside and returned with a rockery plant catalogue, that she showed to the interested neighbour. She nudged Jack, compelling him to play up.

" You're digging deep," remarked Mr. Burman facetiously. " Going to bury yourself in the rockery ? "

" These little trees they talk about—you have to dig deep for them," said Jean, swiftly, moving so as to protect Jack's extreme pallor from the other man's curious gaze. She was afraid to go indoors, to leave him again, lest in desperation he blurt out the whole dreadful story. Fortunately, Mr. Burman did not remain long, and after he had gone she tried to put fresh heart into her husband.

" It isn't as if you were guilty," she argued. " And you said yourself it'll be hard to make any one believe the truth."

" It's a queer sort of life I'm fighting for," muttered Jack.

" It isn't only yours, it's mine and Meg's," she retorted. " You've known about it all these years. . . ."

"When I was a kid," said her husband slowly, "I used to wish I could believe in ghosts. But I never could. I believe all right now, and I'd give anything if I didn't."

At last the digging was finished. A deepish trench had been prepared and lightly filled in. Jack had left the spade concealed by an adjacent tree. Jean was thinking for both of them. It was well known to their neighbours that on these warm June nights she and Jack often meandered round the little garden after dinner, so no one would be surprised to hear movements and voices there. Mostly the other windows were dark by the time they came in. They must pray that this was the case to-night.

"Dinner's spoiling, Jack," she called at last in a hearty tone designed to be heard by the neighbours.

Jack struggled to produce a semblance of his usual voice. "I'm spoiling for it." He left the spade where it was and came up the path.

All through that dreadful meal Jean strove to keep up some sort of conversation on normal topics. Come what might, she must prevent her husband brooding over the appalling ordeal that faced them both after night had fallen. She knew that time was the essence of the affair. Since Terry's visit she had shuddered each time the gate swung wide.

"They can't search without a warrant, can they?" she asked suddenly.

"They'll get that, easy enough, if they think they're likely to find anything."

It seemed to Jean that he deliberately prolonged the meal, almost as though he would welcome the advent of the police, to render unnecessary the grisly thing they had set themselves to do. Determinedly she talked of this and that, but the success of her manœuvre could be measured by Jack's sudden irrelevant exclamation, " It's going to be a moon to-night. Look at her."

" People go to bed," urged Jean, and to her horror Jack began to laugh. At first he laughed on a low sustained note, but presently this rose and rose like a fountain.

" Stop that," she said quickly, " stop it." He laid his head on the table, shaken to pieces by that dreadful mirth.

" It's what you said," he gulped. " It—was—so damned funny. People have to go to bed. And Beatrice, too. To bed—in the rockery. The queerest bed she's ever known—and she's known a good many."

The whole of this speech was punctuated by bursts of gurgling laughter. Jean filled a glass with water and flung it suddenly in his face. The shock of that sobered him at once. He put out a hand and caught hers.

" Jenny, I'm frightened. Frightened as hell."

" So am I," she told him calmly. " That's why we can't afford to make any mistake."

After she had cleared away the meal they sat together and tried to speak of the thing they had to do. It wouldn't be anything like so difficult a task as if the woman were only recently deceased. There could not, after so many years, be anything left to dispose of but the steadfast and enduring bone, some rags, a jewel or two—remains that could be packed into a small suitcase.

" There's Brown Miggs," said Jack. " How can I explain her being down there ? "

" We can drag that back to the boxroom, and I'll clean up the buckles. I've done that sort of thing often enough before. That part of it you can leave to me."

She knew that if she for one instant withdrew her support he would throw up the sponge, admit the facts and possibly—most probably—pay for a crime of which he was innocent. It did not occur to her simple mind that cowardice is the crime most bitterly punished by the gods. She didn't think of Jack as a coward. She only remembered the superhuman courage he had displayed for years in bearing this secret alone.

Even so it took all their nerve to unlock the cellar door and descend those dark and ominous stairs. Jean's mind was filled with a picture of Jack, nine years ago, dragging the trunk—and how heavy it must have been then !—down those stairs, the sweat pouring off his forehead, wondering desperately whether the neighbours heard the dull clatter, whether their curiosity would be aroused, what explanation he could conceivably give if questions were asked or he were discovered at this gruesome work. And no wonder he had sometimes seemed half-demented in the months that followed, knowing what lay in the cellar and the consequences to himself, should any one come to share his secret !

They went down, carrying a suitcase belonging to Jack. In the minds of both was an emotion entirely divorced from reality. It was as though they watched themselves stealing down the steps and opening the cellar door and turning reluctant eyes on the horror that lay pushed into the darkest corner. Jean carried an electric torch, and she had a pair of candles in the other hand. Not until she had actually approached the long hamper did she seem to realise what it was that they were proposing to do.

It was her husband who voiced her thought: " We can't, Jean, we can't."

" We must." Her tone had the firmness of a nature torn between resolution and terror. Had she been more widely read she might have remembered Lady Macbeth, that dominant woman whose strength only survived the crime, and whose future was black despair ; but she knew nothing of Macbeth, and in any case would not have considered that he and Jack Barton had any qualities in common.

The hamper was thickly encrusted with cobwebs and heavy black dust ; in one corner a great black spider had made his web, like a net, and he watched them malevolently, like some spirit of evil. Jack put out his hand.

" Don't kill it ! " cried Jean sharply. " It's not lucky."

" Lucky ! " Did he say that, or did the dreadful whisper come from the thing inside Brown Miggs ? Jean hardly knew. She saw her husband put out his hand and begin to wrestle with a mildewed strap. The spider stirred slowly, came walking across the lid. As the man flung this back, the insect slipped over the rim and let itself down on to the Thing the box contained.

" Take it off quickly ! " cried Jean ; but it had scuttled into some safe crevice of bone and watched them from there.

And now even Jean was not proof against their circumstances. For, oh, what horror was this that they beheld ? What horror beyond all imagined horrors ? This crouched and rigid shape of bone, with tatters of cloth clinging to it, with a ring on one curved finger, a trace of red-gold hair fallen across the skeleton breast ? Those long bones of tibia and shin, the bent shoulders, the dropped skull, the great sockets where Beatrice Barton's unforgettable eyes had flamed ten years ago, and whence now that black monster watched them with unswerving glance. What madness of hers had it been to suppose that they could, in cold blood, lift those bones, wilfully destroy that structure and bundle it into the black earth under cover of night ? Jack had spoken the truth. The thing was impossible. Besides, illogical though it might appear, utterly devoid of spirit or of life as this grim ruin was, the dead woman seemed uncomfortably near. Jean felt gooseflesh all along her skin. Looking at her husband, she saw that he was about to collapse.

" We can't," he said.

" No," she agreed at last. " I didn't dream . . . I dare say they would have learnt the truth, anyhow," she added, a feeble palliative to conscience that derided her for lack of courage. Even to herself she did not pretend that there was any nobility of motive in her altered decision.

" Lock up the trunk," said Jack. But he drew nearer and stared with fascinated eyes at what that trunk contained. It was appalling, thought Jean, to reflect that to this must even the haughtiest and most glamorous flesh descend. Had Beatrice ever thought of herself as she must one day lie in the tomb ? Could the dignity of humanity endure it, if it could see clearly through its prevailing tissue of skin and bone ?

Then, as they took either end of the lid to cover up this horror, they heard a new sound that left them petrified with dread. There fell upon their appalled ears the creak of the garden gate that they had forgotten to oil, and then footsteps coming deliberately up the path. The cellar was under the front steps ; they heard those feet like the clods of earth on their own coffins. Then a knock sounded on the door.

" That'll be the police," said Jack, with the awful resignation of despair.

" You don't know."

" We soon shall. There it is again. You'd better go."

" Shall I say you're not back ? "

" Not safe. Burman knows I am."

" You might have gone out since dinner."

" No good, if they mean to search the house. Supposing they do. They'd only wait, at best, and I should look a pretty fine fool, squatting here with . . ."

She caught his arm.

" No, Jack. Look, I must go up or he'll get suspicious. You can come in a minute. I'll keep him that time at the door."

She turned away, stumbling up the stairs, reaching the hall as a second knock sounded on the door. She braced herself for the greatest effort of her life, wondering crazily how to hold the visitor at bay while Jack re-fastened the hamper and came up from the cellar. Suppose he insisted on examining the house at once ? She clenched her hands desperately, and, as the door opened under her touch, put on a fine casual air, ready to change to one of grave welcome, if circumstances warranted. Then she heard a sound, once so familiar and so dear, but now grown hideous in her ears, the sound of the letter-flap rising and falling. Was it possible—her eyes dilated—that this wasn't the police after all, but the brown man returned at a critical instant to prove his vile theories ? Passionately she resolved not to open the door.

The tapping continued ; then a voice came, a little muffled, through the slit :

" Mrs. Barton ! "

It wasn't *his* voice. She knew that. It spoke again : " Is that you, Mrs. Barton ? "

She forced herself to open the door and found their neighbour standing on the step, a spade in his hand.

" I've been calling at the back," he told her cheerfully, " but I couldn't make you hear. The rain's begun, and I know what your husband's like about his gardening tools. Some of these chaps would leave a spade out all night in a thunderstorm, and then blame it for being rusty ; but Mr. Barton's got a proper respect for such things. I suppose he didn't think it might rain. So I just leaned over the fence and brought it along for you." He handed over the spade, his honest, uninterested face beaming with good nature.

" I didn't know it was raining," murmured Jean faintly. " That's kind of you. Jack'll be grateful, I know."

" He won't get those plants in to-night," the neighbour went on heartily.

" No. Well, there's no particular hurry, I suppose." She wanted him to go. She wanted him to go quickly. She felt that in a moment she would faint, her knees sagging under her. She heard Jack's step in the passage. He was coming in their direction.

" Hallo," he began. And then, " That my spade ? I must have left it in the garden."

The neighbour began to explain all over again about the rain. Jack saw his wife was trembling and put his arm half about her. The neighbour said in jocular tones, " I thought your wife was never going to open the door. Did you think I was the police ? " He grinned with the air of a man who has said something amusing. The last vestige of colour left Jean's cheeks.

Jack said, " She's not feeling too good to-night, and that's a fact. Thunder in the air, perhaps. I'd ask you in, but . . ."

The neighbour excused himself volubly. He'd got a lot of work on hand. He was a keen stamp-collector—he said philatelist with conscious pride—and he expected to be up late as it was. When he got back he told his wife that he wouldn't be surprised to hear that, after all this time, the second Mrs. Barton was furnishing her nursery.

CHAPTER EIGHT

NOTHING HID THAT SHALL NOT BE REVEALED

THE next morning, before Jack started for his work, the gate creaked again, and this time there could be no doubt as to the identity of the man coming up the path.

" It's the police all right this time," said Jack, peeping from the window.

" Don't admit anything," Jean warned him quickly.

" It won't be any question of what I do or don't admit. The facts 'ull speak for themselves. One thing, Jenny: You don't know anything. Remember that."

" If you think it'll help you——"

" It's the only thing you can do to help me now. Come on, we must go down."

It was Madden himself who had called. He said, " You'll have heard about those anonymous letters that have been going round, Mr. Barton ? We think you may be able to help us."

Jean left them to it. She went into the kitchen, that was as spick and span as usual, and rearranged the cups and jugs on their hooks. She walked softly down the hall, trying to catch some of the conversation that rose and fell in the parlour. When that proved useless she went upstairs and looked out of the bedroom window. There was a man standing by the gate, with his back to the house. He might have been a casual loafer, but Jean knew quite well he was nothing of the kind. He was there to make sure neither of them attempted to stage a getaway. Not that even a start was much use these days, with wireless and the flying squad and every other person in the country so mad about detective stories they believed they could beat the police at their own game.

The two men came out of the parlour at last, and she moved down the stairs to meet them.

" Everything cleared up ? " she asked, forcing a smile to her pale lips.

" They just want to take a look round," said Jack. His voice conveyed absolutely nothing, not fear or resignation or defiance. It was just a thread of sound.

" Does the inspector want to see my kitchen ? "

Madden grinned. " Not quite an inspector yet," he said. " No, thanks, Mrs. Barton. That'll be all right. Sorry to put you out. It's just a matter of routine."

She watched them going upstairs. How much did the man know ? Was it just spinning out the agony, going through those upper rooms ? Surely, if he suspected anything near the truth, the cellar would be the first place he'd look, and the garden the next, so perhaps she was frightening herself for nothing. Why, he hadn't even brought a spade.

She heard their feet overhead, and then they came down again.

" What's below here ? " inquired Madden.

" That's a cellar, but we don't use it."

" Not even for coal ? "

" No. I've had a shed put in the garden. It's more convenient. These chaps that design houses don't think of the women who have to lug the coal upstairs. It's enough to break any one's back."

The inspector casually put out his hand and touched the door.

" Locked ? "

" I dare say it is. As I told you, we never use it."

" Got the key on you ? "

" I'm afraid I haven't. I must have had one some time, of course. . . ."

The inspector bent to look at the lock. " Oughtn't to be hard to force," he said. " I've got a chap in the front. I wonder if you'd mind giving him a hail."

Jack went to the front door. Jean tried to say something, but the words stuck in her throat. Madden didn't attempt to talk. Jack returned with a big fellow, who proceeded to attack the lock in a business-like manner.

" We'll make any damage good," said Madden to Jean. " You know, Mrs. Barton, there's no need for you to be delayed by all this. Your husband can show me round."

That was clear dismissal and as such she read it. She didn't know what to do, so she collected the brush and pan and carried them upstairs. But up there she did nothing, just knelt on the floor of their room in an attitude of prayer, saying nothing, incapable of thought, waiting. . . . They wouldn't be long.

And indeed they were not. When she heard their steps coming up she appeared at the head of the staircase. She saw Jack take his hat from the hook in the hall.

" They want me to go along to the station just to fill in a form," he told her. " Don't worry."

" You'll be back to dinner as usual ? "

" If I'm not, I'll send a message."

Madden turned towards her. " There may be some men coming up soon," he said. " Don't mind them. They won't bother you. It's all a matter of routine."

She watched them go, heard the door shut, and as the clang resounded through the house she felt the last vestige of hope die out of her heart. Before she could move she heard another footstep, and saw that the man who had been stationed at the gate was now in the hall.

" Are you waiting for your friends ? "

The man looked uncomfortable. " It's orders."

" These men who're coming—what are they going to do ? "

" Just the usual routine."

It was no good. He wouldn't tell her anything. She went back to their room and began to sweep the floor as though she would take every atom of nap off the carpet.

It was not long before the police representatives arrived, and were let in by Mason, the man in the hall. They went straight down to the cellar. It seemed to her they were there for ages. They were still there when she received a message asking her to come down to the station. For an instant her resolution stiffened into defiance.

" They want me down there so as they can go through my drawers and cupboards," she told herself fiercely. But, after all, resistance was useless. They were in the grip of the law now, and if she refused to comply with this request she could, she supposed, be compelled to attend.

She wondered whether she would be allowed to see Jack, but there was no sign of him when she arrived, and she dared not ask questions.

Again it was Madden whom she saw. He began, " Mrs. Barton, I want you to help us over one or two points. You've been living at No. 12 Arbutus Avenue for several years, haven't you ? "

" Seven. A bit over."

" During that time did you ever go down to the cellar for any purpose ? "

" No, never. It was always locked, like you saw this morning."

" You never saw it unlocked ? "

" No. Why, there was never a key . . ."

" You're sure you never went ? "

" Quite sure."

" Then can you explain how it is that a footprint found on the floor there corresponds to yours ? "

She looked at him blankly. " No, I can't."

" You don't know what we found there this morning ? "

" No."

" We found a trunk, a hamper-trunk."

" The house is full of trunks. I don't know about a hamper, though."

He looked at her gravely. " Mrs. Barton, if you don't know it, I should tell you that we found the remains of the first Mrs. Barton in that trunk."

" I thought you were coming to something like that."

" Why should you think so ? "

" All these questions about a trunk. Going all

over the house. Taking my husband away. Getting me here. But suppose you did ? That doesn't prove that Jack——"

He stopped her on the instant. " Take care what you're saying. If you wish to make a statement, then we'll take it down. But I should warn you that we are at present holding your husband in connection with the death of his first wife. You're not compelled to say anything that may implicate him. But anything you like to tell us, naturally we'll listen to you ; and if you can help us, it'll clear things up all the quicker."

She threw back her head in a defiant gesture. " What's the good of saying I don't have to talk ? You'll find out if I don't tell you. Yes, I did go down to the cellar—last night. It was the first time."

" Did you know what you were going to find ? "

" Yes. Jack told me—because he had to. But he's only just told me."

Madden nodded. He put a few more questions, and then she was told she could go. She wondered if " holding " was the same as arresting. She supposed it was. Apparently they had no intention of detaining her as accessory after the fact. Only Madden said she mustn't try to leave the district, as she might be wanted. Then he asked about Margaret.

" She didn't know a thing—she doesn't yet," protested Jean. " You're not going to try and drag her into this ? "

" Where is she now ? "

" At her work."

" What's the address ? "

Jean gave it reluctantly. They'd find out if she didn't tell them—twist it out of Jack if necessary.

" You're expecting her back to-night ? "

" Yes." But as she spoke she thought that the news would most likely be in the evening papers that would be on the streets by the time Margaret left her office. " Not that she can help you. She wasn't even in the house when it happened. She was only a kid, staying with her grandmother."

She had to admit the police were fair. They hadn't tried to trap her into any admissions ; they knew she couldn't be forced to give evidence against her husband. But she knew that when the matter came into court, Jack would tell the truth. It was his only chance, and it was unlikely that he'd be believed at that.

Most of the police officials had gone by the time she returned. Photographers, finger-print experts, all the bundle, she told herself bitterly. She was instantly aware of heads at windows, and people standing on the doorsteps as she walked up the street. No sense in holding your head high now. Jack and Bee between them had provided Putney with a seven days' wonder. She supposed they'd taken Beatrice away. The cellar was locked. In any case, she wouldn't have gone down there again for a king's ransom.

Margaret came back soon after lunch. She looked very white and would scarcely speak when Jean addressed her.

" I suppose you knew ? "

" Yes."

" And all the time you've pretended you didn't."

" Jack didn't want you to be worried."

" Worried ? How long did he think he was going to be able to keep this up ? After all, she was my mother."

Jean didn't argue. There wasn't anything to say.

"I suppose this place will be filled with the police." Suddenly her mood softened. "Poor Jean! It must have been awful for you. How could he?"

"How could he what?"

"Keep it to himself for so long. I suppose it was that brown man?"

"Yes. Somehow he'd got to know." She moved restlessly round the room. "Is he actually arrested?"

"I'm not sure. But he's bound to be."

"I suppose so. Doesn't it show you it's no good living a decent life and being kind? You don't know how kind to her he was. He might just as well have hit her on the head and been done with it."

"Don't lose heart now. It's all routine so far. They couldn't help arresting him. It doesn't mean he'll be found guilty."

"I can't even ring up Terry. He wouldn't tell me anything, and it's probably breaking one of the laws to try and coax anything out of him. Like spying in war-time."

Jean heard her go upstairs and start pulling out her drawers and slamming cupboards.

That night the evening papers in Putney went mad with excitement. Nothing quite like this had happened for ages.

PUTNEY CELLAR MYSTERY
LOCAL MAN ARRESTED
WELL-KNOWN PUTNEY MAN TAKEN FOR MURDER
NINE-YEAR-OLD MYSTERY SOLVED
HOW DID MRS. BARTON DIE?

The authorities were more cautious:

"Police this morning discovered a hamper in

a cellar at No. 12 Arbutus Avenue, containing the remains of a human body, believed to be that of Mrs. Jack Barton, who disappeared more than nine years ago. Jack Barton, the husband of the dead woman, has been detained in connection with the affair."

The journalists added their comments:

" Mrs. Jack Barton, whose body was removed from a cellar in the house of her husband, a well-known Putney resident, by the police this morning, was last seen alive on the 28th April, 19——. The following morning her husband informed neighbours that she had sailed in the ill-fated *Empress of Araby*, that was sunk in a collision in a fog on the night of the 28th, all on board being drowned. Suspicion was recently aroused by means of a number of anonymous letters received during the past few weeks by various local residents, which caused the police to examine the house in Arbutus Avenue. It is understood that it is not disputed that the remains are those of the missing woman.

" In June, 19——, Barton married Miss Jean Gray of Putney. There are no children of the marriage, but Barton's daughter, Margaret, by his first wife, lives with the couple. She is engaged to Sergeant Terry Lane of the Putney Police Division."

Next morning everybody knew that Jack had been brought before a magistrate and formally charged with murder, and that he proposed to reserve his defence.

At the Bird In Hand they could speak of nothing

else. Even people who had only known Jack Barton by sight talked of the amazing discovery.

" How was it ? " they said. But nobody knew.

" Well, it wouldn't be easy to tell, after nearly ten years."

" If it had been a bullet . . ."

" No one's said anything. Anyhow, he wouldn't be likely to have a revolver on the premises. He'd need a licence."

" It's rough on a chap, this coming out after so long. I mean, if it had been last week the neighbours might have helped. You can't tell about provocation. Perhaps she threatened him—it might have been self-defence."

" It might have been poison—there'd be nothing to show."

" Can't you tell poison years afterwards ? "

The speculation continued. " It doesn't give him a chance after all this time," was the burden of every one's comment. It was noteworthy that nowhere did you hear a word of pity for the dead woman. Probably he had done it, they decided. After all, it was improbable that any one else could have deposited the body in the cellar. But he'd get the benefit of the doubt, like that other chap whose wife had been found in similar circumstances and who, after enduring the agony of hearing sentence of death pronounced upon himself, had eventually been reprieved.

" He'll have a lawyer, of course," suggested old Peters. " Wonder if he knows anybody."

" The courts help, don't they ? "

It was Mullins who said, " There's a chap called Crook. He might undertake it. He likes these hopeless sort of cases."

" What about money ? "

" I should say Barton had quite a tidy bit put by. They didn't spend a lot, and he had a pretty good job. I shouldn't be surprised if his boss offered to help."

" More than mine 'ud do," prophesied Andrews gloomily.

Mullins said in the same voice, " There's something about Jack Barton, something likeable. No one could want to see him swing."

A little shiver went through the company. It wasn't a nice thought—old Jack being led out one cold morning while they were having breakfast, eyes bandaged, hands bound, to stand on a platform, waiting . . . They shrank from the vision.

" I could see this fellow," said Mullins. " If any one can get him off, Crook will. He's supposed to have cheated the gallows of more men than any lawyer of his time."

" Still, if he thinks he did it . . ."

" That doesn't make any difference. The more guilty a chap is, the better lawyer he needs. Besides, technically none of Crook's clients are ever guilty. Anyhow, he has an uncanny way of persuading juries to say they aren't."

CHAPTER NINE

NOTHING BUT THE TRUTH!

SITTING in his eyrie of an office, like a great watchful spider in a suit of brown dittos, Mr. Arthur Crook, the Criminals' Hope and the Judges' Despair, ran his small, malignant eyes rapidly down the columns of the morning press, pausing every now and again to slash a great blue cross against some significant paragraph. Close by, his ally and employer, Bill Parsons, waited with an air of undying patience that hid a relentlessness even the police had learned to fear. Bill's brilliant criminal career had been stopped in mid-flight some years earlier by a police bullet in the heel, since when he had used his undoubted flair and knowledge on the side of righteousness. It pleased Crook's warped sense of humour to have Bill playing for law and order. Saul among the prophets, he used to say, was nothing compared with Bill among the virtuous.

" See about this chap who put his wife in the cellar nine years ago ? " murmured Bill.

" I've been expectin' that," was Crook's negligent rejoinder, " ever since I heard about these letters. Well, stands to reason, either the chap writing them was a lunatic or, if not, that he knew a bit more than was healthy—for Barton, I mean. Might be something in it."

" For us, you mean ? " Bill knew his Crook, knew that the great man wasted little time on affairs even in the criminal world that were not likely to interest him to a more considerable extent later on.

" It might be, Bill, it might be. After all, however spry the fellow is, it ain't goin' to be too easy to explain how the lady came to be in his cellar. Funny thing, chaps have always found it difficult to explain things of that sort. The man who can find a fool-proof answer to that one isn't going to have to do any more work for the rest of his days ; he's going to draw a pension from the Murderers' Guild and loll round in a Rolls till it's time for him to go to the churchyard in a gold coffin."

Bill produced a platinum cigarette-case that had once belonged to somebody else and that he had removed without its owner's permission, and offered it to his companion. This was a mere matter of form, because Crook never smoked cigarettes. " I don't like middle-class qualities," he would say. " Upper or Lower Ten—they're all right. But these folk that are neither one thing nor the other—you can buy 'em." Which was his elaborate way of saying that he could smoke a pipe in a pub or a Corona Corona in a king's castle, but not a cigarette anywhere with any one.

" Suppose he did dump her there ? " Bill was asking placidly.

" I'd lay three to one on it, Bill, even with us lendin' a hand, and forty-three to one if we don't."

" Going to take a hand ? "

" My father used to tell me that the law was a gentleman's profession, and I've never forgotten it. Drunk or sober, always a gentleman—that's a lawyer. And gentlemen don't butt in where they ain't invited. Besides, this is going to be a hell of an expensive case. We'll copy that grand old gentleman, Mr. Henry Herbert Asquith, my boy, and wait and see."

His eyes narrowed to such an extent they became

almost invisible. He looked like one of the less desirable exhibits in the Birds of Prey Aviary at the Zoological Gardens, though Bill didn't say so. Crook wouldn't have minded if he had. He said he always went and prowled round there before any big case came on—and by big case he meant something in which he himself was involved ; no other cases existed so far as he was concerned—because there was a certain hooded vulture who looked like the epitome of all the High Court Judges rolled into one.

" No, Bill," he decided, " we fold our hands and wait and know our own will come drifting along on the right tide," he wound up, loosely paraphrasing that poet whose work is universally loathed by all Sixth Forms, who have to learn his philosophy by heart. " Besides, what about this chap who's been doin' the writing ? Either he's actuated by the true public spirit that likes to see another fellow suffer for his misdeeds—and that's called Morality, my boy—or else he was interested in the lady himself, and wants his revenge. That'll come out sooner or later. And sooner or later we'll come in."

So it was that, when Mullins approached his man, he found him, like the cohorts of the righteous, ready for the fray.

" Of course, I know it's not much use hoping to show that Barton didn't do it, not after ten years," he acknowledged, " because any clues there might have been in his favour will have disappeared a long time ago."

" And contrarwise," interjected Crook.

Mullins looked surprised. " I should have thought the body in his box in his cellar was about all the clues the police 'ud want."

" I ain't the police," returned Crook comfortably,

" and I want a hell of a lot more than they do. Oh, their case is as easy as pie. Barton comes back, finds a lot of funny business going on, goes for his wife heavy-handed. It don't mean he meant to murder her ; the good intentions of husbands never get a fair show in court. But, anyway, there she was, done for, and he'd got to explain somehow. Pity he destroyed the letter, because evidence that only exists on an accused man's word is hardly evidence at all. Well, he had only two alternatives : to go to the police with his story or do what he did. Mind you, I don't blame him. I wouldn't care to tackle the cops myself with a yarn of that kind. There's something very unbelievin' about the police in a case like this. P'raps it's the work they do— seems to sap their faith in human nature ; and, of course, it's common knowledge that when a wife is found murdered, the person with the most obvious motive is the husband. A nice commentary on civilisation, Mullins. Still, there are other pos- sibilities. Some other chap half-mad with jealousy. She seems to have had a string of 'em, like a lady puss ; and not only at the appointed times and seasons at that. Now, let's get this clear : The lady vanished—when ? "

" The 28th April was the last time any one saw her. Next morning we heard about the *Empress of Araby* going down, and Barton told us his wife was aboard. Of course, there was no way of proving she wasn't. . . ."

" I expect he'd thought of that. We might be able to find out who saw her last. A woman like her gets herself remembered somehow."

" I might be able to help there," said Mullins. " As a matter of fact, she came into my shop that afternoon with a watch she said wanted mending.

107

Wanted to know if I could make a snap job of it, because she was going away."

" She told you that ? "

" Yes. But she didn't add for good. She'd been away now and again before. She had an old father. I believe she was awfully good to him. He was in one of those homes for the aged—paralysis or something—and she'd go over and see him, take him something every now and again."

" Anybody ever see the old father—barring the lady ? "

Mullins' brows shot up. " I couldn't say. Jack Barton himself, perhaps. . . ."

" Wonderful how useful those paralysed old codgers can be. Paralysed in both arms, I suppose."

" I don't know. Why should he be ? "

" It 'ud explain why he never wrote. But perhaps he did."

" I wouldn't know the answer to that one, either. Anyway, she wanted the watch back the same evening. I told her I didn't know if it could be managed, but she said it was important. I said I'd do my best. Matter of fact, I got ahead with the job myself. It wasn't finished till almost six. She'd said she would be leaving between six and half-past. She was the sort of woman that people do do things for. There's never anything much doing in my place on a Saturday evening. Regular argy-bargy of girls and young fellows looking in the windows and cracking jokes, but a new glass for a wrist-watch is about the average custom I get. I had an assistant called Abbot, so I left him in charge and went down myself to Mrs. Barton's. I had the car with me, because I was going out that night, after the shop was closed."

Crook said nothing. He had more than an inkling

of the manner in which Mullins spent most of his spare time.

"I got down there about five past six and went up to the door, but I couldn't get any reply. I knocked and rang several times, and I stood back in the garden watching the windows, but there didn't seem to be any one there. I saw a woman in the next-door garden, and I asked her if she happened to have seen Mrs. Barton go out. She said no, she hadn't, but, then, she mightn't notice. 'Well,' I said, 'if you should happen to see her, you might say I've brought down her watch, but I couldn't get any reply.' She said, 'Can't you put it through the letter-box?' But of course I couldn't. I was responsible for it so long as it was in my possession.

"I went back home—about twenty-five past six, that 'ud be—and the next morning I told my eldest girl to leave the watch at the Bartons on her way to Sunday School. She said when she got to the house she couldn't get any answer; but she didn't think they could all be away, because there was a bottle of milk and a newspaper on the step. She didn't quite know what to do, but she left the watch on the top of the milk-bottle. I told her she shouldn't have done that, and I went down myself in the afternoon to make sure it was all right. I saw the woman from next door—she was bringing her children back from a walk—and she said, 'I told Mr. Barton about your watch when I saw him last night. He went out for a bit of a stroll about nine o'clock. I remember it so well because of the news we got later, about Mrs. Barton having gone off with some chap and being drowned.' 'Drowned?' I said. 'What are you talking about?' So she told me. Mrs. Barton had been on this ship, the

Empress of Araby, that had gone down overnight.
I tell you that was a shock. It was difficult to think
of a woman like that being dead. Barton was like
a maniac, she said. I thought I'd best not go in,
so I went back home and told my wife. She'd never
liked Mrs. Barton much, and anyway they didn't
really meet. She wasn't what you'd call a woman's
woman."

" She don't sound it," agreed Crook smoothly.
" Y'know what that chap Egerton used to say ?
Fate always holds the last trick, and she generally
plays it on the side of righteousness." He looked
sideways at Mullins as he spoke, but Mullins didn't
bat an eyelid. " That's a very healthy beginnin',"
Crook went on. " It means that Mrs. Barton must
have died between, say, four forty-five, assuming
she went straight home, and six o'clock. We must
find out what Barton has to say about his movements at that time. Know them well ? "

" I used to meet him, chiefly at the Bird In
Hand. It's more like a club than a pub, you
know."

" I didn't," murmured Crook. " I must take a
peep at it some time. What about her ? "

Mullins wrinkled his brows. " Difficult to say.
I wouldn't suggest I knew her very well, but I knew
a lot about her. It was difficult not to. I mean—
you'd feel her coming before you saw her. There
was something—most men felt it. She was like a
tiger or something ; she couldn't be there and you
not know it. It frightened some people. What beat
most of us was why she ever fell for Barton. He
was such a usual sort of chap."

" He seems to have stood her antics for a good
many years," was Crook's dry comment. " Most
men would have knocked her on the head long

before this. Well, I'll see what can be done. How about the present wife ? "

" She's not having too good a time of it. Well, the best of women has enemies, and someone's started a rumour that she knew all about it, was a party to it."

" Meanin' the murder ? Likely to be anythin' in that ? "

" Shouldn't think so. No, no, the thing's not thinkable. Anyway, if Barton had wanted to marry her, he could have got rid of the first one by constitutional methods any time he liked."

" Ever noticed, Mullins, how most men are like cats : love to take the longest way round to everything. Besides, divorce ain't very common with chaps of that type. And think what a dreadful ass he'd look. Anyhow, a court might have said some nasty things about a man who knew his wife was playing around on the tiles and didn't do a thing about it. There are chaps—I don't say I'm one of them—who think that kind of charity is a bit worse than murder, though clearly the law don't. Still, I don't suppose she was implicated. Ever noticed that these trunk murders are always single-handed affairs ? How about the daughter ? "

" She's staying in London with a girl friend. She won't be able to help much."

" No ? " Crook's casual question was as good as a dismissal, and as such Mullins took it.

" Anything else I can do ? "

" Not at the minute. I'll remember you."

" And you'll keep me in touch with developments ? "

Crook touched the place where his forelock would have been if his hair had not receded so far.

" Sir to you. Well, you're callin' the tune, ain't

you ? " Which was his tactful way of reminding Mullins that eventually there would be a bill to be footed. He used to say it was as well to have matters on a business basis right from the start.

" Neither of those women of Barton's is going to be much use to us," he confided to Bill that same afternoon. " The police know that ; that's why they aren't botherin' with them. They won't talk because they've got nothing to say. You know, Bill, if we're not damn careful this whole case will slip through our fingers. Nobody'll notice it. There's nothing startling about it once you accept the position. And that's not what I'm accustomed to. We've got to get some witnesses for the defence, if we have to make 'em ourselves of plasticine. Meanwhile, I'll go down to Wandsworth Jail and talk to this chap, try and get some sense out of him, and you'd better be ready for anything by the time I get back."

" H'm," he commented cynically, when he had heard Jack Barton's story. " Not exactly helpful, are you ? If you were guilty, you couldn't have done a thing different. What made you destroy that letter ? "

" Would you have wanted to keep a letter like that ? "

" If it had been genuine I'd have had it framed and hung over my bed. Then, if the lady wanted to come back, I'd have had it to face her with."

" She could always have come back," said Jack Barton quietly. " And I didn't keep it, because it never occurred to me I'd want it."

" Very nice from your point of view. But what about mine ? I suppose you see me as the raven bringin' bread and meat in the form of an acquittal in my mouth ? " And indeed there was something of the raven about him, Jack thought, staring with lack-lustre eyes at the bulky figure, that, for all its size and a certain ponderousness of movement, seemed so chock-a-block with vitality that the bare prison walls were kindled by it.

" What would you have done in my place ? " he demanded, with a sudden show of spirit.

Crook smiled at him—a wise, sad smile. " It could never happen to me," he said softly. " I'm not a married man." He crossed his pudgy legs and became more professional.

" You do see it ain't going to be too easy to get any evidence about a thing that happened ten years ago," he pointed out. He didn't believe in encouraging clients too much. Afterwards they got the idea they'd practically got themselves off, and weren't appropriately grateful for all you'd done for them. Most men, he would say, put a quite disproportionate value on the mere fact of being alive ; they don't stop to wonder whether life's worth living, worth, that is, the trouble it involves just keeping alive and paying your way and having a tanner over for a spot of something warm at the nearest public house ; they simply know that it's better to be alive than dead. Well, then, if you've managed to convince the law that they've a right to go on being alive, even if it's only to be a nuisance to themselves and everybody else, they ought to be prepared to pay you a whacking great fee for your trouble. Particularly if, in law, they ought to die, as Crook thought most likely was the case with Jack Barton. He found himself in complete agreement with the Irishwoman who said to her children, " I don't mind yeer being naughty, for I can smack ye for that, but I will not have ye stupid." It seemed to him that in putting this woman in the cellar Barton was asking for precisely the consequence that had now befallen him. Sooner or later everybody hidden in a cellar comes to light ; and if Barton hadn't realised that to date, it was high time someone told him.

" What," he demanded crudely, " were your relations with your wife ? "

Barton's face was ashy-pale. He said, his hands clasped tightly, his face rigid, " I was—very fond of her."

" Did you have rows ? "

" No."

" Did you know about these other friends of hers ? "

Barton nodded.

" And you did nothing about it ? "

Barton gave a great sigh that seemed to tear him in two ; it was almost a groan. He exclaimed desperately, " It's not so easy to make you understand. My wife wasn't like other people ; you couldn't lay down laws and ask her to keep them.

" It's what the law does expect, all the same," Crook cut in.

" In a way, she couldn't help herself," Jack urged.

" Folk that aren't responsible for their actions should be in asylums," his lawyer told him in unsympathetic tones.

" It was nothing like that, but it was a choice I had to make. If I'd told her I wouldn't stand for her men friends, she'd have cleared out, and for me that would have been worse than the truth."

" Don't say that sort of thing in the witness-box," Crook advised him dryly. " Judges—and juries, too, for that matter—have an ugly name for men who sit down tamely under that sort of thing. What

you want to realise is that you've got to get the
sympathy of the jury. It isn't facts that matter in
a court of law nearly so much as the layman thinks.
The average chap is a bundle of conceit ; he has a
thing that lawyers don't recognise, and quite right,
too, that he refers to as instinct. He trusts his
instinct. When his instinct tells him that, in the
face of the evidence, a man or a woman is innocent,
he'll plump for innocence, almost in the face of a
written confession. If you say, ' I know my wife
had lovers, but I just winked at it,' they'll all swell
up like pouter pigeons and say, ' Well, would I let
my wife carry on with another fellow, or several
other fellows, and sit tight and do nothing ? Gad,
sir, I would not ; and if that chap did, there's
something fishy about it. Either it was made
worth his while . . .' No, no, keep calm ! It ain't
going to help you to stand your trial for two
murders. . . . ' Or else he's a chap with a kink
and no damn good to the community at that.' You
knew your wife had a lover—no getting away from
that, because everybody else knew it, too—but you
were constantly urgin' her for the sake of the
chee-ild to give him the go-by and make you a
decent home. See ? Go to sleep saying that to
yourself, and by the time the trial comes on perhaps
you'll believe it."

Barton said in a very low tone, " Perhaps you
don't understand. I loved my wife."

" And that's another thing to keep to yourself.
These boarding-schools nowadays are so smart, they
teach the kids that love and hate are Siamese twins,
and that a man who's in love with his wife is much
more likely to strangle her than a man who just
realises that all marriages are like this, so what's
the good of losing any sleep about it, and there are

other women in the world, after all. That's a man after the jury's own heart. They know that sort of chap isn't going to risk swinging for any woman. Now, let's get down to it. You've destroyed the only proof that she did intend to leave you. What about the chap she was supposed to be going with ? "

" Fryer ? Well, I suppose he went down on the boat, too."

" You don't know ? "

" How could I ? But if she was going with him, it seems likely."

" Likely ? Any one can see you're not a lawyer. You don't know for certain that he is dead ? "

" No. How could I ? Have any proof, I mean."

" It didn't occur to you that perhaps when she didn't turn up he might think the whole thing was off ? "

" Why didn't he come down to find out why she wasn't there ? "

" There might be an obvious answer to that. Oh, yes, Barton, there could be."

Jack started up. " You mean, you think he . . . ? "

" Well, obviously someone committed murder, and clearly it wasn't you."

" You believe that—that I'm innocent ? " Jack flung a look of gratitude at his companion.

" Of course you're innocent. My clients are always innocent. They pay me for no other reason. I never defend a guilty man. If he should be found guilty, then the courts are at fault. But he never is. Though, like other men, I have my enemies, no one can ever say I don't earn my daily beer and board. Now, the point is that at the moment you never heard of Fryer again. He didn't write ? "

" Never."

" You'd know his writing ? "

" Yes. Yes, I'm sure I should."

" Did she have any letters from any one—after her death ? "

" I can't remember any."

" What about her old father ? "

" Oh, I wrote to him. He died a few months afterwards himself—he's been dying for ages—and there wasn't any one else. Anyway, she was never one for letters. I don't suppose a dozen people knew what her handwriting was like."

" I see." Crook's tone was peculiar. " Now, about luggage. Was it packed, ready to go ? "

" I never found any."

" Were there any cases missing ? "

" I didn't think."

" What about her handbag ? "

" I never found that."

" Didn't you think about it after you found her ? "

" I never thought of anything but her—and how to keep it from Margaret."

Crook glanced at the indecipherable notes he had made, and put a few supplementary questions.

" Now, you say you came back about seven. Why were you so late ? "

" I'd been to a Bing Crosby film, after the football. Bee knew I was going. She was very busy, she said, probably wouldn't be in when I got back, anyway."

" Any one go with you ? "

" No."

" Mention to any one you were going to the pictures ? "

" I dare say. I wouldn't remember who, though, not after all this time."

" It wouldn't be proof, anyhow. You got back between seven-ten and seven-fifteen and found your wife out."

" I found her letter——"

" Oh, yes, in the letter-box. Now can you remember how that letter ran ? "

" Pretty well." Jack fixed his gaze on a spot on the wall above the lawyer's head and began, like a child repeating a recitation :

" I am leaving this letter to let you know that I have gone away with Paul Fryer, and I shall not be coming back. I don't think you ever guessed, but we have been meeting ever since he left here—we couldn't help that, though he would if he could—and now the only thing for us to do is to go away somewhere where we can be together for good. So we cross to France to-night in the *Empress of Araby*. Paul has friends in Paris who will help him to find work, and we shall live out there. Perhaps I should tell you that I am expecting his child, and this has finally decided us. I always warned you you oughtn't to marry me. I was never meant to grow in a quiet border and go shopping in the Market on Saturday nights as my chief excitement of the week. Things will be much tidier without me, and anyway I must go. You have Margaret, who will look after you better than I ever did, but even if you hadn't got her I should go just the same. You can tell people what you like—I haven't spoken of it to any one—but probably the truth would be best. I haven't written to Margaret. I thought I'd leave that for you. A card has just come from her (that was a card I found in the box, with the letter, explained Jack), and she wants to come back quickly, so perhaps that would be best. You've always been kind to me, and I'm sorry that wasn't enough.

" And then just her name—Beatrice. She didn't
call herself Barton any more."

" I see. Now, this chap Fryer. Know anything
about him ? "

" He'd lodged with us for about a month when
he first came to Putney. That would be about six
months earlier. Then, at the end of about a month,
he said he had to make other arrangements."

" All quite pleasant ? "

" Perfectly. Of course, I knew why it was, though
neither he nor my wife said a word. I'd seen this
happen before, you see. I thought this meant he
was getting out while it was still all right."

" What sort of a chap was he ? "

" He was a gentleman," said Barton slowly. " I
don't mean to say I agree with those that tell you
it's fatal for a man of my sort to have a gentleman
lodging in the house, if he's got an attractive wife,
because if you've been in the war and seen every
one mixed up the way I did, you know that's all
bunk. And don't make the mistake of thinking
that it was his being a gentleman that made any
difference to Bee. She didn't think of men like
that, any more than men thought of her as not
being a lady—which, of course, she wasn't. Not
in your sense of the word, that is."

Crook maintained an admirable composure. He
knew that his definition of a lady might give Jack
Barton fits. " I didn't think at first there would be
any danger of Fryer falling for Bee. I knew a lot
of men did, but he wasn't so young, and there was
something about him—as if he'd had a lot of life
and it had died down. A quiet chap, a bit foreign-
looking, not handsome but sort of striking, if you
know what I mean. That is, he wouldn't say much,
just sit about looking a bit heavy. He was a biggish-

built man, about forty or not far off it, but somehow afterwards you'd remember he'd been there. It's a queer thing, I never remember anything he said, but he sticks in my memory as a clever sort of chap ; you know, good education—'Varsity, perhaps. He had a bit of French blood in him—I do remember that—and somehow he didn't look altogether English.

" Well, he was with us about a month when I began to notice this change in him. He didn't talk any more than he used to, but he looked as if you'd lighted him up. Not like a flame, not then, but as if there was a bit of fire stirring, and when I saw that, sir, I tell you I began to be afraid. I used to watch them, and though, as I say, it had happened before, I had a feeling it had never been quite like this. There was a play I heard of once, it was called *Yours Unfaithfully*, and that made me think of Bee. I know," he gulped a bit, " she wasn't faithful, but up till then it hadn't seemed to matter so much, because she had in a sense stopped mine. She wanted me, even though she had these other people, but after she met Fryer she didn't seem as if she needed me any more. It wasn't that she was unkind ; she just didn't seem to know I was there.

" I think Fryer tried to play straight. At all events, he got out. He was working at the Moorhouse Bank at the time, and he said he was transferred to another branch. I don't think I believed him, but so long as he got out I don't think I minded what reason he gave. It was queer. I hadn't known him very well or very long, but the house seemed less furnished without him in it.

" We didn't have another lodger, and I was glad about that, too. Then, quite by chance, I discovered that Bee was meeting Fryer outside, and I think after that I realised something was bound to happen."

" You mean, you knew she was going to leave you ? "

" I don't think I put it quite like that, even to myself, but I suppose that was actually what I was afraid of."

" How did you find out about their meeting ? "

" I happened to see them coming out of a Blooms-bury Hotel one afternoon."

" Did they see you ? "

" I don't think so. They hailed a taxi and drove off. He was the sort of chap that takes taxis. I used to take 'em now and again when I was home on leave during the war—they gave me a commission in 1918—but since the Armistice I could count the taxis I've taken, on my fingers."

" Did you ever find out anything about Fryer's past—his people, or whether he was married ? "

" No. He wasn't the chatty kind. I could see he'd come down in the world a bit. A man of his age isn't clerking in a Putney bank in the usual run of things ; but times aren't too easy, especially when you're not a young man any more, and there's no doubt about it, there aren't enough jobs to go round, and there's always someone waiting to bounce you out of yours. I thought maybe that's what had happened to him."

" Did you say anything to your wife about having seen her with her boy friend that afternoon ? "

Jack Barton winced. " No. What would have been the use ? She wouldn't deny it, and if I'd said I wouldn't stand for it she'd just have gone off."

" Had she any money of her own ? "

" People like her don't worry about money. They, so to speak, live from hand to mouth."

A remarkably polite way of putting it, thought

Crook in his vulgar fashion. He could have phrased
it equally accurately and with considerably less
elegance.

" So you said nothing ? "

" No."

" Was that what you usually did ? I mean,
hadn't you ever had a word with her about her pals
before this ? "

The accused man's face turned a deep, dreadful
red. " Yes, once, a long time ago, when I first began
to realise there were others. She was perfectly
honest about it. That only made things harder.
She said she was fond of me, but it wasn't any use
me trying to hold her. She was my wife, I know,
but she was more than that. I mean, that wasn't
enough for her. She had a zest for life I've never
found in any one else. If you'd met her you might
know what I mean. She had to keep the fire roaring,
and I wasn't enough. Do you understand ?

" I've always said she was a good wife to me,
though people think I'm crazy ; but, then, I
understood her. I don't mean I didn't feel it, but
I knew I'd rather have what she'd got to give me
than anything I could get from any other woman.
If I had to keep her on those terms—well, then,
I'd keep her. Even so I'd get more than I could
get in any other way. If it had ever come so that
I'd felt I couldn't stand any more, it would have
been me that I'd have put out, not her. But there'd
be months on end sometimes when everything would
be all right, and I learnt just to live for the day.
Anyhow, that's how most people live these days.
A week's a long time. And I've said before, and
I'll say it again, that I got more out of my marriage
than many a man who's so sure of his wife that he
knows next year will be just the same as this."

He fetched up short at the sight of Crook's, quizzical eye, and turned his own away.

" Spill all that to me if you like," the lawyer assured him, " but remember, the jury don't like a man to be out of the ordinary run. And remember, too, that they're just a lot of ordinary fellows whose wives are like the mackintoshes hanging in the hall, part of the house decoration, and they aren't going to fall for a chap whose wife is anything else. And when it's a wife who wasn't even faithful, they'll think it's disgustin'. You've no idea," he added earnestly, " never havin' had the chance of standin' a trial for murder before, how important respectability is. Let these chaps think you're the least out of the ordinary and they'll start whitewashin' the shed for you. That's a worse crime in their eyes than stranglin' half a dozen women. Now, I'm going to outline to you the case for the Crown and give you some idea what you're up against."

He proceeded to carry out this promise with a thoroughness that made Barton appear to shrink under his gaze. " One thing you're not to do, and that is let any one guess you had proof of her carryings-on. I take it you hadn't ? "

" Not actual proof, but I knew all right."

" All that matters at the Old Bailey is proof. Just remember that. Y'know," he added thoughtfully, " you were asking for it, thinking you could manage everything off your own bat. Amateurs are like that. Any one with a bit of experience would have told you that your one hope was to get the police, and get them pretty damn' quick."

" That was simply putting a rope round my neck," objected his client. " What could they have done, except arrest me for murder ? "

" Examined the trunk for fingerprints ; examined

the house ; taken prints from the letter your wife left ; looked for fingerprints on the door-handles ; looked for footprints anywhere where footprints would register. Check up with the neighbours to find out if any one had been seen comin' into the house that night. Checked up on your movements, given you a sportin' chance. And you might have had one then. Now you're expectin' me to work a miracle for you, as if I was one of the chaps with long beards in the Old Testament." He paused a moment, then added, " I suppose you didn't hear any gossip about him comin' to the house or anythin' that night ? "

Jack shook his head. " Not a word. And if any one had seen him it 'ud probably have leaked out. This place is as chatty as a village."

" You mean me to earn my fee, don't you ? " Crook congratulated him ironically. " I suppose every one believed your story ? "

" Of course."

Crook nodded. Then, almost as if it were an after-thought, he added, " Is it true, by the way—your story, I mean ? "

The other man stared. It was as though he could not believe his ears. " You ask me that ? But— but you're defending me, aren't you ? "

" That's why I asked you. I don't suggest you should put your cards on the table for any one's benefit but mine ; only if you were thinkin' of sleevin' an ace I wanted to warn you. Only a fool thinks he knows more than the law."

" I can take my oath, if you like," cried Jack fiercely.

But Crook shook his big, cynical head. " Keep that for the courts," he told him. " That kind of thing weighs more with a jury than it does with me."

CHAPTER TEN

A SNAPPER-UP OF UNCONSIDERED TRIFLES

" NICE case," said Crook cheerfully to Bill Parsons.
" Of course, every one will believe him guilty. Why
not ? Who else had any conceivable motive ?
What's more, we're goin' to have even more of a
job than we generally do cookin' up a motive in
another quarter. Why the hell should Fryer have
done it ? And if he's dead, which foot do we get
off on ? It's a pity Englishmen are so damned
sentimental. If you ask me, I don't believe that
Latin tag about speakin' no evil of the dead ever
started with the Romans. I believe they heard an
Englishman say it and turned it into their own
damned language afterwards. No other nation,
bein' such damned prigs, could be so damned dis-
honest. Why, a dead man's the only man ninety-
five per cent of the English ever dare malign. The
libel law in this country is too strong for anything
else."

Bill nodded sympathetically. " You would think
they'd have the sense to realise that you can't do
a corpse any harm, whatever happens, unless he's
the sort of chap who's been buried in the Abbey,
and then it's his relations and not himself who'd
mind if they turfed him out and shoved his head
—or whatever was left of it—on Tower Hill, or
whatever the proper procedure is. But they'll
simply start throwing cats if you suggest this was
his little job. And there's nothing to show, anyhow."

" Well, I know one thing : I'm not goin' to have

the police force goin' round sayin' they put one over on Arthur Crook," returned the lawyer explosively. " We'd better see what we can unearth about Fryer. After all, we don't even know that he's really dead. And if he ain't, and he did put the lady out of the way, you can't blame him for lyin' low ever since. Meanwhile, there's the girl— not that I anticipate gettin' anythin' useful out of her—and there's this nigger chap. He might be our trump card, even yet."

A single glance at Margaret Barton assured Crook that she would make the worst witness conceivable. Her aggressive determination to admit nothing that might further involve her father, her obvious bitterness against the dead woman, her caution and her inward doubt of her father's innocence, all of which were clear enough to a man of experience, would create a hopeless impression in the witness-box.

" What's the use of asking me any more questions ? " she demanded at once. " The police have been here already. I can't tell them anything, and I haven't anything to say to you."

" Sure ? " murmured Crook, thinking, " If this were my girl, I know where she'd get it." " Remember, I'm not the police. I'm out to see your father acquitted."

" But I wasn't even in the house. I never knew anything about my mother going till I got back on the Monday afternoon and my father told me she had gone."

" Quite so. But you'd been livin' there for years. You know a lot of things about your mother that no one else, perhaps not even her husband, knew."

" What do you mean ? "

126

" When you came back, had your father got rid of any of her belongings ? He said he intended to."

" No. He hadn't had a chance. It was Bank Holiday week-end. He'd only started collecting them, and I helped him to pack."

" Well, in the light of what's happened since, can you recall anything that struck you as odd ? I mean, supposing your mother had gone, as you naturally believed she had, did she leave anything behind you'd have expected her to take ? Did you notice any particular case being missing ? Had she packed all the clothes she'd be likely to want ? "

Margaret's attitude softened slightly. " I see what you mean. Well, as a matter of fact, I do remember saying to Father, ' I wonder what hat she wore,' because all the hats she had, so far as I knew, were still in the house. He seemed so distracted ; but that didn't surprise me, because the whole thing was such an appalling shock. He said, ' Perhaps she bought a new one.' There were other things, too, though. She had a fur coat that Father had bought for her. He knew a man in the trade. You'd be surprised if you knew the difference between the trade price and what they ask in the shops."

" It takes a lot more than that to surprise me," Crook assured her. " So she left that behind ? "

" Yes. I thought perhaps this other man was going to buy her one, or had bought one for her already. So that didn't surprise me so much. It was when I opened the drawers of her dressing-table and found that she'd left nearly all her creams and powders behind that I thought she must have gone off in a terrific hurry. Some of the pots were barely opened, and it wasn't like her not to think of them.

I don't mean she put on such an awful lot, but she took a lot of trouble. Anyway, any woman thinks of those things first."

" But still it didn't occur to you that perhaps she hadn't gone as far as the Continent ? "

" No, not even when I found her washing-things in a bag on the wash-hand stand. I just thought that something had happened to make her go off more suddenly than she meant, and she had decided she could buy new ones when she arrived. She was like that. It's called having no money sense."

" You're telling me," said Crook politely. " What about hairbrushes ? "

" They had gone. All the things off the dressing-table had gone. The brushes and the mirror and the clothes-brush."

" Was there anything particular about them, so that you'd know them again ? "

" They had pictures of shepherds and shepherd-esses on them, what they call a Watteau pattern, and Father had her initials worked into the pattern on the handle. Double B, all intertwined."

" Do you remember if there was a suitcase missing ? "

" Yes, a rather small one with a soft lid. I thought perhaps that was why she had left so many of her things, because they wouldn't get in ; but I should have expected her to take a hatbox as well."

" Do you remember any of the clothes that *were* missing ? "

Margaret considered. " Well, not all of them, of course. But there was a green georgette blouse with crimson silk embroideries like dice on the collar and the cuffs. That sounds rather gaudy, but actually it was lovely. And there was a green dress, too.

She loved green. Red-haired people generally do."

" What was the dress like ? "

Margaret began to describe it. " I could really draw it better," she suggested. " She made it herself ; and her dresses were never quite like any one else's." With a pencil she made a sketch on a bit of paper and handed it across the table. " I don't think I remember anything else specially. It's rather a long time ago," she added.

" So long that both the blouse and the dress are as dead as mutton by this time, but you never can tell when trifles will help. What happened to her other things ? "

" We sent them to some people who were asking for clothes for poor clergy or something."

" Anyway, that wouldn't help us now, so long as you're sure the green blouse and dress weren't among them."

" I'm quite sure."

" Right. Now. Can you remember what time you arrived on Bank Holiday afternoon ? "

" About three o'clock. Father wasn't expecting me, and he seemed surprised and, more than that, put out, as if my coming had upset some plan of his. I remember I asked him what was the matter, and he seemed to pull himself together, and said it was all right, he'd had a shock, and I must be prepared for a shock, too, and then he told me about mother."

" Was it a shock to you ? "

" Not as much as to him. I'd felt it couldn't go on like this for ever. You see, I was bound to hear the gossip that went round about her, and even if I hadn't, the girls at school would have told me. There was one girl who said she couldn't ask me to tea, because my mother was a bad woman and her mother wouldn't like it. I asked Father what she meant, but he only said that a woman who loved other people and made other people happy couldn't be really bad, and when I was older I'd understand better. And later on there was a boy I used to go for walks with, and there was another girl who had wanted him, and she came and said I'd stolen him, and I was just like my mother. And after that I think I knew what they meant."

"This chap Fryer," continued Crook, without comment. "Remember anything about him?"

"Not much. He was there such a little time I didn't know about her meeting him afterwards. In a way, I think, I was glad when she did go. I thought when Father got over it he'd be able to settle down. Because, up till then, it had been awful for him, never being sure."

"And did he seem to settle?"

"No. At first he was like someone who's half out of his mind. Of course, now I understand why. How he stood it, knowing she was down there . . . But nobody ever guessed. I thought he was crazy because she'd gone with this man, but I just waited, and felt presently he'd accept it; because, you see, they were both dead, we thought, which made it easier for him than if she'd been alive. And it was something that she couldn't suggest coming back— ever. Then he married Jean, and he got better, and I think sometimes he'd forget about her for weeks on end. Jean did want him to leave the house and take another, because she thought he wouldn't remember her so well then. But he said, ' No, no. That's impossible. Never ask me that again.' And I don't suppose she ever did."

"She didn't attach any special meanin' to that?"

"I suppose she thought, as I did, that he didn't

want to leave *her* house. He was awfully fond of her, in spite of everything. Oh, how he bore it . . ."

" Human nature's surprisin'ly adaptable," Crook assured her grimly. " Most likely he was chiefly bothered in case any one ever dug her out. Now, did you go all over the house as soon as you got back ? "

" I went in and out of all the rooms. I didn't go down to the cellar, if that's what you mean."

" Supposin' the suitcase with the brushes in it had been in the house, could he have hidden it ? "

" Only if it had been in the cellar."

" Of course, he might have got rid of it earlier."

" That sounds as though you think he might have done it. He didn't, he didn't."

" Well, all right. I'm goin' to tell the world he didn't. Only, if by any chance he did, I've got to be prepared. Look here, don't you open your mouth about any of this. In a murder trial it's the things that aren't said that are quite as important as the things that are."

And, leaving her inarticulate with rage, he took his leave.

The police had taken no definite steps against Mr. William Jones, although they had him under surveillance. He was not any longer looking for employment, one of the more enterprising organs of the Yellow Press having offered him a retaining fee to write up his story of Beatrice Barton's death, so far as he knew anything about it, should Barton find himself condemned for murder. If Barton were acquitted, then the paper would cut its losses, but the odds in favour of the Black Cap were about forty to one. Mr. Jones, for business as well as for personal reasons, clung to his assertions of the prisoner's guilt, and openly hoped that he would hang for the crime. He made no secret of his attitude to Crook, nor did he attempt to conceal his fury at being interviewed by the Defence.

At first he shut up his thin mouth and refused to answer questions.

" No sense in bein' that sort of a fool," the lawyer assured him. " You're one of the chief witnesses in the case."

" I do not think so," contradicted Jones resentfully. " Now that the fellow has admitted that he put the woman in the cellar, my evidence is not required."

" It may not be required by the Crown, but it's goin' to be required by the Defence," Crook told him in robust tones.

" I do not understand. You cannot force me . . ."

" Can't we ? You just wait. We'll utter a subpœna on your account, and if you don't appear you can be committed for contempt of court."

His companion, who had little knowledge of the intricacies of British law, although he had suffered from its action, looked at him in a sulky silence.

" So you've got that straight ? " suggested Crook, with cheerful brutality.

" What is it that I am supposed to do ? "

" Just answer a few questions, and don't spend your time thinkin' up any fancy bits. I'm a plain man and the plain truth's good enough for me. Now, then, I know the first part, about you lookin' out of the window like one of these film stars and seein' my man handlin' his lady-wife, so we can skip that. You told the police you could see clearly into the room."

" I could see most clearly," protested Jones huffily.

" And you saw Barton at the window ? "

" Yes. I saw him so well that I knew him **again** at once."

" What was the next thing you saw ? "

" I saw him with the woman in the box. . . ."

" Half a minute. Did you see him open the box ? "

Mr. Jones hesitated. " You're goin' to be asked this on oath, so you'd better make up your mind," Crook informed him.

Mr. Jones replied with dignity, " I am telling only the truth."

" Very wise of you. I mean, you'd be a fool to try anything else with me. Well ? "

" I saw him open the box."

" You must have quite remarkable powers of eyesight."

" He had the light on, and I was a little higher than he."

" Meanin' you were on the window-sill, wondering if it was safe to make a bolt for it ? "

" That does not matter."

" Everything matters," Crook assured him truculently. " Now, then, you saw him open the box, and you saw the woman in it ? "

" Yes."

" You didn't see him put her in ? "

" No, she was already there."

" And what happened next ? "

" He seemed to be trying to take her out."

" I wonder what he did that for. I mean, you would think, having got her safely parked, he'd have left her there. Was the box unfastened ? "

" He undid a strap. That I also saw."

" D'you believe in Providence ? " asked **Crook** unexpectedly.

" In Providence ? "

" That's what I said. Because if you did, you might think Providence had sent you there on that particular morning."

" That I might see him and know what he had done ? "

" It could be," admitted Crook, " it could be. Now, then, he tried to lift her out of the box. Did he get her right out ? "

" No. After a minute he pushed her back, and he closed down the lid, and he strapped it and then he began to pull the box away."

" En route for the cellar, presumably ? "

" That is what I should suppose."

" H'm. It sounds a bit queer to me."

The Eurasian stiffened. " If you doubt my word, sir . . ."

" I didn't say so." Crook's voice was as smooth as milk. " But, you know, if I'd laid a lady out on Saturday, I wouldn't be sleeping in the room where she was boxed up, and I wouldn't want to open the box again nearly forty-eight hours later. You say you saw very well. Could you see his face ? "

" I tell you, the light was on. I saw everything."

" What should you say his expression was like ? "

" He was—horrified. He was like a man who cannot believe what he sees."

" Not like the face of a man who expects to find the body of his wife in a box ? "

His companion said sulkily, " I do not know. I cannot say."

" Did he shut the box at once, or did he put anything in ? "

" He put nothing in that I could see."

" And you say you saw everything, so the odds

are he didn't put anything in. Anyhow, they didn't
find anything there, except her."

" Why should he put anything in ? "

" Why should he open the box at all ? Why
should he lug the lady into the boxroom, instead of
lugging the box along to wherever the lady was ?
It's a queer story, Jones."

" I know nothing of that. I know only what
I saw."

" Quite. By the way, you didn't think of mentioning this to the police at the time ? "

" It was not my affair."

" That shows the democratic principle carried to
the nth degree. What you really mean is there
wasn't anything in it for you at the time. Or
weren't you really sure ? "

" I was quite sure."

" And when you came out of chokey you didn't
see why you shouldn't turn your knowledge to some
account ? Enterprising, ain't you ? "

" I do not understand."

" I suppose it didn't occur to you that they might
have taken you as accessory after the crime ? It
happens to be the law in this country that if you
see a fellow involved in a murder you're supposed
to lend a hand. That's what good citizens do. Know
the good citizen's catechism, Jones ? What is your
duty, N. or M. Answer : My duty is to assist the
police in all possible ways, whether to my own
detriment or otherwise. Y'know, you're lucky not
to be standing in the dock for the second time."

" This is a waste of time," cried Mr. Jones angrily.
" I can tell you nothing, nothing at all."

" You've told me a whole heap," Crook assured
him. " In fact, I wouldn't be surprised if you were
my star witness. It's lucky for me you were pinched

that day, because it establishes the date beyond all doubt. And that may be the turning-point of the whole affair."

The next witness on his list was Mrs. Lewis, the neighbour who had occupied No. 10 Arbutus Avenue at the time of the murder, but here he met with an unexpected check. Mrs. Lewis' husband had died some five years previously, and she had disappeared. No one knew anything of her. Another neighbour believed that her only daughter had married and gone to Canada. It was possible that Mrs. Lewis had accompanied her, or gone out later to join her. On the other hand, she might be in the cemetery, in some other man's house, under another name (Crook's way of saying she might have remarried), or be in an asylum. There didn't seem any way of finding out, although he employed scouts to track her down. They all came back, as he observed, like Noah's dove on its first excursion from the Ark, without bringing so much as an olive-twig in their hands.

Nobody else seemed able to tell them anything at all. Still, Crook did his best. He found Harvey, the man who had been present when Barton made his spectacular announcement in the Bird In Hand on that momentous Sunday morning, and Harvey said that every one knew how good Barton had been to his wife, and how devoted he was. If he'd wanted to knock her on the head, she had given him plenty of previous opportunities. Also, the dead woman had been of muscular build, whereas Barton was a little chap who had never been known to kill so much as an earwig.

" Now, then," said Crook to his ally, Bill Parsons, when he had made all these inquiries, " let's see what we've got."

He laid out his results, his facts and his theories, like a woman coming back from the Sales with all manner of bits and pieces from the bargain counters.

" If I had anything to do with the making of laws—only, naturally, they wouldn't think of consulting a lawyer—I'd let any man who'd got away with a crime for more than five years have a free pardon. It's putting too much of a strain on us to expect us to unearth evidence after that time. Still, as we don't live by the law of common sense, we must make the best show we can. In Barton's favour are his feeling for his wife and the fact that on Monday, two days after she was killed, she still wasn't in the cellar. If I killed a woman, or if you did, and we meant to put her underground, we'd do it right away. And we certainly wouldn't open a window of a room that we knew could be over-looked and put on a light and then open up the box containin' the corpse. If he'd wanted to swing he couldn't have staged things better. You'd have thought even a romantic chap like Barton would have disposed of her in the dark. He'd had Saturday night and Sunday night to do it. Anything else in his favour ? "

" This chap, Mullins, couldn't get in at six o'clock. That sounds as if she was out of the way by then."

" Barton can show that he wasn't in the house then. He says he went to the pictures ; but we can't check up on that, not after ten years. That don't help us much."

" The toilet articles weren't packed."

" The Crown will argue he was in such a stew he forgot about them. The suitcase had to be disposed of as soon as possible. He might have done something with it that evening. He wasn't actually seen till nine, when he came out of the house."

" He wasn't carrying the suitcase then ? "

" No, but, then, he hardly would be. He had Sunday."

" Not so much of Sunday. He wasn't up at ten-thirty."

" Meaning he'd left the milk and paper on the doorstep ? That's probably right. A chap like that would automatically take them in, even if he was going out. He'd do it without thinking. Well, they were there at ten-thirty, and he was at the Bird In Hand at twelve. Suppose he'd packed the case overnight, supposing it wasn't all packed for him— and it couldn't have been, or she'd have put in the creams and spongebag—he could have carried it out any time after half-past ten and lost it before twelve. If you wanted to hide a suitcase, Bill, what would you do with it ? "

Bill considered. " You could put it in a station cloakroom ; but if you'd murdered its owner, the odds are you wouldn't in case you were recognised as the chap that took it there. You could drop it it out of a train window ; but you wouldn't do that either, because it 'ud be found on the line. You might take it out and drop it in a quarry, and it might never be found there ; but there ain't so many quarries round about Putney, and he'd be afraid of being seen with it a minute longer than he could help."

" There's the river, of course." Crook took up the tale. " Putney's handy for the river ; but, 'smatter of fact, that sort of thing happens more often in fiction than in fact. If you're trying to shy away a key you might get rid of it without bein' noticed, but a suitcase is a different affair. If you drop it in from the bank the odds are that it'll be washed up on the next tide and questions will be asked—uncommonly inconvenient questions, too. She may not have had her name stitched into her cami-knicks, but there were those brushes, with her initials on them, and the famous green georgette blouse with the crimson facings. And you can't shy a bag off a bridge without someone seeing you. Putney's such an occupied part of the river, too. Nicely lighted, with plenty of craft on the river, and nosey parkers all over the place. " Why, you can't put yourself in the river, unless you're lucky—not in London, I mean—without a dozen chaps hopping in after you to pull you out. And if he walked along the bank carrying the suitcase he might be remembered. It was a Sunday, y'see, when none of his pals were at work. Dessay a lot of them were lounging round waiting for the Bird In Hand to open. And when it gets a bit less crowded, there are the anglers. Considering how difficult it is to lose a piece of luggage, it's amazing how many do contrive to get lost in the course of a year. Well, that only leaves one answer. Of course, he could have tried hiding it in the garden, but he don't seem to have had much opportunity for that. He wasn't back from Harvey's till four o'clock, and it began rainin' after that, and it went on rainin' all night and all the next day. No, I can only find one answer. Where does a wise man hide a leaf ? In the forest. And where does a wise murderer hide a bag ? With a lot of other bags. It was Bank Holiday season, remember. Dump your bag on the platform and leave it there, and it won't be recognised as lost luggage till evening. Then it'll be jammed in the Lost Property Office. After a time, when it's not claimed, it'll be sold off. Well, you might find out who bought it, but the proverbial needle in the bundle of hay is child's play by com-

parison. Still, there is the trump card that Providence likes to play on behalf of Justice so we could
put out a few flies. There are the brushes ; though
how it'll help us to find them I don't quite see yet.
Still, I've never had a piece put on the board I
couldn't use, somehow, so you can get ahead, and
I'll see what can be done about Mr. Paul Fryer.''

" There's another point that struck me as queer,"
contributed Bill, " and that was the letter in the
letter-box. You've have expected to find it on
the table."

" If she'd written it and put it out, you would.
But she didn't get as far as addressing the envelope.
You know what a blank envelope conveys to most
chaps. Another of these damned advertisements of
money-lenders or breakfast-foods, and into the
basket it goes. Whoever's responsible for this little
job meant to be sure that Jack Barton found that
letter. Being in the box, he'd be more likely to
open it. That explains that, I fancy. Well, Bill,
you do what you can. I don't mind who you
implicate, not if it's one of the Crowned Heads of
Europe, and it won't take you long to run through
those. Roll, bowl or pitch, every time a blood
orange or a good cigar. Only find me someone to
take Jack Barton's place while I go after this
fellow Fryer."

Bill grinned. " Nice case," he observed. You're
after a stiff and I'm after a set of brushes with a
double B on the handle that nobody's seen for
nine years. Well, I'll say we earn our keep."

His lame foot dragging a little behind him, he
crossed to his desk and began to draft an
advertisement.

CHAPTER ELEVEN

THE LONG TRAIL

At the bank where Fryer had been employed for a couple of months the manager said in patronising tones that it was improbable that any one would remember him.

" If he was only one of the temporary clerks . . . staffs change so much and so often," he pointed out. " The man who was manager at that time, a fellow called Barstow, died a couple of years ago. Even so, I doubt whether he'd recall him."

" I suppose you keep records," snapped Crook. " And if you've never heard his name before, believe me, you're going to hear a hell of a lot about it now. Now, then, what staff have you got now that was here then ? Perhaps their memories ain't so mouldy as some I know."

The manager was furious. " He almost demanded my marriage lines," Crook told Bill with a chuckle, for he is a man who is wedded to his work and has little use beyond it for women. Besides, except where beer is concerned, he is apt to be mean, and women are so damned expensive, even the least assuming of them.

One of the clerks, himself a middle-aged man, said he remembered Fryer quite well.

" There was something about him," he said impressively. " A queer chap. Always thought he had something on his mind."

" He didn't confide in you ? " suggested Crook.

The clerk—his name was Willoughby, and it was the only aristocratic thing about him—said he wasn't

141

one for being nosey ; but if you were a student of human nature, as he, George W., was, you put two and two together.

" Confound this free education," fumed Crook. " Before there were any Board Schools every fool who could afford himself a bowler hat didn't imagine he was a mathematical genius. Why, the number of men per cent who can add two and two correctly can be counted on the fingers of one hand, and that's obeying the Biblical convention that ' the greatest of these is charity.' Why can't these chaps be satisfied with foozling other chaps' accounts and leave proper arithmetic to the few that understand it ? "

But for all that, he listened with apparent courtesy while Willoughby unfolded his deductions.

" There was something fishy about him," he declared. " I knew it from the start. To begin with, what was a chap of that age doing in a junior job at a bank ? He was forty, if he was a day, a sullen, haunted-looking chap. You see his kind on the pictures in these psychological crime films. I wouldn't be surprised to know that the police had heard of him in another name. Don't ask me how he got his job here. Pulling strings, I've no doubt. He was competent, too—too dashed competent. And about as communicative as an oyster. You know how it is with most fellows—after a time they do open up about themselves. But to hear him talk, he might have been born last week and have no history at all. Married ? I've no idea. He might be a bigamist, for all I know. He was more like a machine than a man, just turned up on the dot and knocked off work as the clock ticked the hour. Didn't take any interest in anything, so far as you can judge. I thought myself he had a queer look, as if he was always hiding something. And I dare say he was. Anyway, he didn't stay long. Some trumped-up yarn about getting a transfer. Don't tell me. I've been in the bank all my life . . ."

" And never got further than polishing your pants on a high stool," reflected Crook, but not maliciously. Crook is kind to those whom he despises ; he considers them unworthy of anything else.

" He got out because he had to get out, and he got out damned quick."

Crook paid his man the compliment of looking a little surprised.

" What d'you mean by that ? Something wrong with the accounts ? "

Willoughby coloured quickly. " No, no."

" Well, then ? "

" What I mean is that he'd been monkeying with this chap's wife, and I dare say he found the going a bit hot."

" So you knew about him and Mrs. Barton ? "

Willoughby sniggered. " He wasn't the first lodger the Bartons had had."

" Nasty bit of work," decided Crook, adding aloud, " Never thought of lodging there yourself, I suppose ? No, I thought as much." He grinned at the fellow's angry discomfiture and marched out. Nothing that Willoughby had told him amounted to a row of pins ; but he had rather better luck with a less obtrusive member of the staff, a man called Thomas, who knew the address where the missing man had lodged after leaving Arbutus Avenue. These rooms were over a chemist's shop in the High Street, and thither Crook repaired.

The landlady was a harried, dried-up woman with a dyspeptic complexion, who stared at the

big red-faced stranger and said, " Fryer ?   Fryer ?
I don't know any one of that name."

" He lodged here some years ago."

" How many years ago ? " She did not invite
him in, but kept him on the well-trodden mat
outside the front door.

" In 1930."

" Well, he may have done, but I don't remember
him. People come and go. . . ."

" A big dark chap, employed at the bank. A bit
of a foreigner."

She shook her head. " My sister might have
remembered him. She had a better mind for faces
than I have."

" Then perhaps I could see her."

" She's gone to her rest these three years."

Crook reflected ungratefully that heaven had an
inconvenient knack of abstracting the useful witnesses and leaving the fools.   " You perhaps have
the Visitors' Book for that year ? "

" My sister had one, of course. You have to, by
law. But now . . ."

" Of course, you would have had a new one since
then."

She passed a thin hand over her lined forehead,
automatically smoothing back her dry, colourless
hair. " I don't know. I didn't carry on with the
lodgers after I lost her. Just one lady, who boards
with me. . . ."

" Cheerful for the one lady," thought Crook, and
asked again if she thought she could unearth the
record of visitors.

Grudgingly she invited him in and put him in
the bleak passage with its green pottery vase of
mauve and white everlastings, while she went
through a grained wooden door and began tossing

papers about. Crook decided that there must be something in the old proverb that Providence looks after fools and children ; otherwise this woman would long ago have had her sticks sold up, through sheer incompetence and lack of method. After a long time she came out, carrying a tatterdemalion book in her hands.

" This seems to be it. When did you say it would be ? "

" Some time in February, 1930."

Miss Grover turned the pages with maddening clumsiness. She was short-sighted, and when she reached the approximate date she pored over the pages as if she were trying to lick up the signatures, as her companion inelegantly put it.

" Paul Fryer," she said at last. " Would that be the man ? " Then she looked at him. " Why do you want to know ? " she asked breathlessly. " Who are you ? "

" We are trying to trace this man Fryer," Crook told her with commendable patience. " We don't know for certain whether he is dead or alive. I am a lawyer representing his wife . . ."

" But even if he was alive in 1930, that doesn't mean he's alive now."

" Sure it doesn't," Crook agreed, " but you might have some address for him—some link—something I could get on to. This is the last definite address I know. He's believed to have gone abroad."

She said in her sad voice, " If only my sister were here. She was always the business head. I miss her so much."

" What is your record of this chap ? " Crook dragged her back to the present.

" Just Paul Fryer. He seems to have come on the 2nd February and left on the 4th March."

" You've no note where he went ? "

" There is something here against his name. I don't know what it means."

Crook took the book out of her hands. Against the man's name was a scrawl in his own writing, " Gorleston House Hotel, W.C."

" Was that the address he left for his letters ? "

" Perhaps it was. Yes, it was. I remember now that Maud said I ought never to have let him put it in the book. She was very particular, was my sister. But he put it in in case we forgot. It happened that Maud was away for two or three days when he left—I remember now—he had to go very suddenly, and he paid me a week's lodging instead of notice. Wait a minute. It's coming back." She stood with both hands pressed against her forehead, like an impromptu prophetess. " Something about a job," she said. He was a very strange man. Even Maud couldn't get him to talk. But there was something about him. . . ." She brooded.

" There must have been," Crook agreed heartily.

" What do you mean by that ? "

" It's almost ten years since you saw him, and you remember him, though you must have had a lot of other lodgers passing through your hands."

" I remember about that address. He said if any letters came I was to be sure to send them on, but not tell any one where he had gone. I remember Maud didn't like that. She said honest people didn't have to cover up their movements like that. And she said she wouldn't be surprised to know that he was wanted . . ."

" By the police ? "

Maud seemed to think so. " You're not the police, are you ? " Her eyes widened in acute apprehension.

" I told you . . ."

" Oh, yes, I remember. His wife. I didn't know he had a wife. Perhaps that's what he meant about not giving the address. . . . You don't think we shall have the police here, do you ? "

" I doubt it. But you wouldn't mind, would you ? I mean, it's not your fault if he got into queer company."

He had thought her colourless before, but now she seemed to turn paler yet.

" I don't like the police meddling in my affairs. It's—it's un-English."

" If they did come they'd only ask exactly the same questions as I have. But you needn't worry. They won't. They're not interested in him, whatever he may have done, not after all this time."

" You're sure ? "

" I'm sure."

" Interesting life," he told himself as he thumped down the stairs and turned towards the station. " You wouldn't guess a woman like that had a thing to hide, but there's something, or I'm a Dutchman. Wonder if she bumped Sister Maud off ? I should say she was a damned unpleasant woman to live with."

However, as no one was paying him to inquire into this mystery, he put the lady and her affairs out of his mind and turned his face towards Bloomsbury, where Fryer had presumably concealed himself.

Gorleston House Hotel was one of those boarding-houses that like to describe themselves on their prospectuses as select private hotels, with which London W.C.1 is honeycombed. It had the usual terra-cotta porch supported by pillars, the usual deep basement with bars at the windows, the usual narrow hall with dubious shiny wallpaper smooth with the dirt and smells of years, the usual bead curtain that concealed the entrance to the kitchen quarters without neutralising the odour of smoking fat and stale vegetables, the usual grained wooden doors, the everlasting hair carpet secured by cheap wooden rods, the inevitable lithographs over the worst stains on the walls, the mahogany hatstand that has become a period piece. Crook could have described it backwards in his sleep.

This house had changed hands twice in the last twelve years, and nobody here knew anything about Fryer at all. Crook pursued his inquiries in vain. The present owners were a fat, shiftless couple, probably a butler who had married the house-keeper on joint savings and perquisites, and they carried the business on in a slipshod manner that allowed of no interest whatsoever in their boarders or their concerns. No, they said, they hadn't got the Visitors' Book for 1930. They'd only taken over in 1937.

" There might be somebody among your boarders," Crook suggested, but they said sharply that they had taken over nothing from their predecessors, neither boarders nor servants.

" A clean sweep," said the greasy, fat proprietor. " That's what we decided on, a clean sweep. It's always best."

They didn't know the names of any of the boarders of that period or the servants.

" Nothing for it but the press," Crook assured himself, hailing a taxi, since he wouldn't have to pay for it ultimately, and driving to Somerset House. Here, after some labour, he learned that Paul Theodore Fryer had married Kathleen Valentine Hope in 1925.

" What we've got to do now is find out if she's

in the land of the living," he told Bill Parsons. " That's where the press can lend a hand. Something short and snappy, but allurin'—that's what we've got to aim at." " Sounds like an advertisement of ladies' underwear," was Bill's languid comment.

Then they got down to it, and after some discussion prepared an advertisement that subsequently appeared in the agony column of three of London's leading papers :

" Information sought regarding KATHLEEN VALENTINE FRYER, wife of the late PAUL FRYER, believed to have been drowned on board the *Empress of Araby*, April 28, 1930. Information to Box No. ——."

" There's a smell of money about that," Crook said complacently. " P'raps someone's left this chap a legacy, and it 'ud go to his next-of-kin."

" Always supposing he has any."

" The chap isn't born that hasn't got a next-of-kin. The luck don't run that way even for the best of us. I've got a married sister myself. Sends me little tracts about Wine is a Mocker, Strong Drink is Raging, and diagrams of a drunkard's stomach in three colours. Thinks I'm such a fool I don't see through her. A fat lot she cares about my immortal soul. It's my mortal money-bags she's got her eye on. And she watches them so hard, her eyes are half poppin' out of her head ; and I don't like those bulgin' eyes, Bill. They give me bad dreams. On my sam, they do. Well, well, to come back to what I was saying. Some eye will fall on that paragraph and 'ull see money there. Human nature's the same, whatever shape it wears. Don't tell me people don't care about cash. I'm too downy a bird to be caught like that these days. Ever noticed that it takes a rich man to be a philanthropist ? Well, well, what more d'ye want ? "

On the third day after the advertisement had appeared, a reply was received at the offices of the paper.

" If the inquirer for Mrs. Paul Fryer will state his reasons for wishing to hear more of her whereabouts, he may learn something of advantage. Address reply to Box —— "

" Regular cat-and-mouse game," observed Crook. He took two thick sheets of blank paper, placed them in a handsome square hand-made envelope and addressed them to the box number in question. He then installed a scout to watch the inquiry desk and report developments. The morning following the receipt of the letter a young woman in a neat black dress called at the offices of the paper and asked for any correspondence marked Box No. 189. The scout trailed her to a block of flats in Marylebone, and saw her vanish into a door on the second floor. On consulting the register he saw that this flat was rented by a Mrs. Kathleen Hope.

" Sounds like our bird," Crook told Bill Parsons. " She's gone back to her maiden name. Either there was a divorce or a definite split and she dropped his surname. Perhaps she was afraid he'd sponge, or she may just be one of these strongminded women. Well, we'll soon know."

The same afternoon he called in person at the flat, and the neat young woman opened the door. Crook asked for Mrs. Hope.

" What name, please ? "

Crook produced his card, and after a momentary hesitation he was admitted into the hall. The flat, he decided, was worth about a hundred and fifty a year. If this was indeed Paul Fryer's wife or widow, she either had private means or a private backer. He had reached this stage in his speculations when the young woman returned to say that Madam never saw visitors unless they stated their business.

" Tell her it's in connection with the letter you fetched from the offices of the *Morning Record*," replied Crook blandly.

The young woman looked startled, but said nothing. As Crook had anticipated, this reply brought the lady of the flat on the scene. Or, rather, she gave instructions for Crook to be admitted. It was obvious at once that she did not care greatly for his appearance. Mrs. Fryer, like her husband, according to reports received to date, was a striking-looking woman, tall, severe, and full of a brooding vitality. She had a long, thin hand that gripped like whipcord, and an incisive voice that cut like a knife.

" But a well-bred knife," reflected Crook, privately thinking this pretty good, for he has none of the fine shades of education. Nor, indeed, does he desire them, holding that education is responsible for five-sixths of the ills to which mankind is heir.

" Mr.—er—Crook ? " Crook bowed. " I haven't, naturally, the slightest idea why you thought it necessary to play this very childish trick on me (by which she meant the blank sheets), but perhaps you will tell me why you wish to get into touch with Mr. Fryer ? "

" Mrs. Fryer ? " queried Crook.

She took him up sharply : " My name is Hope."

" Once married to Paul Fryer ? "

She hesitated.

" There are records," suggested Crook delicately.

She shrugged. " Very well. But I still don't understand . . ."

" We're tryin' to trace him. You might be able to help."

" What do you want with him ? "

" Just to know if he's livin' or late."

She stiffened at the frivolity, the unprofessional note of the conversation.

" Why do you wish to know ? "

" Important case pending," Crook told her. " He'd be an interested party, unless, of course, he's where there is neither sorrow nor pain."

" Which case is that ? "

" If you haven't proof that he's alive, the matter wouldn't arise."

" Do you know anything about him at all ? "

" I know he was scheduled to sail on the *Empress of Araby* about nine years ago. If he did—well, that's that. But if he didn't, then he's an important man. Seein' you've assumed your maiden name, it may be safe to suppose he's livin'."

She was startled by that implication. " What does that mean ? "

" Ladies generally do that when they want to disown a livin' husband. Dead, it don't matter."

He was aware that his companion was simply ravening with curiosity.

" I take it you mean you are being employed as a private inquiry agent." She rapped out the words, and Crook knew she was thinking that men engaged in that capacity should have at least a superficial appearance of gentlemanliness, and not look obvious bookie's touts.

" It could be," he allowed, " it could be."

" Who is it who's so anxious to know about my

husband ? " She was the kind that has to be wrung like a damp cloth to get anything out of her.

" Me," said Crook simply.

" I shall send for the police," she began in an indignant voice.

" I would," Crook agreed. " They mostly know me."

That called her bluff, as he had anticipated.

" You can't expect me to discuss my husband with you until I know a little more about things," she urged in more reasonable tones.

Crook suddenly tossed his cards on to the table. " I'm a lawyer representing Jack Barton in the Putney cellar crime, and your husband, if he's alive, will be called as one of the witnesses."

He saw the red come furiously into her check. " What has my husband to do with that ? "

" He was elopin' with the lady."

" Ridiculous ! "

" Most of Putney knew about it. Oh, we haven't given that to the press yet. Don't do to treat the press like a favourite kid and feed it cake all the time. But it's a fact, and everybody's goin' to know soon."

" But—since she didn't sail . . ."

" Because she couldn't. Well, we want to know why she couldn't."

" She was dead. I've read the case."

" She was dead, all right. We want to know a bit more about it, though."

" You're not suggesting my husband could have had any hand in the murder ! "

" It was you that suggested that, remember, not me."

" If you don't mean that, why are you here ? "

" Because he knew her rather better than any

one else at that time, and he might be able to suggest someone. . . ."

" I thought the husband had done it."

" So do the police—at present."

" And you think you know better than the police ? "

" It wouldn't be the first time I'd wiped their eyes. Oh, it's all right. That's what I'm paid for."

She set her mouth in a line like a slit in a pie, as Crook put it to himself.

" I can't tell you anything."

" Too bad," agreed Crook, taking up his appalling billycock hat. " P'raps you'll remember a bit more when you're on oath."

" What do you mean ? "

" You'll be subpœnaed at the trial."

" But it's nothing to do with me."

" He's still your husband."

" I've told you I don't know where he is."

" I haven't asked you where he is—only if he's still alive."

" Even if I did know he was alive two years ago, that's no proof."

" It brings us seven years nearer. Where was he then ? "

" I hadn't seen him for years, and it was the merest chance I saw him then."

" I'm always telling the world that chance is the ace of trumps. Where was he ? "

She clenched her fist and brought it thumping down upon the table. Crook's sympathies, which had throughout this interview been for the missing husband, increased tenfold.

" I don't intend to be involved in this affair."

" That's one of the snags about marriage. You

never know where it may land you. Still, if you had the gumption to tell me anything you know as to his whereabouts you could probably fade right out of the picture. After all, I see your point. There's no question about it that Fryer was Mrs. Barton's lover. And people ain't kind, no—I have to hand it to them for that—they're not kind. Things may have changed since Shakespeare's time, but my experience is that the quality of mercy is strained like a violin string in ninety-nine cases out of a hundred."

She threw in her hand, still scarlet with rage. " I'll tell you what I know. It isn't much. I had no dealings with my husband for three years before he disappeared ; that is, before he was supposed to be going on board the *Empress of Araby*. And I saw nothing of him for seven years afterwards. But I do know he wasn't drowned on board, because two years ago I saw him in London, in Park Lane. He was in a big car, turning out of Park Lane into Greatorex Square."

" You didn't speak ? No, I suppose you couldn't if he was a passenger. Or was he driving ? "

" He was driving."

" Alone ? "

She said in very distinct tones, " He was driving—in uniform. There was a woman in the back of the car."

" Notice her at all ? " But of course she had. A woman always noticed any other woman her husband was with.

" A very showy kind of person." No words could describe the disdain of Kathleen Fryer's voice. " A very showy outfit altogether, a crimson car, and Paul—my husband—wore crimson livery, like a commissionaire outside a picture-house. It

155

was deplorable, the whole thing. I only trust he wasn't using his own name."

" It was after that you changed yours ? " suggested Crook astutely.

She looked sullen, opened her mouth as if to reply, and then closed it again.

" Would you know the lady ? "

" I should hardly think so."

" Nothing special about her ? "

His companion lifted her long, aristocratic nose. " She was one of those people that like to wear very ostentatious jewellery. I dare say it wasn't real ; but if so, it was all the more ridiculous to flaunt it."

" It's always more foolish to flaunt the real thing," Crook assured her soberly. " The real jewel thief always knows a fake piece, and no one's going to risk a rope neck-tie for the best imitation that was ever made. What was this piece ? "

Mrs. Fryer opened her hands in a gesture of disgust. " Oh, an enormous affair like a fountain, all green stone and paste, like something out of a cracker."

" You didn't happen to notice the number of the car ? "

" I am neither a policeman nor a book-keeper."

" Or whether the car stopped in Greatorex Square ? "

" Certainly not. I was not interested."

" Well, I am ; and the odds are it did, because the Square happens to be a cul-de-sac. Well, I'm very grateful to you, and I hope I shan't have to bother you again."

" In any case, I am going abroad shortly. . . ."

" You'll leave me your address ? I mean, it's expensive enough bringing witnesses back, but when you have to find them first. . . ."

" What could I do ? I've told you everything
I know."
" Well, you might have to testify to your hus-
band's character. There's no knowing. . . ."

" And when I said that she reared up like a cobra
preparin' to strike," Crook assured Bill later. " If
she hadn't been such a lady she'd have spat in my
eye, though I dare say she'd have missed. I wouldn't
say accuracy was her strong suit. Well, well, no
good blaming her. No woman could be expected to
like the position. A real lady, Bill, middle name
Vere de Vere, and her husband's fallen for a Putney
Queen. Makes it worse than if she'd been a
duchess. No doubt about it, Bill, women are the
social sex. I've put Ellison on to keep an eye on the
lady. She's quite likely to make a bolt for it. Now,
then, let's get down to brass tacks. This emerald
and diamond pendant—rouse any memories ? "
Bill, who had been the Jewel King on the wrong
side of the legal blanket for many years, considered :
" There were two or three I always wanted to handle,
but they may have changed hands by now. Lady
Kay had one, I remember."
Crook hauled up the Red Book and turned to
Greatorex Square. " Got it first time, Bill, my boy.
18 Greatorex Square—Lady (Frederick) Kay. That
sounds like the goods. The next thing to do is to
discover how long she's had her present chauffeur.
That's a little job you might tackle."
Bill nodded. He seldom asked questions. He
held that speech is golden, and if a man's not going
to pay you for what you say, why waste your
breath ? Anyhow, he had his own methods.
" Any news of the missing suitcase ? " Crook
remembered to ask.

" Not yet. I've got notices out to all the dealers at the various markets, with descriptions of the brushes and the clothes the girl can swear to ; and I've circulated the second-hand dress shops—that green blouse sounds a bit spectacular—and the second-hand shops that might know anything about the brushes. But nine years is a long time. Even if any one remembers buying the gear, it's all odds against his identifying the customer who took it off him."

" That's not his job," replied Crook dryly. " That's ours. Of course, if Fryer took the case aboard the *Empress of Araby*, it can't be traced. Even I don't pretend to be able to work miracles."

" About the passport," said Bill. " The lady took that out a few days before the *Empress of Araby* sailed. Naturally, that's what we expected. Whether Fryer meant to cross to France or not we don't know, but the lady doesn't seem to have had any doubts on that score. She gave her own name and address, so presumably she chanced her husband seeing the envelope."

" A woman that can manage a harem the way she did wouldn't find a little job like that too much for her ingenuity," grunted Crook. " Well, we'll hope for the best, but if we don't get it there's always the great British press—the great Yellow Press of Britain—always only too anxious to lend a hand to the puny forces of law and order."

" You'd be a gift to Fleet Street," was Bill's casual retort, as he made his preparations for tracking down the evasive Mr. Fryer.

" Even in the Temple I have my uses," claimed Mr. Crook modestly, and made his preparations to spend the evening at the dogs.

CHAPTER TWELVE

GREATOREX SQUARE is one of those haughty residential roads that have not a good word to say to
honest poverty. The houses reek of money, though
in the most elegant manner conceivable : tremen-
dously long cars, at whose wheels sit the most
negligently expert chauffeurs in the world, stand
before each house ; the morning sun catches a
veritable Crystal Palace of plate glass and intensifies
the colour of the lavish window-boxes on the
first-floor balconies. Here servants and beggars
know their place, the one in the basement and the
top storey and the other in the gutter, and even
there the cars give them little encouragement.
There are notices everywhere prohibiting street
cries ; all the most highly polished vans of the
most exclusive shops deliver their goods to the back
door ; at night the whole square is alight with
diamonds. A very grand place indeed. Paul Fryer
might well have argued, " Better to be a chauffeur
in Greatorex Square than a pen-pusher in Putney."

Bill lounged against the doorway of a house
almost opposite, that inhabited by Lady (Frederick)
Kay, and thought of that great army of men who
have found their paramours a nuisance and have
immured them in walls and cellars and the like.
Wainwright and Crippen and Mahon . . . the
details of each case came back to him. The astonish-
ing thing was the success that had for a time
attended each effort. Wainwright put the rope

159

round his own neck after a year, through sheer carelessness ; Crippen lost his head at the moment when his security was practically assured ; Mahon committed a major blunder by leaving incriminating evidence at the station cloakroom. Barton, if he were guilty, had been the victim of sheer ill-luck. He could not have foreseen the onlooker from over the way, though you could argue, if you were fussy, that he would have been wiser to draw the curtains or, at least, extinguish the light. Bill had reached this stage in his cogitations when Lady Kay's chauffeur brought his car round to No. 18 with a fine flourish. It was a striking, not to say an ostentatious, car, but it was not crimson. It was dead white picked out with gold, and looked as though it were part of a stage property for Mr. Ivor Novello's latest musical comedy. The chauffeur wore a uniform that made him look like the leader of a beauty chorus, a position for which neither his face nor his build had designed him. He seemed aware of his noticeable appearance and to resent it, for his manner was sulky in the extreme. He was a little wiry man with dark hair and a dark, sullen face. Bill decided that he had originated in the stables and regretted his evolution. The fact that the car was the wrong colour did not trouble him at all. Lady Kay would be unlikely to keep a car for more than two years. Also, she probably wouldn't keep a chauffeur for a longer period. She seemed the sort of lady who would like to ring the changes. All the same, it would be as well to make certain he was on the right track.

He stuck a cigarette in his mouth, threw an empty matchbox into the gutter and crossed the street.

" Got a match, pal ? " he murmured.

The chauffeur, who had been looking the car over for imaginary blemishes, straightened up and handed him a box. Bill offered him a cigarette.

" Goodish car," he suggested casually.

The man's face did not lighten. " If you care about that sort of thing," he allowed, in the grudging tones of one to whom a ten-pound wreck and a Hispana Suiza are alike so much damned machinery.

" Who doesn't ? "

The man shrugged. " Where's the sense in it ? Tooling along at a funeral pace, never seeing anything but the backside of the car in front of you when you're in London, and making up for it by hogging it in the country, so that you might as well be travelling through a quarry ? What's the country for ? I'll tell you : for the nobs to live in. That's what they think, anyhow." His tone was extraordinarily bitter.

" Horses ? " drawled Bill. " Thought as much. Still, not much doing in that line nowadays—unless you keep a riding school."

" I've tried that," said the man. " I'd have bin a murderer if I'd stayed there another month. Why, these chaps you meet nowadays treat a horse as I wouldn't treat a car. Only do it for swank because the lords do it." He lifted a meditative foot.

" I wouldn't," Bill advised him. " Not if you care about your job."

" Oh, jobs ! I can stay here as long as I please."

There was a slight commotion behind them, and the speaker became in an instant transformed from a bitterly disappointed human being into an automaton. A lady was standing on the top step, a maid and a companion in attendance. She spoke to her servants as even the ex-jockey wouldn't have spoken to a car.

" Bet she gives him hell for talking to his common friends in front of her house," Bill reflected, slouching away. He watched the woman get into the car, assisted by her chauffeur, the meek companion and the far-from-meek maid, who wore her hat and coat and was obviously receiving final instructions as to a number of commissions she was to execute for her employer. The soul of charity could not have pretended that Lady Kay's manner to her servants was an ingratiating one. The old north country saying, " I'm not rude, I'm rich," came into Bill's mind. These people were so much servile capacity that she had bought, and she meant to have her money's worth.

Bill heard her talking harshly, with a casual disregard of humanity, to the girl. The companion was so much depressed that probably by this time she did not feel anything but a sort of dull expectant misery at her circumstances. The lady's maid, however, was a different matter. She was a high-spirited young woman of about five-and-twenty, with a full-lipped mouth, a head that could toss resentfully, even when it was her employer who had caused that resentment, a fine buxom figure, a vitality that nothing had so far suppressed.

" It's my night out, my lady," Bill heard her say in obstinate tones.

Lady Kay brushed that aside. " You can have some other night instead. I will arrange it. To-night I need you. You should have realised that."

The girl smouldered with rage. Her air of sullen strength had a certain fascination about it. She might be both dangerous and attractive when opportunity offered. She said something else that

Bill did not hear, and Lady Kay snapped out, " Don't dare to argue with me. Any girl who took a grain of interest in her work would have realised I should require you to-night. I suppose some other night will do for your excursion to the pictures, or whatever your engagement was. I'm not accustomed to this kind of thing. If you're not satisfied with my service you can leave."

Bill had the curiosity to glance at the companion. She was watching the little scene with an expression that was part amazement, a spark of jealousy, but mostly with resignation. If she had ever rebelled, it must have been so long ago that neither she nor any one else remembered it. Lady Kay dropped back into her seat, the maid stood away, the companion leaned forward and whispered to the chauffeur, the chauffeur took his place at the wheel of the car, and the great monster purred away as swiftly as though someone had pressed a spring.

The slighted lady's maid stood in the middle of the road, staring after the car with an expression of such hate that Bill found himself thinking, " I wouldn't much care to be her ladyship if this sort of conversation happens any time there's a knife handy." There was foreign blood, he thought, in that dark, subtle face.

He waited another instant, then moved towards her. " I beg your pardon."

She flung round tempestuously ; but when she saw who it was her mood changed a little.

" You are speaking to me ? "

" If you don't mind. It's about the chauffeur."

He saw the sudden colour run into her dark cheeks. " The chauffeur ? "

" What's going on here ? " Bill wondered, but aloud he said, " Yes. I didn't think. I'm afraid he may get into trouble. It didn't actually occur to me that any employer would object to his speaking for a minute to a chap he met during the war."

" You don't know her," returned the maid passionately. " She wouldn't think you had a tongue given you for any purpose but to say, ' Yes, m'lady,' and ' So kind of you, m'lady.' " Fury had robbed her of any discretion she had ever known. Even as she spoke Bill could see her trembling with the force of it. He thought it strange, no matter what Lady Kay had said. If she had been for any length of time in this employer's service she must have endured many similar scenes. Why should this one have kindled in her such a storm of rage ? Obviously the engagement had been an important one.

The girl glanced at his lame foot meaningly. " The war ? So that's where you met him ? Well, next time you'd better not talk to Harvey or any one else in front of the house."

" Queer to find him at the wheel of a car," Bill ventured.

" He's got to live, like the rest of us. And jobs aren't so easy."

He thought, " She may be a human fiend, but she probably pays well. It's the only way women like that can keep servants."

" Was he always such a devil ? " the girl went on. " One of these days I believe he'll run the car into a lamp-post or something, for sheer spite."

" You don't like her, do you ? Isn't her ladyship ever nervous of being driven by him ? "

" She wouldn't think God Almighty would dare go against her. Besides, what's Harvey but a machine she's bought ? And she can buy another, can't she, with all her money ? "

" These rich women think they can buy anything," Bill agreed. "How long has Harvey stuck it?"

" Six months."

" Is that the average for her chauffeurs?"

" The last one stayed the better part of two years." Her tone changed insensibly as she spoke. " But it was too much for him. He had patience, though. He said he must wait . . ."

" Until he'd saved enough to emigrate?"

" Emigrate? No. To start his own business. Now no one can ever tell him what he must do, that he must break his engagements. . . ." She simmered. " If I were not a fool I would go, too," she muttered.

" So that's why she blushed when I spoke of the chauffeur," reflected Bill shrewdly. " Keeps up with him, I should say. Was that why she was so enraged about being kept in to-night?"

It seemed to him improbable that a young woman of passion and enterprise would allow herself to be so easily frustrated. He set himself to learn a little more of the position. He didn't find women the problem the magazines and novelists represented them. You only had to remember they were intensely personal creatures, with no sense of proportion and naturally introspective, and play up to their sense of their own personality. You couldn't go wrong.

He learnt that Lady Kay was attending a large charity ball that evening. She was one of its initiators and most substantial backers, and it was clear that she would throw her weight about from the opening of the proceedings until the exhausted musicians had packed up their instruments and departed.

" I suppose this girl's got to stay behind and

button her ladyship's pants," he reflected inelegantly. " If anything happened to that creature and she lost her brass, she'd be bound to go nudist. She doesn't know how to put on her own chemise. All the same, I fancy our young friend is a match for her."

He could not wring from the girl—whose name was Suzanne Lamarre, as he subsequently discovered—any admission that she had remained in touch with the late chauffeur, but he did discover that this man had been known in Greatorex Square by the name of Hart. A little later he parted from her, leaving her to execute her commissions, and reflecting that it was as well for tyrants that the law has now made it extremely difficult for disgruntled employees to buy deadly poisons. He didn't think Suzanne would have the slightest compunction about putting prussic acid into Lady Kay's morning tea, provided she could be sure the crime would never be traced to her.

" I'd be a nervous wreck in that woman's place," he told himself, hailing a taxi and watching that erect, stubborn back moving in the direction of the shopping centre. " All the people in that house hating her. Wonder if she's got any family, or if she's driven them out, too."

He decided that Lady Kay would hardly arrive at the ball before ten o'clock, and would certainly be among the last to leave, so that after ten the lady's maid could regard herself as off duty until the small hours. Of course, when her employer returned she would be expected to be as trim and lively as a young winkle ; but no doubt Suzanne could attend to all that.

It was a few minutes before ten that Lady Kay left the house, still driven by the chauffeur, Harvey, whose hours seemed as elastic as his employer's ideas about servants' rights. Twenty minutes later the basement door opened and a dark figure stole up the steps. She walked rapidly, head up, in a northerly direction, and Bill followed on the farther side of the street. Even at that distance he obtained a distinct impression of her quality, fiery and magnetic, something that would always give her power over men. In a way, he thought, she was not unlike the dead woman. Her retinue would always include a man of some kind, and it wasn't likely she would have to go out into the highways and hedges to look for him. He found himself becoming engrossed in her and her probable future, until he shook the mood from him in instinctive disgust.

" I'll be writing psychological novels next," he told himself dourly, having no use for novelists, who were all satisfied with talking about what some other fellow had done, and never went out and did anything themselves. They even accomplished their work under a dry roof, and without the smallest element of risk.

He followed at a casual pace, his keen eyes under their mock-lazy lids noting the eagerness and storm of her movements, as though she could not arrive soon enough at her destination. Presently she turned into the street where the shops were locked and in most cases barred against night-thieves. The ladies of joy paraded here, incredibly perfect as to complexion and hairdressing, standing in shop doorways, holding neat, coloured umbrellas over jaunty little hats, for the rain had begun again, watching with lynx eyes the passing of rare possible clients, who walked, head down, hands in pockets, against the teasing rain. Suddenly she seemed to melt into a doorway. Bill saw that a man had been

waiting there, and after a moment the two of them
turned into a side street and came to a halt in the
doorway of an empty shop. The lights here were
dimmed by the rain, so he could not see the man's
face. Anyway, he had no photograph, nothing on
which to check up ; but he clung doggedly to their
trail, following them into another and narrower street
until, to his relief, they turned abruptly into a
brightly lighted little public house called The
Running Horse. Bill followed them and sat at a
small table with a huge yellow ash-tray and a fern
on it. The man and the girl were seated a little
distance away. Bill gave his order and leaned
back. Presently he drew a pencil from his pocket
and began idly to sketch that hard-bitten face.
Embittered, disillusioned, it scarcely softened even
in his present company. It was not a face easy to
forget. Dark eyes sunk under a brooding forehead,
long, bitter mouth, a fierce chin, a nose that jutted
out at an abrupt angle, yet gave character and
unity to the whole at the expense of symmetry.

He heard the woman's voice, low, fierce, pleading.
" Paul," she said. " I tell you, we need not wait.
I do not mind. . . ."

The man said nothing. He had a dogged, burnt-
out look. The woman went on speaking ; she
caught her companion's hand and crushed it between
her own until with an abrupt movement he drew
it away. The situation was common enough : here
was a woman, desperately infatuated, making the
running, working so tirelessly that it would need a
man exceptionally subtle or exceptionally brutal to
escape her. He thought, " Was he like this with
Mrs. Barton ? Had she at last met her match, she
who had played all her other men as if they were
instruments over which she had complete mastery ? "

At half-past ten the Running Horse shut down, and the three returned to the damp and cheerless streets. The woman was reluctant to part, but the man said something, inaudible to Bill, that proved he wanted to go home. Then came a few words in the woman's higher-pitched voice.

" It is also my life, Paul."

Bill reflected, " I've been a fool in some ways, but thank God I've kept clear of women. It's not so much that they won't see your point of view as that they can't."

A few minutes later the pair separated, reluctantly on the girl's part, with a final slow, unwilling loosing of hands. After she had gone the man stood watching her mistrustfully for a moment, then thrust his hands into his pockets and turned in the other direction. Wary as a cat and almost as invisible in the unwelcoming night, Bill followed. He saw him turn at length into a drab road, a good half-mile distant from their rendezvous, and vanish down the basement steps of one of those tall bleak featureless houses so common to London streets. He let himself in with a latch-key, and a moment later the light flashed on in the basement. There were bars here to keep out thieves, and for an instant his quarry came to the black glass and stood staring into the night. Bill thought he had never seen a face so expressive of overwhelming despair. He lifted his hands in a gesture that was empty of hope, then slowly let them fall.

" The more a chap's like a gorilla, the more the girls fall for him," reflected Bill, watching those hungry arms slowly relax. " He don't care a row of pins for her. She's just a female bit, and a chap's human. Queer cuss, though. I wouldn't like to find myself up against him." He shrugged and turned towards the tramlines. The conductor was one of those pert, cheerful young men, whom no weather can put out of countenance.

" Nice night for the ducks," he said.

Bill suppressed the obvious lewd retort and took his ticket without comment. It had turned into a beast of a night ; the rain was coming down in torrents now ; even the houses seemed to drip water. Bill walked on slowly, remembering Fryer—if it was Fryer—a dreadful, lost, embittered face staring into the night.

CHAPTER THIRTEEN

OLD SINS HAVE LONG SHADOWS

EARLY next morning he was at his post in front of the house in Roland Terrace. The rain had cleared, but the sky was a thick dirty grey and it was clear that a further storm was in the offing. At about eight forty-five the basement door clicked and the stranger came out. A brisk walk brought him to the Red Triangle Garage, where it appeared he was employed. Bill saw him go on duty, then walked slowly back to Roland Terrace.

The landlady at No. 6, in response to his request for rooms, said she hadn't one vacant at the moment, but her basement lodger had told her only that morning he would be going at the end of the week. He was being shifted to another depot, he said.

" Basement ? " repeated Bill dubiously.

" It's a good room," she urged. " Mr. Hart's been there for months, and he's never complained once of the damp. And well furnished, too."

" Could I see the room ? "

" Well, I haven't quite set it to rights yet, but you could come down, if you liked."

She led the way down the narrow dark flight of steps into a room that was surprisingly light and comfortable. There was a bed in one corner, with the covers thrown back, the usual table and chairs and pictures on the walls. The unusual was represented by a large empty photograph frame and some books. Bill strolled across and glanced at the titles. *Anatole France*, a volume of American short stories, some *Plays of the Year*. Mrs. Prince's gaze followed him. He was looking now at the empty photograph frame.

" Funny thing about that," she said chattily. " He used to have a picture in it—a woman. A beauty, she must have been. His wife, he said. ' I suppose she's dead,' I said to him. And he said, ' Yes, she was drowned.' A bit Irish, if you ask me—the lady, I mean—lots of go about her, but hasty the way the Irish are. Then one morning I came into the room as usual and I found the picture torn to bits, lying in the fireplace."

" Did he say anything about it ? "

" Well, he didn't, and I didn't like to ask. I thought perhaps he was thinking of marrying again. There was a young lady he used to go out with ; I saw them together once. And I suppose he wouldn't particularly want to keep the picture of the first."

" I suppose you threw the pieces away ? "

" Well, I meant to, and that's a fact, but my little grandson—he lives with me since his mother was killed in a coach crash—he asked to have them to play with. I didn't think there was any harm, so long as he kept them out of Mr. Hart's way."

" Of course not," agreed Bill, luring her to talk

171

about the child. Before he left the house he had
contrived to see not only the little boy, but also
the fragments of the photograph.

" It's a pity it's been torn," he said.

" I can make it good again," said the little boy
defiantly, piecing the scraps together.

" A pretty lady," Bill agreed. " But perhaps I
can do even better than that." He brought out his
pencil again. The small boy approved of the result.

" For Joe," he said firmly.

" I'll swop it for your bits of picture," Bill
suggested.

The little boy hesitated, but succumbed when
Bill added sixpence to his offer.

" You shouldn't give him so much," protested
the woman, but it was obvious that she only spoke
from convention. Bill laughed. " I've got a kid
that age," he said inaccurately, and went off to see
Crook.

" As nice a couple as you'd meet anywhere
outside the Wildcats' House," observed Crook
approvingly, looking from one sketch to the other.
" Who do we get to identify these ? Don't say Mrs.
Fryer. The less truck I have with that dame the
better. After all, no one's paying us to preserve
the sanctity of the home."

" To say nothing of the fact that Fryer might
quite well commit suicide if we reintroduced him
to his wife. He'd have my sympathy if he did.
No, no, what about Mrs. Barton No. 2 ? You can
bet she'd know Fryer by sight. Anything that concerned Barton would concern her."

" I don't much care for these single-track women,"
Crook confessed.

" Are there any other kinds ? " queried Bill.

" Come to think of it, Bill, I believe there aren't.

You're right there. The great difference between the male and the female is that the average male has a mind like Mr. Arlen's hero, that was like Clapham Junction and went all ways at once, and the female scurries along to her self-selected destination, regardless of any other interests."

Jean was not having a very good time of it. Most of her correspondence these days took the form of anonymous letters, some of them of an altogether incredible vileness, accusing her of helping to dispose of her predecessor's corpse. The police guard, that she had at first been inclined to resent, now seemed to her more of a protection than a menace. Anyway, she didn't go out much, and they wouldn't allow her to visit Jack. She didn't blame them exactly, but her hunger for him and her dread for his safety robbed her of all vitality and all love of life.

When Bill Parsons came to see her she didn't at first understand what he wanted, until he produced his two sketches. Then she said at once, " Those are Beatrice, and Paul Fryer. Do you mean that he's alive ? "

" Seems like it. We're going to get you to make sure, though."

She thought for a moment. " Then, if he is, what does it mean ? "

" I wouldn't worry about that," Bill advised her. " That's Crook's job, and he'll do it better than any one else. I suppose you are sure ? About Fryer, I mean ? It's a long time ago."

" He isn't a person it would be very easy to forget, particularly in the circumstances."

" You knew he was running around with Mrs. Barton ? "

She nodded. Then she said, " I've remembered

something. The top joint of one of his little fingers was missing."

" We'll check up on that," said Bill promptly. " See here, I'll pick you up in the morning and tell you what you're to do."

The next day he called for her in a car and drove her to the Red Triangle Garage. As they turned the corner he looked over his shoulder.

" Your escort's very faithful," he observed. " Does he always shadow you like this ? "

She shivered a little. " I try to get accustomed to it, and in a way I have. I can't believe I'll ever be able to go out without someone watching, just be a free woman again. While as for Jack . . ."

" You don't have to bother about Jack," he told her. " Crook's handling his affairs."

" What's my husband to him but just another case ? " she broke out passionately. " Oh, I know he'll do his best ; but if he isn't successful, he'll just shrug his shoulders and go on to something else. I suppose you couldn't expect anything else. If he was going to get worked up over every client, he'd never get any peace at all. But it's all my life to me."

They turned another corner, just getting through on the lights that held up the taxi behind them. Bill generously slowed down.

" Are we there ? "

" Give that fellow a chance," suggested Bill. " If he thinks you're trying to make a getaway he may turn nasty, and he hasn't been—say—difficult to date, has he ? "

" What does he think I might do ? " she wondered.

" Make for the open road, I dare say."

" With Jack in prison ? "

" You must remember they're only police officers.

If they see a primrose by the river's brim, it's only a primrose to them."

His manner intimidated her. She hadn't expected lawyers or their assistants to be like Crook and Bill Parsons. Stately, dignified men, probably with silvering hair and monocles—that was how she had seen them in her mind's eye.

Arrived at the garage, Bill got out and went in to see about a mythical repair to the car. He came back in about a minute with Fryer, and plunged into a mass of technical detail. Apparently whatever it was was quite simple, for after a few minutes he came back to the driving seat and they returned to Arbutus Avenue.

" That was Paul Fryer," said Jean. " He's changed a bit—got hollower. But I'd know him anywhere. It was only while he was with Beatriec Barton that he ever wore that ' released ' look."

" Next chap to see is Fryer himself," remarked Crook. " I'd better take that on. The fact is, Bill, you're too well known at that house. Wonder how much trouble he'll give us. From all I've heard, I should say a devil of a lot."

He waited at a spot conveniently near the Red Triangle Garage, being of those unconventional creatures who like to do what they call the plummy bits of work themselves. This fact, that was well known in the profession, was a thorn in the sides of many of his brethren. When Fryer emerged, fortunately walking alone, Mr. Crook padded amiably over to him.

" Mr. Fryer, I think ? "

Fryer turned an expressionless face towards him. " I'm afraid you're mistaken."

" Don't you believe it. I could get half a dozen witnesses to swear to you. I want a few words . . ."

" I've told you you're mistaken," said the man more roughly. " I don't know who you are . . ."

" My name's Crook, and I'm by way of defendin' Barton in the Putney cellar murder. I expect you've read about that in the press."

Fryer preserved a poker face. " I expect so ; but it's no concern of mine."

" I wouldn't be too sure. After all, you're the Other Man, as the movies put it."

" What other man ? "

" The chap she was going off with. You can't escape that. Any number of people know it."

" You mean Paul Fryer's the man she was going off with. . . ."

" I wonder how you knew his Christian name."

" It was in the papers."

" I must have missed that one ; and I thought I'd got 'em all. Oh, it was, was it ? Well, then, Mr. Fryer, seeing you know so much . . ."

" I tell you, I don't know anything."

" You don't really think you're going to get away with that, do you ? "

His companion stopped abruptly. " Look here, I don't know whether you're mad or just drunk, but if you don't leave me immediately I'll hand you over to the police."

" Jolly good idea," applauded Crook. " There's a bobby over there. Let's go across and you can give me in charge."

The other man hesitated.

" Of course," Crook continued, " I shall go on telling my story about Fryer and Hart bein' identical, and as it's a capital charge, they'll have to put through inquiries, and it may be a bit difficult for you to explain how it is so many people have already recognised you—even the top joint off your little finger, too ; that's a coincidence, if you like—and your wife could probably suggest other marks of identification. . . ."

Suddenly his man threw in his hand. " All right, have it your own way. I'm Fryer. Officially I've been dead for ten years."

" Officially so has Mrs. Barton. The queer thing is that both of them were supposed to have been on board the *Empress of Araby*, whereas in actual fact neither of them was."

" What is it you want with me ? "

Crook looked up and down the street. They were in the act of passing a public house called the Goat In Boots, and he drew his companion within.

" I never was much of a lad for hiking," he confessed. " I should say whisky. Wouldn't you ? I thought so. Now, then, you knew the late Mrs. Barton pretty well, didn't you ? "

" I lodged there for a short time."

" I don't fancy your acquaintance with the lady stopped when you changed your quarters. Come, now, we know you were going off together. She left a letter for Barton telling him as much."

" Then why was she not on board ? "

" That's what we're all tryin' to find out. The police have one answer and I have another. You might be able to throw a little light on the situation."

" I tell you, I do not know. I have never known. I expected her, I waited for her. I went on board and paid for a cabin, that we might be together. And she did not come. At least "—he hesitated— " she had not come to within five minutes of the boat's sailing. After that . . ."

" And so you didn't go on board ? "

" I was only going for her."

177

" And after the boat sailed, did you go down to Putney to find out what had happened ? "

" I made inquiries, and I learned that she had been drowned on that boat."

" But you said you watched and she never came."

" I watched until five minutes before the boat should sail. Then I became frantic. I ran out to look to see if she were coming. It was not that I minded so much about missing the boat, but I was afraid she had been prevented. I ran across the road, thinking I saw her in the distance, and a car swerving suddenly struck me and threw me to the ground."

" That was a bit of luck for you," commented Crook. " And then they say there's no goodness in the motorist."

" Luck ? You can say that ? "

" Well, if you'd gone on board you'd have been drowned. Why didn't you fill the papers when you heard what had happened, though ? You could have had a magnificent run for your money. Lucky survivor. The ha'penny press would have loved you."

Fryer's grim face refused to relax. " You understand nothing," he said fiercely. " When they told me that the boat had gone down and that no one was saved—no one—I thought, of course, that she had been on board. I wished that I had been there, too."

" And—when did you change your name ? "

" I became Hart after that. Every one whom I knew, whom I had told, would think me dead. I need not go back to that life."

" Any particular reason why you shouldn't ? "

" I tell you, she was dead, or so I thought. What was there to go back to ? "

178

"Hell!" thought Crook. "That jane certainly could hold her men."

"What about the hospital where they took you?" he went on. "Didn't they find letters or anything on you?"

"I had put my overcoat and my luggage in the cabin. My tickets, everything, were there."

"How did you expect to get back to the boat?"

"I had said to a sailor, 'My wife has not come. I am going to look for her! He would have let me return."

"I should have thought it would be a lot easier to keep your passport on you," Crook said ungraciously."

"I did not think," said Fryer. "I was anxious."

"What was the name of the hospital?"

"The Grosvenor Hospital. I have been in Dover since. It was burnt down three years ago."

"And all its records with it. The gods do seem to be on your side, don't they?" Could any man really expect to tell such a story and be believed?

"When did you last see her?" he wanted to know.

"On the Thursday. I gave her her ticket and told her to be careful."

"And you didn't suggest meeting at Victoria?"

"She thought the boat. There might be someone who knew us at the station. It was her husband she was thinking of."

"I love these solicitous wives," Crook muttered *sotto voce*, "so much that I'd like to black their eyes for them. And it's a pity Barton didn't try that instead of all this Christian meekness. Women don't understand that kind of thing. By the way, what happened to her luggage? Did you put that in the cabin, too?"

179

Fryer looked startled. " Luggage ? I saw no luggage."

" She wasn't travelling without any, I presume ? "

" I tell you, she did not come."

There was nothing more to be done with the man. " You were seeing a good deal of her then, I suppose ? "

" When I could."

" Was there any one else—any one besides the husband, I mean—who might have been pestering her ? Any one who might try to prevent her coming ? "

" She never said a word."

" Would she have told you ? "

" I think not. She would have been afraid I would have done some desperate thing. . . ."

" You'd got it badly, then ? "

Fryer turned his head towards his interlocutor. His dark eyes were black ; under the swarthy skin of his face an ugly pallor showed. There was no light in that face, no peace, no hope.

" You didn't know her," was all he said.

" I wonder if any one did," Crook observed to himself, after they had parted. " With a bit of luck this is going to be a star case. Messalina of the Suburbs all over again. And will they eat it ? Can a duck swim ? And it won't be only the suburbs, either. Mayfair's going to love it."

CHAPTER FOURTEEN

BILL was in the office when Crook stamped in, tipped his hat on the back of his head and began to savage the latest delivery of letters.

"Any news about anything?" he demanded, disembowelling an envelope with one thick thumb stuck under the flap.

Bill sounded even more languid than usual.

"I've got a line on those hair-brushes at last."

Crook laid down the letter he had just opened and, solemnly taking off his hat, bowed slightly in Bill's direction.

"Me to you," he observed grandly. "Who's got 'em?"

"I can't tell you that, but a chap who has a stall at the Caledonian Market, one of those female foolishness stalls, remembers buying a suitcase from the Railway Lost Property Office years ago at one of their auctions, that contained brushes like that."

"And he sold 'em?"

"In the Market."

"Does he know who bought 'em? He's a smart chap if he does."

"In the first place, it was his lady friend . . ."

"His wife?"

"He's a Scotch Jew," explained Bill, "the sort that doesn't go chucking three half-crowns away for a thing he can get for nothing."

181

" I'd like to meet that chap," said Crook, a note of real admiration in his voice. " I feel we could do business together."

" You're probably going to. Meet him, I mean. I dunno about business."

" Has the lady still got the brushes ? "

" Not that one. After a bit her fancy changed, and she found a boy-friend she liked better, so she got this one to give her a price for the brushes—which Moses seems to have done. He took 'em along to the Market and sold 'em again the following week."

" Was the next lady one of his team, too ? "

" No. But though he doesn't know her name he knows her. She's there every Friday fresh as paint and regular as Big Ben. He reckons he's dressed that woman and her household for years."

Crook brooded. " And how far does that get us ? "

" As far as the lady. To-day's Thursday. I'm going down to the Market to-morrow, and he's going to introduce me. How about Fryer ? "

" He's not a fool, either. He's told just the sort of story that nobody can prove. We ain't going to get him by hook, Bill."

" What are crooks for ? " asked Bill negligently.

" I've heard that one before," returned his companion in momentarily sour tones, " and it wasn't funny the first time." He returned to his correspondence. Barton, whatever he himself might feel about it, was by no means the only man in London who was in trouble and was looking to the Criminal's Hope to pull him out with as little scathe as possible. Suddenly he looked up.

" Here's something else," he said. " That woman who lived alongside the Bartons in 1930 and who moved without leaving an address—she's turned up again. I've had scouts out after her. You'd better get along and see what you can do."

Bill took the letter his companion offered him. " Mrs. Lily Morris, Saffron Walden. Married again. So that's why we didn't get her." He glanced at the very elaborate watch on his wrist. " I could get down there to-night by car. May as well try every avenue."

" You remember the chap in the Old Testament : Blessed is the man that hath his quiverful—full of nice sharp arrows, Bill, and the more the merrier."

Bill arrived at Saffron Walden at the unpopular hour of eight twenty-five. Mrs. Lily Morris had a nice little modern villa, with electricity throughout, and furniture that looked exactly like the furniture of all her neighbours. The house was called Mione. Bill tried pronouncing it several ways before he hit on the subtlety of that title.

Mrs. Morris, very smartly dressed in a short velvet coat over a printed silk dress, came to the door, saying something about the girl being out. When she saw Bill she softened at once. It was a boast of hers that she did know a gentleman when she saw one. If Crook had come in person she'd probably have called her husband to throw him out.

" Mrs. Morris ? "

" Well ? "

" I believe you were at one time Mrs. Lewis, and lived at No. 10 Arbutus Avenue."

Her voice sharpened. " What's that to do with you ? "

" You were living there when Mrs. Barton disappeared in 1930 ? "

" Suppose I was. I couldn't help it."

" It might have occurred to you that the authorities would want to get into touch with any one who could throw the smallest light on the matter."

" And what do you think I can do ? "

" You're the last person who admits to seeing her alive," Bill pointed out reasonably.

" You mean—because I saw her go in that night ? "

" And saw Mullins afterwards. It's of first importance to fix the time of death as near as possible."

" Where do you come in ? " she asked him in the same suspicious manner.

" Oh, that was stupid of me. I should have explained. I'm Mr. Barton's legal adviser."

She calmed down a little. " You didn't tell me that."

" I know you'll give us any help you can. After all, a man's life is at stake."

" I never would have believed it of Mr. Barton," she confessed. " He was such a nice little man, wouldn't kill a mouse. He told me once that when he found one in the trap he opened the back door and let it out. Can you beat that for being soft ? "

" Not the sort of man you'd expect to find murdering his wife," agreed Bill mendaciously, knowing that a tenderness of heart towards animals had, like the Gilbertian flowers that bloom in the spring, nothing to do with the case.

" Well, that's what I thought. Of course, she led him no end of a dance. It's a wonder he put up with it. My husband wouldn't. Harry—that was Mr. Lewis—used to say, ' Well, perhaps he has his fun, too,' but I never heard any one else suggest it."

" There's never been an iota of evidence to support that theory," Bill told her with outward pleasantness and an inward desire to wring her neck. These chattering women! They had no sense of propriety, didn't realise the harm such a rumour even coming from this obscure quarter could effect.

A door on the right of the little hall opened with a jerk and Mr. Morris shot out. He was a thin man with the wrong kind of moustache, and was dressed nattily by the forty-five shilling tailors.

" What's all this ? " he buzzed, blowing the overhanging moustache this way and that as he spoke. It was like a bead curtain over some domestic entrance, thought Bill. " We don't buy at the door ; and, anyway, this hour of the night . . ."

" It's all right, Leonard," his wife cheered him. " This gentleman is Mr. Barton's lawyer. You know—the Barton that's supposed to have killed his wife and put her in the cellar."

" That has nothing whatsoever to do with us."

" It has to do with the whole community," said Bill unexpectedly. " You can't hope to shirk your responsibility."

Mr. Morris puffed till the moustache looked as though it might be blown off.

" My responsibility ? " he fumed.

" The jury that will try Barton represents the country—you and me and every one. If he's condemned, he's condemned by the country. As a matter of fact, I don't suggest that you could help us, but it's possible that your wife could."

" All poppycock," panted Mr. Morris. " Don't care about my wife getting herself mixed up in this sort of thing."

" I'm afraid she was mixed up in it before she became your wife."

" Shut the door, Lily," ordered Mr. Morris magnificently.

185

Bill advanced his foot. " I wouldn't. I wouldn't, really. She'd only be subpœnaed."

" You don't understand," Mrs. Morris told her husband. " The gentleman thinks I might be able to help."

" You women ! " growled Mr. Morris. " See yourselves in the witness-box wearing a new hat. That's as far as you know how to think."

" You ought to be ashamed. Haven't you got any sympathy ? "

" You wait and see how much sympathy you have when someone finds you buried in my cellar and I'm waiting to be swung. Serve him damn' well right, you'll say."

" It's that tinned crab," explained Mrs. Morris. " It always takes him this way. Come in, won't you ? "

Bill came into one of those rooms that, if any are allowed to survive the pseudo-civilisation of the twentieth century, will surely make a more artistic generation colour with embarrassment. Bright fringes on all the uneven lampshades, medallions of colour on the fat kapok-stuffed cushions, tassels on the chesterfield, strips of patterned material running like a disease up the curtains, unframed mirrors with uneven edges, machine-turned fire curb : the eye saw nothing simple, nothing fine or direct or clean-cut wherever it turned. Even the vases were made of shaded plaster of no symmetrical design.

" Take a pew," invited Mrs. Morris familiarly. " Now, what is it you want me to tell you ? Mind you, I didn't know any more about Beatrice Barton's affairs than any one else, though I must say she didn't take much trouble to hide them. Still, you couldn't help liking him, as I say, and the girl was nice, too, though if I was a man I'd be afraid of marrying into that lot. You know what they say about bad blood, and she was that woman's child. I know when I heard she was drowned I thought, ' It's a pity this didn't happen ten years ago. Might have given the girl a chance ; but as it is . . .' "

" Coming back to that evening," said Bill firmly. " Now, would you tell me everything you remember from the time you saw Mrs. Barton going into her house ? "

Mrs. Morris hesitated. " What exactly is it you wanted to know ? "

" Everything," repeated Bill firmly. " And you'll find it easier if you tell it in your own way than if I keep pulling you up with questions. Besides, there may be some detail that appears quite trivial to you that is actually very significant."

The last word had the desired effect. He could see Mrs. Morris trying it over in her own mind.

" Well," she said pleasantly and a little importantly, " I'll do what I can, of course."

Mr. Morris intervened. " How he expects you to remember something that happened nearly ten years ago—it's not right. It's all a trick, Lily, if you ask me. You didn't ought to talk with him, not without your solicitor being present. The next thing you'll find yourself in the witness-box, and that'll be a pretty kettle of fish."

" Don't be silly, Leonard," retorted his wife in scornful tones. " The gentleman's not trying to make out I had anything to do with it. It's just he thinks I might be able to help. As a matter of fact, I do remember very well. I mean, what with her being drowned, as we thought, the next day, it sort of got printed on my memory. It was a Saturday, I remember, the 28th April, it was, young Ernie's birthday. I remember that, because I was married on the 26th and young Ernie was born two days later. Ernie was my sister's first, and when her second was born she didn't seem able to get over it. Her husband married again, the way men generally do. Well, you can't really blame them, can you ? I mean to say, a baby is a woman's job, and me not having any of my own, I didn't mind when Herbert used to ask me to have them for a bit. When his wife was having hers, that is, and she had them long and regular for nine years. Well, as I say, April 28th was young Ernie's birthday, and my husband—my first, that is ; mad about kiddies, he was—he'd bought young Ernie a bow and arrow set. Just like a man. Why couldn't he have given him a clockwork lion or something ? Because you couldn't make Ern put that bow down. He played all over the garden, till he'd lost one of the arrows, and then he played in the house. I remember he shot my grandmother through the eye. I was angry about that. Ever such a lovely photograph it was, and all coloured by hand. My mother paid any amount to have it done when Grannie died. Out of respect for the dead, you see, and after she passed away, well, I had it. Naturally. And I was that careful of it. And what does that young limb of Satan do but shoot off one of his arrows, and it went right through the glass. Ruined it, as I told him.

"Then he shot another arrow into the cuckoo clock. I told Herbert, my first husband, that is, ' That's not a suitable gift for a child,' I said. ' He could do a lot of harm with arrows like those. Suppose it was his little brother he'd shot ? ' Why, that arrow went so deep into the clock, it stopped the works, and it went on saying a quarter to seven for years afterwards.

"Then he shot his little brother's Dismal Des-
mond. And after that I said, ' Now, my lord, you
go straight up to bed.' He yelled, of course, but
I took him upstairs. ' One more sound from you
and you'll be glad to eat your breakfast standing,'
I told him. Well, you have to be a bit firm with
children.

"By the time I came down I was feeling I'd had
about enough. I opened the door and went on to
the porch for a minute. I heard a car door slam,
and the next moment a man came to the gate and
opened it and said, ' Excuse me, but do you happen
to know if Mrs. Barton is out ? ' I said, ' I really
couldn't say.' I know she was in, because we came
back the same time, and though I wouldn't care to
go far with a woman of her sort, I'm all for civility
between neighbours. So I said, ' Good-evening,'
and she said the same, and in she went. That 'ud
be, say, five o'clock, as near as I remember. ' She
might have gone out again,' I said. ' I wouldn't
know.' He said, ' I've been knocking and ringing
for five minutes, but I can't make any one
hear, and I've got a parcel for her. Do you
think she'll be in again later ? ' ' Well,' I said,
' she generally goes to the Market of a Saturday,
but perhaps she and Mr. Barton have gone out
together.' ' Well,' he said, ' if you should see either
of them later, perhaps you'd tell her I brought
her watch. I'll send it round in the morning.' Very
civil-spoken he was.

"I didn't see her that night, but coming back
from the Market I saw him. He was just coming
out of his gate. There's a lamp outside my door,
and he looked as if he was going to faint. ' You're
not looking well, Mr. Barton,' I said, and he told
me he'd been to the pictures, and it was stuffy. I

189

said, ' Is Mrs. Barton in ? ' And he looked queerer than ever and said, ' No, no, she's gone away for a few days.' ' Well,' I told him, ' you ought to have gone away yourself over the Bank Holiday. You look as if you could do with a change.' Then I told him about the watch, but he didn't seem to take it in much. Still he did say, ' I'll send for it ; there's no hurry,' and he went on. I didn't see any more of him that night, but I do remember that she wasn't at the Market like she generally was."

" You didn't hear anything strange in the house ? "

" You couldn't hear anything over the noise young Ernie and his little brother was making," returned the one-time Mrs. Lewis grimly.

Bill came away soon after that. " Will they want me to come into court ? " pleaded Lily Morris.

" I shouldn't be surprised," said Bill.

He was at the Caledonian Market next day before the doors were open. He saw a member of the police force going the rounds. " Looking for stolen goods," thought Bill with a grin.

A lot of stuff found its way here, as he had reason to know. The little men, the ones who didn't bother with a stall, but just dashed in and turned a caseful of rubbish higgledy-piggledy on the stone flags, were crowding round the entrance. They came early and went as soon as they'd disposed of their stuff. Anything did for them—petticoats, bloomers, old children's-clothes, babies' wear, blouses, ragged evening dresses. They just held up each article in turn and shoved it into the hand of the first bidder. Threepence, sixpence, eightpence, those were their prices. On the barrows you could discern all manner of junk : enormous ancient bedsteads, rugs, harness, old chairs, gramophones with chipped horns, books tied up in parcels, old magazines, china of every quality and kind.

The bigger men came with cars or motor vans ; they set up their stalls under cover and sold new stuff : cheap artificial silk underwear, stockings, furs, new rugs and little carpets, bed-quilts, curtain net, cheap blouses, second-hand evening clothes.

You could furnish your house and your wardrobe from the Caledonian Market, he reflected, looking at some gaudy electric fittings being uncovered.

There was the usual rush when the gates opened, and he strolled casually in, looking out for his man. Even when he saw him he didn't approach him. The fellow gave nothing for the Law and less than nothing for Jack Barton. His job was to set up his stall and encourage and entice customers. Bill gave him plenty of time, then strolled up. The man recognised him at once.

" She's not here yet," he said. He was a swarthy, middle-aged fellow, very heavily built, and spoke with a pronounced Jewish lisp. " I'll tell you when she comes."

Bill smoked his inevitable cigarette and waited. He had to wait till after eleven o'clock before a woman in a long blue coat and a black hat walked up to the stall. Even then Bill didn't hurry. She wouldn't be able to give him her full attention until she had made her purchases. But at last Moses said, " This gentleman "—(it was almost " chentle-man ")—" would like to see you."

Bill explained his business. She understood him at once.

" Well," she said grimly, " I'm sure I don't know what you're trying to tell me. That they were stolen property ? It's no concern of mine if they

191

were. I bought them fair and above-board off Mr. Moses here."

" And Mr. Moses bought them fair and above-board at a sale at the Railways' Lost Property Office. That's all right. The point is, I want to know whether they're the ones I'm after."

" I haven't got them in my pocket."

" Perhaps I could call some time. . . ." Bill's suavity was more dangerous than all Crook's bluster.

" What's odd about them ? "

" Strictly in confidence," murmured Bill, " we believe they may have been the property of a lady who was murdered."

" You see," struck in Mr. Moses, who, like so many of his race, seemed able to conduct business and listen to quite irrelevant conversation, " you got a real bargain if that is so. Not many ladies brush their hair with brushes with such a history."

" You ought to be called Bluebeard," said the lady —her name was Mrs. Perkins—with some asperity. " Well, I suppose if you want to see the brushes, I can't stop you. Not if you're the police, that is."

" Mr. Barton's legal adviser."

" But they're not for sale—not yet."

Bill said nothing as to that, just asked Mrs. Perkins when it would be convenient for him to call.

" I shan't be away till four," she told him, " and my husband won't want a stranger in the house when he gets back to his tea. You better come in the morning."

Bill noted the address and left the Market. He went to the flat where Margaret was staying, and told her that she would be wanted to identify some hairbrushes the next day.

" We think they may be your mother's."

Margaret stared at him with hostile eyes. " Suppose they are, how does that help ? "

" I haven't the least idea," returned Bill candidly. " But I'll want you just the same."

Mrs. Perkins' house was at once ambitious and resourceful. Everything in it had once been something else and retained some hint of its original character. This made it an unusual house to be in. Mrs. Perkins herself wore a striped cotton blouse that had once been one of her husband's shirts, a skirt she had cut down from a velvet curtain and a house-cap fashioned of scraps of vari-coloured materials once used for her children's frocks.

She looked at Margaret with unaffected curiosity.

" This young lady will be able to identify the brushes," Bill explained.

" I've brought them downstairs, but I'm sure they look to me like any one else's. It's a pretty design, of course, but I dare say there have been others—like them, I mean."

" It's a matter of the monogram," Bill explained patiently.

Mrs. Perkins led the way into the parlour. The brushes were laid out on the table. Margaret, still without speaking, took one of them up. Then she nodded to Bill.

" Those were your mother's ? "

" Yes."

" How can you be sure ? " demanded Mrs. Perkins inquisitively.

" It's the monogram. A double B."

Their hostess took up the hand-mirror. " So that's what it's meant for. I've often wondered. Doesn't look much like a double B to me. Well, then, what are you going to do now ? They're mine, you know."

" You won't part with them until after the trial,"
said Bill. " I don't know that we shall want them
as evidence at all, but as they did belong to Mrs.
Barton, they prove that her luggage never got as
far as France."

" Oh, that's who they belonged to ? Well, she
didn't get to France, either."

" She might have sent her luggage in advance."

" You mean, she probably never meant to go to
France and the husband . . ." She stopped, her
quick mind racing ahead. Then : " I thought you
were for him ? "

" I am."

" Then I don't see how the brushes are going to
help you."

" Nor do I, at the moment," confessed Bill.
" But you can't afford to let anything slip."

" This is like a jig-saw puzzle with the best bit
missing," Crook remarked when he heard Bill's news.
" You know, I think we might go and talk to Bruce
about this. P'raps he'll be able to supply the missing
link."

CHAPTER FIFTEEN

HOW MANY BEANS MAKE FIVE ?

" Despite wars and rumours of wars and the gradual suppression of the middle classes to which I have the honour to belong," observed Aubrey Bruce, K.C., to his companion of the moment, " life still has its piquancies. Here, for instance, is Arthur Crook, whose methods are uncommonly like his name, proposing that I shall defend his client at the Old Bailey on the not unusual charge of wife-murder."

" Pretty clear case, isn't it ? " suggested his companion. " Question of—who else could it be ? "

" Any number of people, now Crook's on the scene. I admire that man, I admire him more than I can say. I'm not sure I don't envy him, too. He's got a magnificent absence of principle that must simplify while it undoubtedly enriches all his dealings with the law. You know, it was once said to him that if Adam had had him for advocate he'd never have been thrust out of Eden."

The result was that a few days later a meeting was arranged that was attended by Bruce, his junior, Marshall, Crook and Bill Parsons, Mullins (who might be able to answer additional questions put by Bruce and who was getting anxious about his man), and, rather unexpectedly, Jean Barton, the latter at her own urgent request. It seemed to Crook improbable that she would be called as a witness for either side. The Prosecution could not use her, and the Defence, so Crook believed, would not, since she had nothing useful to contribute.

195

A greater contrast than that presented by Bruce, that spruce, red-headed, green-eyed fount of wisdom, and Crook, the bookie's tout in everything but profession, would be hard to discover. Their very rooms emphasised the difference between them. Crook's always overflowed with papers, so that Bill once said it reminded him of a washerwoman's shed before the day's work began, while Bruce's was as neat as a Harley Street consulting-room.

" That may be all right for the swells who come to see Bruce," Crook said, in his casually genial way, " but my clients like to feel they're getting value for money, and if I sprawl a lot of papers and files all over the chairs, they know I must be a damned important chap."

This was the first time that the two men had been associated on the same side. Bruce, who had a delicately reckless temperament, welcomed the opportunity. You could never tell with Crook what middens you might be expected to overturn, but at least you wouldn't spend your time in the cramping refinements of a suburban drawing-room.

Crook and Bill arrived a little early and went over the outlines of the case, while they waited for the others.

" I've got a fine outsider for you," was Crook's characteristic greeting. " 100-1, no takers."

" All the more glory when he romps home," suggested Bruce, not to be outdone in enterprise.

Crook grinned. " It could be, Bruce. (He never bothered with prefixes. He said it was a middle-class tendency, and, unlike Bruce, he disliked the middle classes ; he said their initials really stood for Muddle and Caution.) " It could be. Y'know, everybody's goin' round saying this chap 'ull never be able to prove he didn't do it, but he don't have

196

to. If he's guilty, he's thought up a damned good story and deserves to be acquitted. He's goin' to get the jury on the raw. Suppose, gentlemen of the jury, you'd come back and found your wife dead in a box, would you have gone for the police? Wouldn't you have felt a bit apprehensive? Are you quite sure you wouldn't have done what he did? Shake a jury's confidence in themselves, and your verdict's half won."

" It 'ud be as well to have some suggestions as to the murderer," suggested Bruce. " Who else is in the field? "

" There's the lover," suggested Crook casually. " If there's a case against the husband, there's generally more of a case against the kind that are only married in the sight of heaven. Sometimes," he added with that cheerful irrelevancy that characterised him, " I could find it in my heart to envy heaven. The things it must see. . . ." Then he came down to facts, spreading them before Bruce as a man at the Market spreads his wares before you, not urging you to buy so much as dazzling you with his merchandise.

Bruce listened, asked an occasional question and fell to drawing fishes, his unique way of stimulating the brain processes. By the time Mullins and Mrs. Barton arrived, the place looked like a study for an aquarium of unusual catholicity.

Crook did the introducing and, standing back, let Bruce take the field. Bruce explained briefly what the law would demand, and what he and Crook considered the best policy to adopt.

" When it's a matter of producing an alternative murderer," he pointed out, " it's not easy in a case like this. Mr. Crook has made the somewhat startling discovery that Paul Fryer, who was admittedly the dead woman's lover, is still alive. I'm afraid it's not going to be very simple to trace his movements on that particular Saturday afternoon so long after the event, but we feel that if we outline the case in considerable detail you, Mrs. Barton or Mr. Mullins, may be able to detect some weak point only obvious to those who knew the deceased and the prisoner, and who were living in the neighbourhood at the time of the tragedy. Now, to come to this man Fryer. From what we can learn, and from his own account, he was sufficiently infatuated with Mrs. Beatrice Barton to throw up a safe position and to leave the country. Now, that does argue considerable infatuation, or else very considerable representations on the part of the woman. In law, unless her husband brought an action for divorce, no claim against him on behalf of the alleged child could be made. The husband in these cases is presumably the father and is, in fact, regarded as such in law, and the child may bear his name and look to him for entire maintenance. Now, Mrs. Barton, I believe you knew Fryer ? "

" I went to the house once or twice while he was lodging there. Once he was there and once he came in with Mrs. Barton, just before I went in."

" Did you know anything about their relations ? "

" I knew he was in love with her. I could only guess the rest."

" When he left the house, why did you think that was ? "

" Because he was in love with her and he wanted to do the decent thing."

" Did you know anything about their meeting afterwards ? "

" No. But if he'd been in love in January, it wasn't likely he'd be out of love by April."

" Why do you say that ? "

" Because her men never were. Anyway, I'd seen them together. It was just as much his side as hers."

" You know, perhaps, that he asked his landlady not to give any one his new address ? That looks as if he wanted to get clean out. Who else would be likely to ask for it but Mrs. Barton ? "

" Well, if he wanted her to know where he was, he'd tell her himself."

" Exactly. So if he asked the woman not to tell any one, it does look as though he wanted to cut the whole connection. Nobody else would be likely to ask. According to himself, he had no friends in Putney."

" He wasn't what I'd call a friendly sort of man."

" Have you any idea how deeply it went with her ? She never spoke to you ? "

" No, never. But if she says there was going to be a child, and if it was true, then she was pretty far gone. Because there had been others, and she didn't have any children by them ; and she would know how to prevent it. So she must have wanted his child. And she wouldn't have wanted that if she hadn't cared. Besides, she said she was going away. She'd never said that for any of the others. Oh, there's a story by Rudyard Kipling that I once read. It was called *The Wish House*, and one of the women in it says, ' Either you're theirn or they're yourn.' I think up till then they'd all been hers to do what she liked with, but when she met Mr. Fryer she was his."

" A man might find that infatuation inconvenient, particularly as he wasn't in a position to marry her. Or he might resent the attentions of other men. Being in love is as good a motive for murder as any."

" Meanin' that Fryer might feel the lady had put

one over on him," contributed Crook. " Of course, we don't know how far she'd go when it came to getting what she wanted. She could ruin him with his employers if she told her story there, and they believed it. He had a job with an ecclesiastical bookshop at the time, and they were more rigid than the Pope. I went to see them a while ago, said I was trying to trace the fellow on behalf of the widow, and they said he'd told them he was goin' abroad to join his wife. The chap I talked to looked like all the ushers in Dickens rolled into one. Added D.V. to every other sentence. So tragic, he said, that just when Fryer was on his way this terrible disaster should overtake him. But there was some reason in it we couldn't understand. D.V. Still, he did throw in his hand, put in his notice, arrange to go overseas. Our trouble is we don't know if he did it willingly or if she coerced him. Luggin' a lady that's not your wife, especially with a Little Stranger on the way, round the Continent isn't every fellow's idea of Paradise. Besides, he's not like the orang-outang or whatever ape it is that mates once in a lifetime."

Bill said unexpectedly, " I think it's a goldfinch," and Mullins laughed suddenly on a queer, harsh note.

" There's another dame in the picture now," Crook went on. " And, if you ask me, it's history repeating itself. Goodness knows why. I've never been much of a target for the girls myself, but there's no guessing at their fancies. If you'd asked me, I'd have said that Epstein might have taken a fancy to Fryer, but not many other people would. He's got a face like the Tragic Muse after a night out, and hands like baulks of teak. But this girl's fallen for him all right. It wouldn't surprise me if you saw another little paragraph in the papers one

fine morning : ' Girl found strangled in a doorway.'
These clinging females. You know "—he spoke
confidentially to Bruce and Mullins—" the trouble
about women is they don't seem to realise there are
some men would prefer to face a judge and jury
to getting penal servitude in a two-by-four top-floor
back for the duration."

Mullins interjected with a question : " You don't
mind me asking, but I feel we're all in this. What
was Fryer's reason for letting every one think him
dead ? I mean, the reason he gives."

" He says that when he believed Mrs. Barton was
dead he thought he might as well fade out, too.
I suppose he thought there was Barton, who might
turn nasty if he'd managed to stay safe while the
lady was drowned, and there was Mrs. Fryer, who
might put in an oar at any time, and, for all we
know, there were other reasons—female and otherwise. Besides, once it had come out that he wasn't
dead, he'd have had the whole press round his
bedside. The story would have come out all over
the country, and there's some kinds of limelight a
chap don't exactly court."

" But—do we know he ever was in hospital ? "
Mullins sounded doubtful.

" We've got Fryer's word for it—the word of an
English gentleman. We can't get at the hospital
to check his story, because it was burnt out subsequently, and even if we could find the nurse who
held his hand, which is remarkably unlikely, she
wouldn't remember one accident case nearly ten
years ago, not unless Fryer made passes at her,
which is a bit steep even for him."

" He's a clever devil," Mullins admitted. " Of
course, he's had plenty of time to think it all out ..."

" If he'd been just a little cleverer we couldn't

have touched him," Bruce responded grimly. " He had only to say he'd never made súch an arrangement, and he'd have been absolutely safe. Barton had destroyed his wife's letter, there wasn't an atom of proof against the fellow. Even if we could have known they'd been meeting on the sly, there wasn't evidence that they were planning an elopement. Or, if he was, that the lady concerned was Mrs. Barton."

Jean intervened gently. " Margaret says you've traced her mother's hairbrushes."

" We have, but actually that don't help us, except that it proves her suitcase couldn't have been put on board the *Empress of Araby*. And as it didn't go down with the ship, Barton might just as easily have got rid of the suitcase as any one else.

" That's the Prosecution's case. Of course, he might have done it, even if he was innocent, if his story's gospel. Only, if he had found the brushes and the luggage, to say nothing of her handbag on the Saturday, he must have realised she hadn't gone. And yet it was on the Monday that he was seen looking at her in the trunk, and Monday's the day he gives his own version as the one on which he found her. If he'd known she hadn't gone, surely he'd have hunted all over the place—after all, it's not a palace—that same night, and if he'd found her then he'd have dragged her down to the cellar at once. In any case, in view of the girl's postcard asking to come back earlier, he'd have got her underground as soon as possible. The odds are he'd do it on the Saturday evening after dark. Anyway, he wouldn't wait till broad daylight on Monday. If he didn't find her till Monday, it's because he had nothing to give him a hint that she hadn't gone with Fryer—I suppose he didn't notice about her washing things—and that means that the handbag and the suitcase had been removed. Which means that the chap went down to the house on Saturday afternoon. He could easily do it without being seen. The women would be busy in their own homes or at the shops, the men would be at football or out somewhere or other. Anyway, the average man and woman see very little more than kittens before their eyes are opened, all the years of their lives. Ask a man for a description of the chap next door and he'll be flummoxed. He not only won't know if the fellow's eyes are green or blue, he won't be able to swear on oath that he has any eyes at all.

" Oh, Fryer wasn't taking many risks. Mind you, I don't say that he went down there intendin' to finish the lady off, but the circumstances and their own temperaments and the precariousness of their situation—for neither had any cash, so far as we know—everything taken together, they were probably on a knife-edge of nerves, and he may have hit out and done for her before he knew.

" Another thing in Barton's favour," he went on, " is the finding of the body in the boxroom. If he was goin' to put her in the cellar, why put her in the boxroom at all ? It's not likely the row took place there ; she'd got her luggage out. So you'd expect him to take the box to the body rather than the body to the box. Then, if he lost the suitcase, when did he lose it ? According to himself, he wasn't back till after seven o'clock. It takes a little time to murder a lady and dispose of her, and when he was seen leaving the house at nine o'clock he wasn't carrying anything. That woman is sure of it. I've seen her, as well as Bill, and she says his hands were empty. On Sunday he didn't get up till late ; of course, he could have got rid of it on Sunday evening, but, again, you'd expect him to dump it somewhere right away, or else put her clothes back in the drawers and chuck the suitcase into the boxroom. He was going to get rid of her clothes, and he could have packed them into the various boxes and sent them off before any awkward questions were asked. Her handbag, too. We've heard nothing of that. The passport naturally would be destroyed, and any personal belongings, but not the bag. It could be shoved in a dustbin ; but, if so, the housemaid might rescue it. I'm not assuming any murderer would be fool enough to put it in his own dustbin—or it might be recovered somehow and recognised. . . ."

" Only if it were hidden in the neighbourhood," amplified Bruce. " If the case were deposited in London, the bag might be deposited there, too. Empty bags are constantly being found in pieces of waste ground ; it's a way the thieves have of disposing of them. I've even known them packed up and sent to post offices."

They debated that a little and then Crook went on to the next point. The sponge-bag and toilet articles. Was it likely, he said, that a man who knew his neck was in danger would forget about things that would be immediately obvious to any woman ? And he was expecting a woman in the person of his daughter in the course of the next day or two. Of course, if an outsider did the job, then he'd be panic-stricken ; his one idea would be to get out as soon as possible. He mightn't notice the washing things or think about them and even if he remembered them afterwards it would be too late.

Mullins, looking puzzled, said, " There's one thing

I don't understand. Suppose Fryer did do it and he went off with the luggage, how is it he didn't put the bag on board the boat ? "

The three men looked at him gently. " There could be an answer to that," murmured Crook.

" Supposing Fryer didn't intend to travel by the boat himself, then he wouldn't be likely to go down to the docks," Bruce explained. " This story of putting his coat in the cabin—who's to verify that ? Nobody can, now. If the ship hadn't gone down, we might have got hold of some of the crew or a steward, someone on board, to help us, but we're working absolutely in the dark. We can only conjecture."

Crook joined in. " Talk about the ancient Egyptians havin' to make bricks without straw ! If you ask me, they were a grumbling lot. Look what we're expected to do. Make a building as snug as Buckingham Palace with no more than a handful of mud."

" What next ? " asked Bill as, having shaken off their companions, the pair were returning to the office.

" Ever know me do a job any one 'ull do for me ? " returned Crook coolly. " No, we do a spot more waiting. Let patience have her perfect work. Why do you suppose I allowed Mullins to attend to-day's conference if it wasn't that I thought he might be useful to us ? "

Crook's wisdom was justified. Mullins, who was genuinely anxious about the progress of the case, proceeded to take a much more energetic part than before, with the inevitable consequence that he also began to attract the limelight. Four days after the meeting of the Powers, a lady called to see Crook.

She was tall, thin, not with a fashionable slenderness, but with the haggardness that excites no admiration, no longer young, her eyes discontented, her mouth drooped. Sick and sorry, thought Crook. Another of these dames come to complain about her husband romping with some other jane. And can you blame 'em? I'd as soon go to bed with a wet broomstick as this specimen.

The lady gave her name as Mrs. Mullins, and said she was troubled about her husband.

" What's he up to ? " asked Crook.

She stared haughtily. " You should know."

" Ah ! " said Crook wisely. " You mean our Mr. Mullins."

" Of course I mean him. He's in danger, and he won't listen to me."

" What do you want me to do about it ? "

" You must tell him to stop this business. Whoever is responsible for the murder is dangerous and desperate. He won't hesitate at anything. It stands to reason that a man who has killed one man won't hesitate about killing another."

" Actually, that's not terribly good logic," Crook warned her. "A man who committed a murder nine years ago and got away with it is likely to be precious careful how he jeopardises his neck again. Still, let's get this straight. You think the real murderer of Mrs. Barton is threatenin' your husband ? But how ? "

" There are mysterious telephone calls, and this morning there was a letter addressed to myself." She drew it out. " It came from the postal district W.C.1, and it says : ' Tell your husband that discretion is the better part of valour. Let him attend to his own affairs and leave the police and the lawyers to attend to theirs.' "

" That's a rum sort of letter," ejaculated Crook.
" What do you take it to mean ? "

" Well, of course, it's this Mrs. Barton case. He's
been neglecting his work for days on that account.
I've spoken to him about it. ' We have ourselves to
think of,' I've said. ' Businesses don't run themselves,' I've said. But he's beyond reason. It's
become a point of honour with him now. I don't
know whether he really believes Mr. Barton is
innocent, but that's the kind of man he is. Having
come out in public and backed him, and got you to
take up the defence, he feels this man has got to
be vindicated. ' What's it to do with us ? ' I say
to him. ' We've got to think of ourselves, haven't
we ? ' But he's like a fanatic, Mr. Crook. Can't
you do anything with him ? It's your job, I suppose, to take risks in connection with your work,
but it isn't his."

" He's not doing it under my instructions,"
Crook assured her. " In fact, I'd much rather he
kept out of things. It's not good policy or even
good sense to keep a dog and bark yourself."

" Couldn't you tell him that ? " she urged. " I
can do nothing with him."

" Have you tried ? "

" I spoke to him yesterday, but it was absolutely
useless. He got so angry, told me I didn't understand. He's right—I don't. I don't mean I want
her husband to hang if he didn't kill her ; I don't
know anything about that. Anyway, I don't think
he ought to hang, if he did do it, because I'm sure
she drove him to it. She was that kind of woman.
She couldn't leave any man alone. When my husband told me that Sunday morning that she'd gone
down on the *Empress of Araby*—because, of course,
at that time we never dreamed she hadn't sailed—

I was almost glad. And I should think a lot of other wives were glad, too. You never knew whose man she would try and take next. She had no conscience. If ever a woman deserved to die, she did."

" I'm afraid that's not the law," Crook told her. " The ordinary citizen hasn't got the power of life and death, even over an unfaithful wife. And by all accounts, Barton was rather attached to his."

" He was mad about her ; we all knew it. He wouldn't have put up with her behaviour for so long if he hadn't been."

Crook was thoughtful. " What makes you think that Barton didn't kill her ? "

" I didn't say . . ."

" Well, who do you imagine is threatening your husband ? "

" He says you've found this man Fryer she was supposed to be going with. Tom—Mr. Mullins—is watching him . . ."

" Very good of him," exploded Crook. " Does he imagine I don't know my job ? If he wants to carry on, let him tell me to get out. What chance does he suppose I'm going to have of pulling off this ticklish business if amateurs are going to butt in ? "

Mrs. Mullins leaned forward eagerly. " Tell him that. That might stop him. But, oh, tell him before it's too late. I warn you, I'm frightened. If this man knows you're after him, he'll become desperate."

" Has he had any of these letters ? "

" He hasn't told me."

" Would he, if there were any ? "

The slow, unbecoming colour mounted to her sallow cheeks. " I don't suppose he would. He says he hates being fussed over. That any woman who understood men would know that. But he's my husband, and it's natural I should be anxious."

Crook sighed. He rang for a clerk and told him to bring Mrs. Mullins a cup of tea. " You're looking all in," he told her frankly. " You know, your best course would be to persuade your husband to take you away for a few days. Could he ? "

" I don't know if he could. I know he wouldn't. He's like that. Once he gets interested in a thing he doesn't let go till he's got bored with it. And this is a new rôle for him."

" Curse the films and the various Crime Societies of this country," observed Crook, but without heat. " They've made every little pot-bellied clerk think he can pit himself against Scotland Yard and win. You go back to your husband, Mrs. Mullins, and tell him from me that he's doing neither himself nor Barton any good by playing at Sherlock Holmes. Ask him if he's lost his confidence in me. . . ."

She shrank back. " You won't tell him I've been here ? "

" Not if you say not, but . . ."

" He'd never forgive me." Her face was pale with terror. " He'd say that was the last straw."

" It's a pity when any lady feels the way that one does about her husband," Crook remarked to Bill, when the haggard Mrs. Mullins had gulped her tea and left the office. " A pity for him, too. In a way, I'm sorry for the chap. All the same, I'm beginning to wonder if we'll get out of this case without another death."

And here he spoke with true prophetic sense. For within forty-eight hours Fryer, wearying, it seemed, of these cat-and-mouse tactics, and admittedly finding his life not worth the anxiety it had become to him, threw in his hand and made confusion worse confounded.

CHAPTER SIXTEEN

DEATH OF A GENTLEMAN

IT was Cartwright, Fryer's assistant, who made the discovery, made it by sheer chance, one of those coincidences that life likes so much more than the average publisher. Cartwright had been spending the evening with a friend who mentioned that he wanted a second-hand car, and, knowing his companion's mode of employment, asked if his boss had had anything up to his (Turner's) weight—his financial weight, he meant.

" There's a decent little Morris Twelve going dirt cheap," Cartwright told him. " We're selling it for the owner. He wants a quick sale because he needs the cash. You'd get it at bargain price. If it isn't sold, that is . . ."

" Well, if it wasn't sold when you left the place to-night, the odds are it's still available."

" Can't be certain. Some chap telephoned Hart this afternoon about a second-hand car. I don't know if that was the one, if he'd seen it, or if he just wanted to know if there was a car. Anyhow, Hart was staying to-night to see him. He said he'd be coming in about eight."

" Who is he ? "

" Don't know. I didn't take the call. I was outside with a customer, and when I came back Hart told me in that you-be-damned way of his that he'd had a call about a car, and he'd be staying late. I cleared off at six."

It then occurred to him that they were no great distance from the garage, and it might be worth their while to make a slight detour and see whether the car had disappeared from the showroom. Cartwright had a key with which he admitted himself each morning. When they reached the garage they found the main door unlocked, and a crack of light showed under the door leading to Hart's office.

" They may be still there," Cartwright murmured to his companion. " Wait a shake."

He moved across the floor, hesitated a moment, said, " No sound of voices," and opened the door. An instant later he had staggered back, his face greenish, his eyes sick with shock.

" What's up . . . ? " Turner looked startled. " Has someone staged a murder ? "

" Something like it," muttered Cartwright. " Holy Jake ! That's why he stayed to-night, I suppose. I thought he'd been looking queer, but I didn't dream. . . . I don't suppose there ever was a telephone call. Come to think of it, I don't remember hearing anything. I say, Joe, look out and see if you can spot a copper. If not, I'll have to telephone. My oath, I haven't seen anything like this since the war."

Joe Turner, moving to the door, said, " You don't mean he's done for himself ? "

" Looks bloody like it. And bloody's about the right word, too. The place is like a butcher's slaughter house. It turned me up for the minute."

" It is your boss ? "

" Why—who else ? Not that you can tell much from the face. Gawdamighty, there isn't any face worth mentioning."

Turner told him sharply to pull himself together and went out into the street. Cartwright stayed where he was. His friend came back with the news that the street was empty.

" You ought to get a doctor."

" The police can do that."

" Where's the telephone ? "

" In there."

Turner pushed open the door, took one glance at the Thing lying mutilated over the table, and grabbed the receiver. While he talked he kept his back to the body.

" Funny no one heard anything," he said, returning to the outer room.

" Well, there's not many round here would be likely to, this hour of the night. It's hardly what you'd call a residential neighbourhood ; the nearest people are some wholesale dress manufacturers, and they shut up about seven."

" No night watchman ? "

" Never seen one. Anyway, if he did hear anything, he'd probably think it was a bursting tyre."

Turner nodded. " This is bad luck for you," he suggested. " Jobs aren't too plentiful."

" I'll find something. Lord, are the police never coming ? "

A car swept round the corner of the street and stopped in front of the garage. Several men got out. One was a police sergeant, another was the doctor they had thoughtfully brought with them.

" Red Triangle Garage ? "

" That's right. He's in there. You'd better come in."

The doctor gave one glance at the body, said, putting his hands in his pockets, " The Archangel Gabriel couldn't help him now," and then, removing his hands, bent over the wreck.

" He's made a certain job of it," he observed with a kind of grim humour. " Where's the weapon ? Ah ! "

On the ground, lying a little to the right of the chair in which the dead man sat, was a revolver. The sergeant said something to his assistant. Nobody touched the gun.

" How long ago did you find him ? " the sergeant asked Cartwright.

" Just before I telephoned. My friend and I came in to look at a car that was for sale . . ."

" How did you get in ? "

" I have a key. I'm employed here. But, as a matter of fact, the door wasn't locked. We came right in."

" Isn't the door generally locked at night ? "

" Mr. Hart told me he was staying to see a customer about a car."

" Know who the customer was ? "

Cartwright shook his head. " I only have his word for it that there was a customer. It may just have been an excuse for staying late."

The sergeant came back into the front office. The usual routine as to fingerprints, etc., would have to be observed. Meanwhile he continued to examine Cartwright. " Who are you ? " he asked Turner.

Cartwright explained the position.

" What do you know about him—the dead man, I mean ? "

" His name's Hart—Paul Hart—and he's had this garage about six months."

" Know anything about his private life ? "

" Not much. He was as close as a clam. A queer chap. Liable to blow up at any minute, but all right as employers go. Knew his job, too."

" How long have you been here ? "

" Nearly six months. I came about the time he opened the affair. I don't know who had it before that."

213

" Was he a married man ? "

" I gathered so. Not that he ever talked about his wife. There was a girl, though . . ."

" What girl ? "

" A Miss Lamar, or some such name. She used to ring him up sometimes, and once she came and waited outside for him. He wasn't half rorty. ' This I will not have,' he said. And she got all worked up and said, ' Paul, why cannot you understand ? ' A bit foreign, I thought."

" You don't know where she lives ? "

" I couldn't say that. He was a queer bloke, had a sort of down on women, I always thought ; though there's no question they fell for him. I've seen 'em when they came in here about their car or with their menfolk, the way they'd look. . . ."

" When did you last see him alive ? "

" Just after six when I shut the place up. He said he'd stay for this fellow, there was nothing for me to do."

" Did he say who the man was ? "

" No. Perhaps the chap didn't give a name. Or perhaps there wasn't a chap at all. Perhaps it was the girl again. That's all guesswork, though. Still, Thursday was her evening out, and I suppose they hadn't many other places to go to."

" Where did he live ? "

" Roland Terrace—No. 6."

" You can't suggest any reason for that ? "

" I tell you, I didn't know him very well. The business was going all right ; doing very well, in fact. He knew a lot about cars, and he never seemed to spend a bob on himself. I suppose everything he got he put back into the concern."

It was obvious that Cartwright could be of little assistance. Possibly, when the news was made public, a wife or some friend might come forward with supplementary information. In any case, there seemed nothing very unusual about the affair. In these days of crises men were perpetually finding the strain of modern life too much for them, and when their business or personal affairs began to go wrong they took the easy way out.

The doctor came in, saying that the man had been dead an hour at least, possible a little more. Death was instantaneous and due to a gunshot wound in the head. The shot had probably been fired by the revolver found beside the body, but there would have to be official confirmation of that. The wound was consistent with suicide. He said, " If there's a wife or any near relative, she'd better be told."

" He only seems to have a landlady," said the sergeant. " I'll go round there and see if she can tell us anything. Something may come out at the inquest."

He made the necessary arrangements for completing the records and removing the body to the mortuary. He left his subordinate in charge, took Cartwright's name and address, asked Turner for similar information, added that they'd be wanted at the inquest, and made his way to Roland Terrace. It was by this time almost eleven o'clock, and Mrs. Prince was in process of undressing. Jenkins had to ring several times before she came to the door. When she saw who he was she looked startled.

" You've got a lodger of the name of Paul Hart ? " he began.

She fired up at once. " You're not going to tell me a quiet-spoken man like that's in trouble with the police ? "

" Why should you think so ? "

ANTHONY GILBERT

" What are you here for, this hour of night ? I've
never had the police come to my house all the time
I've been here, and that's fifteen years and more.
Only once, and that was the time when one of my
lodgers lost her cat. A lovely cat it was, wore a
collar and used to go walks with her, and one day
it went for a walk by itself and got run over by
a car. A policeman came to tell us about the
accident. Ever so upset, she was . . ."

Jenkins, as soon as he could get a word in edge-
ways, said, " I'm afraid it's another case of accident.
Mr. Hart was found shot in his office this evening."

She drew a long breath. " Shot ? You mean, he
did it himself ? "

" The inquest will decide that."

" I always thought there was something queer
about him."

" Do you know if he had a wife ? "

" I couldn't say. He never spoke of her. There
was a girl, though . . ."

" Who was she ? "

" I couldn't be certain. A Miss Lemur or something. Used to ring up when he wasn't here, and
more than once I've seen her walking up and down
the street opposite, waiting for him. It's my belief
he often came back as late as he did to get away
from her."

" How did you know who she was ? "

" Because she came to the door once, as bold as
brass, to ask for him. A bit foreign, I thought."

" Do you know her address ? "

But Mrs. Prince could not help him there.

It did not seem to Jenkins there was much more
he could usefully do that night. The case would
be reported in the morning papers, and any one
concerned with the dead man might be expected

to come forward. This girl—he didn't know—she might prefer to keep out of the limelight. Still, that wasn't very easy. Not that he could see much use in dragging her into the affair. The man was dead. Of course, it might come out that she was blackmailing him. You never knew what lay behind a suicide. Had Jenkins had the faintest idea of the melodrama that had led to this final decisive act, the ancient tragedy in which it had had its root, he might have made his report with less stoical assurance. As it was, his final reflection was that most likely that chap had written to someone explaining his motive. They mostly did, as though they couldn't endure to go out into the dark without some last word. As to that, the morning, he hoped, would show.

The papers carried the news in their first edition :

" SHOT MAN IN GARAGE

" The body of a man, Paul Hart, aged about 50, was found shot through the head in his office at the Red Triangle Garage, Edgware Road, last night at about ten o'clock. A weapon was found beside the body. The tragedy was discovered by Thomas Cartwright, an employee at the garage. The inquest will be opened to-morrow.''

One paper, more enterprising than the rest, had already interviewed Mrs. Prince, and added :

" MYSTERY OF FOREIGN WOMAN IN GARAGE DRAMA "

But even that couldn't say very much.

The staff of 18 Greatorex Square saw the news as they sat drinking their breakfast cups of tea. It

ANTHONY GILBERT

was Cook, who had the *Daily Screech*, who saw it on the front page.

"Well, I'm bothered!" she exclaimed. "I wonder if it's the same."

"What's it all about?" asked Merton, the head parlourmaid.

"It's Hart. Shot himself. Would that be her last chauffeur?"

Merton brightened up. "What does it say?"

"He had a garage. Well, he said he was going into business on his own account. Suzanne, didn't he tell you a bit more than the rest?"

Suzanne said slowly, "I met him once in the street, and he said he was doing well. Is there a picture?"

"No, just a paragraph. Looks like suicide. Place not paying, perhaps."

Suzanne took the paper and read the few lines it contained.

"Foreign woman," observed Merton, over her shoulder. "Well, he was always queer."

"Perhaps they'll want you at the inquest, Suzanne," said Cook encouragingly.

Suzanne put the paper down very quietly. "I don't think so," she said in indifferent tones. "I know nothing more than the rest. But there will be a letter, perhaps."

The postman called late here; it would be some minutes yet before he could be expected. She found some excuse to be upstairs when he came. The butler was sorting the post in the hall.

"Nothing for me, Mr. Fisher?" she asked.

The butler turned a sour face towards her. He disliked Suzanne, distrusted women altogether, and foreigners more than the rest.

"Nothing," he said.

Suzanne walked upstairs with a pale, set face. Nothing ! He hadn't written her a line, and now he never could. Well, nobody knew anything about them. They couldn't drag her into this. She had called at the house once, but surely the woman would never remember her name. He was dead, and there was nothing more to be done. It did a girl no good to be mixed up in a suicide. But under all that her heart was wrung and torn with a sense of loss, a sense that would grow when this first numbness died down. Automatically she knocked on her ladyship's door, carrying her ladyship's post. No need to speak of Hart in this quarter ; *she* wouldn't so much as remember his name. All the morning she waited in an agony for a call from the police.

They came about eleven o'clock, having discovered, in the mysterious way that the police do unearth such information, that the dead man had previously been employed by Lady Kay. They didn't stay long ; there was nothing she could tell them. And then they asked if they might see the servants. When Jenkins heard Suzanne's name he said sharply, " You were a friend of his, weren't you ? "

She looked at him with expressionless black eyes. How much did he know ? How much would it be safe to deny ?

" Called at his house, didn't you, the place where he lodged ? "

She said slowly, " I knew him a little, but I did not know anything of this."

" Didn't have a letter from him ? "

" Nothing. You can ask Mr. Fisher if you do not believe me. He takes in the letters."

They asked some more questions. " Did he ever talk to you about himself ? "

" Not much."

" Did you know about his wife ? "

" Just that he had one and they did not get on."

" Did you know he was leaving his rooms on Saturday ? "

" No."

Jenkins got up. There was no sense in prolonging the interview. If the dead man had had relations with this woman—well, that was no crime punishable by law. A drastic search of his possessions revealed no correspondence between the two. If she'd been blackmailing him, there was no proof. Nothing to show that he'd taken his life on her account. There had been no letter to the police station that morning, either. No information had been received from anywhere. There was still a chance that someone in the country to whom he had written before he put the bullet in his brain might come forward. If not, it would be the usual thing : Suicide while of unsound mind. It wasn't important, anyhow. Too many people committed suicide for that.

But he was an observant officer. " I don't believe she did know," he told himself. " She's taken the knock. I wonder what she expected to get out of it, a married man nearly twice her age."

He returned to the police station to report.

Bill Parsons saw the news about seven o'clock and rang through to Crook's private dwelling in Earl's Court. Crook said, " H'm. I wondered. Well, everything depends now on whether he left any confession or not. When's the inquest ? Right. We'd better be there."

It was a pity, he thought, that British sentiment condemned suggestions of evil intent on the part of dead men. Fryer at least was nicely out of things, but Barton was still in a pretty hazardous condition, and it was touch and go—more touch and go than ever, in fact—whether they could contrive to pull him out of the fire.

Mullins read the paragraph in the *Morning Record* and immediately telephoned to Crook.

" This is our man, I take it ? "

" Looks like it, don't it ? " Crook agreed.

" Does that cook our goose ? "

" Couldn't tell you yet. Shall I see you at the inquest ? "

But he saw Mullins before the inquest. The jeweller called during the morning.

" Well, this lands us in a dead alley all right," he said.

" I've never been in a dead alley in my life," countered Crook indignantly. " Half the time in work like ours you have to hold your thumbs while the criminal dots the i's for you."

" You mean you were expecting this ? "

" I'm not altogether surprised."

" You mean you thought he'd make this get-out. Well, he must have known he didn't stand an earthly."

" Poor devil, he didn't."

" And you let him get away with it ? "

Crook suddenly exploded. " Who the hell do you think you are to talk to me like this ? I've done everything possible for Barton, taken more chances than most men of my profession would have cared to risk . . . and then you have the brass nerve to turn up and practically tell me I don't know my job."

Mullins looked a little alarmed at the storm he had evoked. " I didn't mean that," he said.

" Then what in thunder did you mean ? "

221

" Only that, now Fryer's dead, how do we get on with our case ? "

" Fryer," Crook told him coldly, " was a gentleman. Got that ? "

Mullins considered. " Meanin' he wrote out a confession ? "

" Got it in one."

Mullins looked staggered. " You're not pulling my leg ? You mean he acknowledged he'd done for Mrs. Barton ? "

" He did."

" He did ? "

" That's what I said. It's all over bar the shouting."

" All over bar the shouting ? " Mullins sounded as though he couldn't believe his ears.

" Say, what do you think this place is ? The parrot-house at the Zoo ? " demanded Crook with his customary discourtesy. He would have seen eye to eye with St. Paul on many points, particularly as regards women ; but, unlike that great apostle, he had never even tried to suffer fools gladly, albeit he knew that he himself was wise. " Sit down, if you haven't frozen in your breeks, and I'll tell you the inner history of the Barton murder. " Not," he added vaingloriously, " that it'll tell you much we didn't know already. But it always helps to have it in black and white with a signature at the foot."

" But why you ? Why not the police ? " Mullins' heavy brow was wrinkled.

" Have a heart. Have some sense, too. What do the police know about Paul Fryer ? They've never heard the name, or, if they have, they think it belongs to a man who was drowned in 1930. Sending them the letter wouldn't have done any good, and there'd have been the exhaustin' job of identifyin' the two.

Now I've seen the whole racket from the inside. He won't have to make a lot of troublesome explanations to me. Best of all, I'm defendin' Barton. I'm the chap that can use this sort of thing to the best advantage. Besides, think how we tie the hands of the police in this country. I'm a free agent."

" Do the police know ? "

" They'll know in lots of time," Crook assured him grimly. " I like puttin' one over them now and again. Well, then, like to hear the letter now or wait till the inquest ? "

" I hadn't thought of attending the inquest."

" Well, then, here we are. Bill's seen it already. I've phoned Bruce. He's coming over. That ought to be him now. So it is." He grunted as Counsel for the Defence entered the room. " Well, let's get going. You know, Bruce, these confessions are always damned interestin' documents. It's fine to see where fallible human nature slips up and where it can't resist showin' off a bit."

He pushed cigarettes towards his visitors, picked up a long envelope from among the papers on his desk and drew out what appeared to be several sheets of typewritten matter.

" He's made a long story of it," ejaculated Mullins when he saw these.

" Vanity again. It gets most of 'em in the end. Half a dozen lines would have been enough for a police court ; but they can't resist tellin' you how damned clever they were. Ah, well, it was his last will and testament. You can't blame him for wanting to show off a bit, and he was clever. Nine years is a long time to cover a murder up. However, I warned you, Mullins, you needn't lose any of your beauty sleep. I told you from the start Barton wouldn't swing."

223

CHAPTER SEVENTEEN

A MURDERER SHOWS HIS HAND

THE letter was addressed to Arthur Crook, Esquire, and began without any other formality of address :

"I take this way out because, thanks to you, no other remains. It is impossible that I should go on. Sooner or later—and I think not much later—you will find your missing link, and I prefer to end matters in my own way. For it is true, it is true that I killed Beatrice Barton. Not of my own will or desire, but by one of those accidents in which your police and people do not believe. Ever since they arrested that innocent man my mind has been in a turmoil. Indeed, I am not sorry that it should end like this. All day now I see her, as I saw her that afternoon, lying with her head against the stairs, with that empty look in her eyes. You, who did not know her, could never understand. It was like water on a flame. There was never any other woman like her. Afterwards I only turned to them because of something, some gleam that had recalled her to my mind. But it was useless. Having had her, the others . . ." (The rest of this sentence was so heavily blotted out that it was illegible.)

"As I have said, I never intended to hurt her. This is how it happened.

"It was arranged that we should meet at

Victoria Station. Her husband, she said, would not be returning until late; her daughter was away. But at the last I had a sudden fear that something might happen to prevent her. Mr. Barton might return early, the girl might come home. Since she was my life, and since, also, she carried my life, I could take no chances, and so I went down to Putney to bring her away myself. It was five o'clock when I arrived, and she let me in. She seemed surprised to see me. I had to come, I told her, I had to come. She laughed a little. No one has ever laughed like her in all my life. I said, ' Come, come quickly. It does not matter about luggage. All you need you can buy when we are in France. Just come now. She said she must finish the letter she was writing to her husband. Finish it on board, I urged. We can post it. But she said, ' No. He must find it on his return.' So she finished the letter and gave it to me to read while she went upstairs to complete her packing. I could not rest. I called to her, ' Never mind, never mind, only come quickly.' She came down to me, laughing still. There was something, she •said, that she had forgotten. She put her hand on my shoulder.

" ' You are jealous,' she said. ' Why must men be jealous ? It should be possible to love as one pleases, to love as many as one pleases.'

" I shook her hand off. I said roughly that she was mad, that love is always jealous. ' If you so much as smile at another man it will be a dagger in my heart,' I told her. ' Why, there have been times when to think that Barton might be your lover has made me long to wring his throat.'

" She looked at me strangely. She said, ' No, no.' I told her, ' Of course. You are mine, mine

only.' She drew herself a little away from me.
' I am my own,' she said. ' Always my own. I
cannot be put in a cage.' ' You call my love a
cage ? ' I demanded. And then all in a moment
it had begun, that fatal quarrel. It was not that
I did not love her. I loved her more, I think,
than ever she loved me. I loved her so much I
was mad, delirious with it. She said that if that
was what I meant by love she would not come
with me. If she must forget all that had ever
happened to her or had belonged to her, then she
would not come. ' For,' she said, ' you speak of
breaking off one life and beginning a new life
with you. But lives cannot be begun so easily
as that. Wherever one goes one takes one's past.
That is my history, and I shall take my history
with me. All the things that have happened to
me . . .' It was then that I became mad. I
thought of that past, all the men she had known,
the men who would live with us like ghosts. I
told her she should forget them, that I would
drive the memory of them out of her mind. Then
she said, ' No, no,' and began to move away from
me. And so it happened. How it happened I
have no recollection, only, all in a moment she
was lying at my feet, crumpled, not erect as I
had always seen her. There was a little blood on
her face and on her hair. I looked at her, wondering. I had no memory of touching her, but if
I did it, I must have done it in one of those
moments when the mind is so dark that no light
can enter it. I remember going down on my
knees beside her and taking her head on my arm.
It lolled dreadfully ; that was when I knew her
neck must be broken. Just as I had not believed
her when she said she would not come away with

me, so now I could not believe that she was dead.
I could not. I could not. Only a moment ago
she had been so alive. You could as easily think
of the whole world being paralysed out of all
movement, struck down by some gigantic thun-
derbolt. I walked up and down. Then I began
to realise my own danger. I was a murderer, and
murderers hang. Murderers hang, I told myself
aloud, and I was startled, thinking that someone
else had spoken. The voice was not my own.
Yet there was no one else there.

"All my life I have been afraid of death. There
is no reason, perhaps, or none that I know, but
although she who was my life was lost to me,
that terror remained. I saw her letter to her
husband lying on the table. My mind began to
gather speed like a train, until presently it was
leaping through time. I thought, ' If he reads
that, he will believe she has gone. He will know
she will never come back.' I knew he would not
follow her. ' If he does not find her here on his
return, he will believe what she has told him,
and I shall be safe. Safe.' I kept saying that
word over and over again.

" Suddenly my heart jumped like a fish ; my
flesh crept. I had heard a sound, the sound of
a closing door. It came from upstairs. So, after
all, she had not been alone in the house. I could
not escape. I felt as though I were turned into
something like stone, but horribly, dreadfully
alive, as if all my nerves had been exposed and
were throbbing like violin strings. For a minute
I thought, ' This is what madness is like ! ' But
actually my madness was passed. I forced
myself to brush by her where she lay at the foot
of the staircase and I went up. There was no one

there. The door had slammed in a wind. I looked
into all the rooms. The one at the end of the
passage was a boxroom. I remembered about
trunk murders. There was a man in South Wales
who hid his woman in a trunk for two months,
so that there was not enough evidence to convict
him when she was found. I thought, ' If I could
hide her so . . .' There was no trunk large
enough, but against one wall, under a folding bed
and some rugs and a garden tent, was a long
wicker basket. It must have been six feet long.
I dragged it out, making very little noise. Still,
I could not believe she was truly dead. Then I
thought, ' If I put her here, if the lid will close
(for she was a big woman), then perhaps I could
be safe.'

" I had not known how heavy the dead can be.
In life I had held her so often in my arms, and
now I could not lift her. But somehow I contrived to bring her to the head of the stairs.
There was a glass transom above the door, and
I saw through it men and women passing up and
down the street. I thought, ' If one of them opens
the gate, rings the bell, then I am lost.' I was
transfixed. But nothing happened, and I took
her under the armpits and dragged her into that
little room. Her head lolled against my knees. I
lifted her up and put her into the box, I forced
the lid down ; a piece of her hair that had become
loosened caught in the buckle, and I found myself
tearing at it. I broke one of my finger-nails
before I got the buckle free. Then I replaced the
box and all the lumber on the top of it, leaving
one of the rugs to trail down, so that the box
itself would not be noticeable. As I passed her
room, I saw that the door was open, and her bag,

her handbag, lay upon the bed. I thought, ' I must take that or he will know she has not gone. There was a case, too, partly filled with clothes. Others lay on the bed and chairs. I piled them all in, I crammed the lid down. I swept the brushes and pots off the dressing-table. Those brushes—I remember them. How could I know they would ever be traced ? And all the time I thought, ' If someone comes now ? ' I looked at the watch on my wrist. It was almost half-past five. I had no time to spare. No time to think of what I might have forgotten. Downstairs again I saw her letter ; she had left an envelope on the table, but it was unaddressed. I dare not write on it, so I put the letter into the envelope, and put the envelope in the letter-box. ' There,' I thought, ' he is bound to find it.' Then I took up the case and I slipped out the back way. The back door shuts very quietly. There was no one in the street, but perhaps there were faces at the windows opposite. I dared not look up at them. I found myself walking very fast, not quite steadily, towards the station, the bag in my hand. Fortunately a mist had collected, the mist that was to develop into a fog in which the *Empress of Araby* would be destroyed, with every soul on board. At Victoria I left her luggage on the platform. There were so many people travelling that I knew it would not be noticed until late that night. Afterwards it would be taken to the Lost Property Office. For myself, I had no plans, but I did not intend to go to France. I could not endure the suspense. I must see the papers, know what was being said. They tell you that fear destroys most murderers.

" The next day I heard that the ship had foundered, that all on board had perished. I saw that I, too, Paul Fryer, must perish. That way I should be safe. I changed my name and my employment. For nine years the world believed Paul Fryer to be dead. I do not know how you discovered me, what you have learned, and now I am afraid. So I prefer to face death, the death I know, to the death that might change me from a man to something less than human. I wonder now why I have fought so hard for my life, except that perhaps life is always better than death, life in any guise."

" And there's his signature, and a pretty poor affair it is," wound up Crook robustly. " Y'know, Mullins, life's queer. A few hours ago, while I was at the dogs and you were——"

" At the New Oxford."

" This chap was writing that letter and then putting a bullet through his brain. All happenin' at the same time. Don't seem to make sense, somehow."

" A lot of life doesn't," agreed Mullins.

" You can take it lyin' down, if you like," Crook told him ; " but that ain't good enough for me. I may be an untidy beggar in the office, and every woman I ever knew told me she could see at first glance I hadn't got a wife to run round after me, but I do like my cases to have neat ends. Once you let 'em fray you never know when you won't be tripping yourself up. And, as I say, this don't make sense."

" What doesn't ? "

" This letter. Just look at that." He passed the envelope across to Mullins.

" What about it ? " The jeweller sounded puzzled.

" Look at the post-mark."

" Ten-thirty."

" Well, now you see what I mean."

" Not altogether."

" This chap was found dead just before ten o'clock. Medical evidence says he'd been dead an hour. There's a post out from the box across the way at nine-thirty. Why didn't the letter catch that ? "

" I don't know."

" It's going to be somebody's job to find out. Y'see, a dead man can't post a letter, and he was dead before the nine-thirty post went out. What do you get from that ? "

Mullins put his hand to his head. " That someone else must have posted it."

" Looks uncommonly likely. Well, then, who ? "

" That chap Cartwright ? " hesitated Mullins.

" Meanin' that Fryer gave him the letter and then, while he crossed the street, put a bullet in his own brain ? "

" Why not ? "

" Two reasons. One, that Cartwright wasn't on the spot till ten—he's got an alibi nothing could shake—and another that, even so, it 'ud have caught the nine-thirty."

" Medical evidence must be wrong, that's all. He must have posted the letter after nine-thirty, so he must have shot himself after that."

" He was good and dead when Cartwright found him. You won't shake the medical evidence on that. Another thing : If he was going to do the decent thing and leave a confession to clear Barton, why didn't he stick to the truth ? "

" What do you mean ? "

" I mean a whole lot of the things in this letter simply can't be true. Take the time factor, for one. He says he got to the house at five, and she was writing the letter, had practically finished it. We know she only got in at five, so she couldn't have done it in the time."

" Perhaps she wrote it before she went out."

" Then why does he say she was writing it when he arrived ? Besides, how about the postcard ? The post in that district on Saturday afternoon don't come round till late—five-thirty, the woman next door told us—so that letter couldn't have been finished before five-thirty, and yet in this document the author says that he was out of the house, with the body disposed of by that time. That's one discrepancy. Another thing I don't understand is about the hair-brushes. How did Fryer know they'd been found ? That hadn't come out. Only the outside ring knew that."

" He may have been trailing you," suggested Mullins.

" It could be, Mullins, it could be. Mind you, I don't think it's likely, but it's a suggestion. It's a fine letter, you know. You're a literary chap yourself, so you ought to appreciate it particularly. I wonder, by the way, what it 'ud be worth to an enterprising journalist." He leaned back and lighted a large green cigar. " You know, if I was going to put a bullet through my brain I wouldn't settle down and write a three-volume novel first. I'd just say there'd been a smash-and-grab and I'd hit her over the head. That's all the courts will want to know."

" Poor devil ! " exclaimed Mullins with some feeling. " Can't you see him, facing death—and he's always been afraid of death—saying the last thing he'd ever say ? Doesn't the thought of that move you in the least ? "

" You sound like an advertisement for Eno's," returned Crook impatiently.

" They say each man kills the thing he loves," mused his companion slowly. " He must have been pretty frightened of death to have put it off so long. I don't like to think of him writing all that and then putting the gun to his temple and . . . They found the weapon on the floor, didn't they ? "

" Yes," said Crook slowly. " And that was perhaps the queerest thing of all. I mean, why a left-handed man should shoot himself through his right temple."

CHAPTER EIGHTEEN

CROOK PLAYS THE ACE

FOR fully a minute after Crook's last words, spoken with that dangerous drawl which characterised all his most pregnant utterances, there was silence, complete, dense as a black curtain in the room. Out of the darkness and quiet came Mullins' voice, soft and hesitant as a mouse emerging from a wainscot.

" What—the—hell—does—that—mean ? "

" Well, what do you suppose it means ? That Fryer didn't write his little piece or conveniently put out his own light. I told you at the start he couldn't post a letter half an hour after he was dead any more than he would shoot himself, using his right hand."

" Then — are you suggesting — murder and forgery ? "

" If you can offer any alternative . . ."

" But who . . . ? " Mullins looked as if he'd got into a topsy-turvy world where he couldn't find the least of his bearings.

" Who would be likely to profit from a cock-and-bull story, do you suppose ? "

" Well, who would ? "

" The real murderer of Beatrice Barton, of course."

" And—who's he ? "

" I could make a damn good guess. I don't think it was Barton, because Barton couldn't have killed Fryer and written out the confession ; and I don't think it was Fryer who wrote this, because he must have known that, however much we suspected him, we could never hope to put him in the dock. He wasn't seen at Putney that afternoon—if he had been, a witness would have come forward long ago—and if he liked to say he'd gone to the pictures or hang about at Victoria Station, who could disprove it ? There was no earthly reason for him to take his own life on account of this affair. He was absolutely safe from us, and he must have known it. Besides, what motive had he ? She'd promised to go off with him. What more could the man want ? If he wanted her out of the way or wanted to be free of her, he could have disappeared and left her to join the unending ranks of Woman Betrayed. I don't suppose she could make any one believe for certain that the baby was his, and he must have known that Barton would acknowledge it, if necessary. That right, Bruce ? "

" Meaning it is murder, after all ? It's a remarkable suggestion, and if it's true it answers one question I asked myself as soon as I heard the news, which was why Fryer didn't lock the outer door of the garage. The ordinary man, intending to commit suicide, at least makes sure he'll be free from interruption, and his normal reaction would be to ensure privacy. After all, the police do go their rounds. A police constable might have tried the door just as Fryer pulled out his gun. But, of course, if it's murder and not suicide, if he was killed by someone who had to make his getaway, then I understand."

" But who is there ? "

" Just what I'm tryin' to find out. I take it the murderer of one is identical with the murderer of the other. That means that whoever murdered Mrs. Barton must have got into the house between five-thirty when the post arrived and seven o'clock when, according to Barton's own statement, he came back. . . ."

" There's no actual evidence of that, is there ? " suggested Mullins. " He may have been back earlier."

" He might," Bruce agreed ; " but, all the same, he couldn't have killed Fryer or written this letter. And whoever wrote this letter was on the spot when Mrs. Barton was killed. It doesn't seem very reasonable to me to suggest that there were two men, of whom Barton was one, in the house at the time of the crime. So for the moment we'll eliminate Barton and try to find out who else could have been there."

He paused, and Crook took up the tale. " One thing stands out a mile," he observed, " and that is that X was pretty mad about the lady himself, and probably knew he had no more chance of gettin' her than the Man in the Moon. Of course, the reason given in the letter is pure punk. Since Fryer didn't write it, she wasn't killed because of her high-falutin' attitude towards love and life and all the rest of it, but I should say X discovered she was goin' off and there was a row, and it ended by the lady passing out. Which wouldn't be a bad ending, if it weren't that it's against the law to put even a wrong 'un underground. Another thing : whoever wrote that letter had read her effusion to her husband, and knew the name of the ship she was sailin' on." Crook made these deductions in a slow, deadly voice as different as possible from his usual clipped, slightly accented speech. He seemed to be arguing each point in his mind before he made it. " You agree with that, Mullins ? "

" I suppose so," said Mullins. " Are you going to spring a completely new criminal on us at the eleventh hour ? "

" There ain't much choice when you get down to brass tacks. Up till now we've taken it that if it wasn't Barton it must be Fryer. Now it don't look as if it could be either of them. Fryer wasn't killed by Fryer or Barton. That's where your evidence is goin' to be so useful. You were on the spot from six to six forty-five the day Mrs. B. was bumped off . . ."

" Not so long as that, I'm afraid. I was back before six-thirty. That gives X half an hour. He must have been a quick worker."

" Too quick to be true," agreed Crook. " Besides, your watch must have stopped. We know you were there till six forty-five, because of Mrs. Morris's evidence. She says it was after the quarter to seven when you knocked her up, and she knows that because her little grandson had shot a dart into the clock and stopped it at the quarter. And you came a few minutes later."

Mullins looked exasperated. " Are you suggesting

that I cooled my heels on Mrs. Barton's doorstep for three-quarters of an hour ? "

Crook blandly played the ace. " Of course not. And I don't believe you were sitting in the car, either, waiting for the lady to return. I think you were inside the house wonderin' how the hell you were going to escape the rope."

Mullins sprang to his feet, but Crook motioned to him to sit down.

" Hear the end of the story. Of course, at this stage, it's not much use givin' you advice. It never is, with murderers. With other criminals it's different, of course. Lots of thieves and embezzlers come out of chokey knowing a damned sight more about their job than they did when they went in. But the tough part about murder is, they don't give you a second chance. If I thought there was any hope for you, I'd point out that in a case like that your only loophole was to go for the police at once. Not that I think you'd have had much of a chance, in any case, not if Barton's story is correct, and the lady was strangled. Anyway, as I say, there's no sense wasting any time on that."

Mullins said, " I suppose you're crazy. You aren't really going to take that story into court. And are you suggesting that I shot Fryer and typed out the letter on his machine ? "

" How did you know he had a machine ? "

" Well, the letter's typewritten, isn't it ? "

" If he didn't write it, it might have been typed anywhere. Actually, it was typed on his ; but if you hadn't been inside his office, how did you know he had one there ? No, no, Mullins, the game's up. I don't suppose for a minute you mean to strangle the lady, but I do believe you got into the house— you couldn't, as you say, have hung about on her doorstep for three-quarters of an hour without any one seeing you—and if you got in, nobody could have admitted you but the lady herself. And we know whoever was responsible must have arrived some time after five-thirty—the postman could vouch for that and so can Mrs. Morris—invaluable woman, our Mrs. Morris—you remember the postman brought a parcel and she had to open the door—so Mrs. Barton must have been in at the time and she'd have opened the door. And if someone else came along, how was it you didn't see him ? I'll tell you : because there wasn't any one else. I do hand it to you," he went coolly, " for the way you played your cards when you realised the whole story was coming out. It was smart of you to come to me and ask me to undertake the defence. It's always the safest position, inside the enemy's front line, so long as your enemy don't see the wolf's teeth behind the lamb's skin. Remember the story of the Cockroach and the Tortoise ? A cockroach was put down in front of a tortoise as an *hors d'œuvres*. The creature knew it hadn't a chance, so, taking one frantic rush, it landed in the tortoise's armpit. You've been nestling very cosy in my armpit for some weeks, and it's suited me to have you there. You see, when you're on a case ten years old, the trail's been cold too long to be much use to you. Honesty and the open road's no good for cases like that. You have to use subtlety. And subtlety means giving a chap enough rope to make his own noose. And you did it, Mullins, you did it very prettily. This letter is a cinch—you do realise that, don't you ? I mean, only Bee Barton's murderer could have written it."

" And when you take your precious yarn to the police, what do you think they're going to make

of it ? " demanded Mullins calmly. " You haven't
got a ha'porth of proof to support you. I wasn't
at the Red Triangle Garage last night ; I didn't
shoot Fryer, I didn't murder Beatrice Barton.
And nothing you say will make anybody believe
I did."

" No ? " murmured Crook. " There is that bit
about the brushes, you know. No one knew about
them but our four selves and the girl."

" I didn't write the letter, so that won't help you.
What next ? "

" This," said Crook, and he leaned across the
table, his wicked little eyes staring into Mullins'
pasty face. " How did you know Mrs. Barton had
sailed on the *Empress of Araby* in time to tell your
wife about it on Sunday morning ? Because nobody
else knew till about twelve-thirty that day, and you
were out of Putney in the morning and didn't come
back till after lunch. Don't say she told you,
because in the letter she left for Barton she said she
hadn't told any one, so as to give him a free field.
Well, what's your answer to that one ? "

Mullins looked indescribably scornful. " Do you
think any jury is going to take my wife's word on a
point like that ? Why should she remember the
particular time I told her something more than nine
years ago ? You're mad, Crook—stark, staring
mad—if you think you can base a case on trifles
like that. No one will believe you."

" On the contrary, the whole of England's going
to believe me. Oh, you thought out a lot of good
stuff, but you have to be a pretty downy bird to
put things over on the police these days. And when
it comes to putting things over on Arthur Crook . . ."

Mullins laughed shortly. " I've no more time to
waste. All right, get ahead with it. Tell the police

it was I who phoned to Fryer asking him to stay late. . . ."

" Did you ? " asked Crook.

" It's what you're proposing to say, isn't it ? "

" Actually it wasn't because I didn't know any one had phoned him. If the police knew that, they kept it under their hats. It isn't in the paper. I'm wondering how you knew."

" That chap Cartwright told them."

" And then came and told you ? I wonder what made him do that ? "

" I haven't seen Cartwright."

" Then how did you know ? "

Mullins made one last terrible effort to pull the game out of the fire.

" All right, all right. Tell your yarn. Say I told you I knew about the message. Then they'll ask me, and I shall say I never heard of any telephone call. It's your word against mine. What's your next move ? "

" I shall just put on my little Dictaphone record— and where are you ? "

Mullins sagged slowly ; his face was a dreadful greenish-white. Before he finally collapsed the long curtains were thrust aside and Sergeant Jenkins emerged. There was another officer with him. The doomed man put up no resistance.

" He can't," said Crook, who knew nothing of the rules of the ring, that prohibit a man from punching the fellow who's down. " He left his gun at the garage last night."

" That was touch and go," observed Crook to his companions when Mullins had been taken away, shambling more like a beast than a man. " To be honest with you, I didn't know whether we'd get him.

I wouldn't have dared take that story into court. Suppose it had been established, as, of course, it would have been, that Fryer wasn't a left-handed chap at all, but as normal as you or me ? It was that that began to shake Mullins' confidence. It was the best I could think of on the spur of the moment, and it worked, as you saw. There's another thing I forgot to remind him about, and that was Mrs. Morris hearing a car door slam just before he hailed her. That must have been when he hid the suitcase under the back seat. And there wasn't any mention in the letter (Fryer's letter, I mean) about booking a cabin. Of course, he didn't know. . . ."

" He thought of a good deal," observed Bruce, who didn't look so happy about the affair as his companion. Bruce had a more orthodox mind. He liked to win his cases by argument and fact, not by trickery. Besides, he couldn't forget so easily the appalling hopelessness of that heavy face. " Probably, if we'd asked him, he'd have produced the counterfoil of the ticket for the New Oxford, and I dare say he did actually go in for a few minutes. They check up on tickets at every show."

" He had some nerve," contributed Bill. " Typing out all that screed with the dead man at his elbow."

" I dare say the door was locked then. I thought of that. In which case there may have been prints on the key itself. But when I asked the police I found they'd removed that, so that was no good by way of evidence."

Bruce stood up. " Well, Crook, you've got your man, and I suppose Barton is practically released. Everything over bar the shouting. A nasty case altogether." He took up his hat and prepared to go.

" It's no use lookin' like a British Museum exhibit

of an English gentleman," Crook assured him.
" Murder ain't a gentleman's game. You've got to
use your opponent's weapons ; and, y'know, he'd
have let Barton go to his death without a qualm.
Funny thing, that if only these chaps could keep
their nerve they need hardly ever hang. We couldn't
have brought a thing home to Mullins if he'd dug
his toes in and refused to budge. Any more than
we could have implicated Fryer if his conscience
hadn't been tender. Of course, no one, not even
Mullins, could guess the body would be found last
night. If it hadn't been discovered till, say 8 a.m.
this morning, no doctor could have sworn within
an hour to the time of death, and then the post-
mark wouldn't have mattered. All the same, he
made a good shot at it. But there you are. Three
men all ruined by women—if you allow Barton's
life is ruined."

" Would you say that Mullins' life was really
ruined by Mrs. Barton ? He doesn't appear to have
been her lover, and really there seems no necessity
for him to have strangled her." That was Bruce,
fastidious, hesitant, scrupulously fair.

" I don't mean Mrs. Barton, in his case. I mean
Mrs. Mullins. You know, it's never safe to tread
on a female. They have stings in their tails. I
suppose Mullins thought of his wife as one of these
poor fish he could do anything with, and didn't
realise that with the weakest of women you're
playing with fire. I wonder if he really did tell her
about the *Empress of Araby* that Sunday morning.
I'd doubt it myself. He was too near the crime to
be indiscreet. But she had wisdom enough and hate
enough to know that if she said so, and if we put
her in the witness-box, she could get a rope round
her husband's neck. Y'know, say what you like,

though they may have had a dashed uncomfortable time in some ways, those old hermits knew their onions when they put whole deserts between themselves and the female of the species."

"You mean she invented that, came here deliberately to throw suspicion on Mullins ? "

"Why else should she be writin' anonymous letters to her own husband ? Oh, they were hers all right—at least the one she brought us was. Only her finger-prints on 'em. I gave her a cup of tea so as to make quite sure. She'd suspected about Mullins losing his head over Mrs. B., though I don't know whether she really believed him guilty, and there was this other dame, and I dare say the night they had their row, the night before she came to see me, he'd said one of those things even meek women don't forgive. I wonder how long it took her to think out that piece about him knowing the name of Mrs. Barton's boat before any innocent man could possibly have known it. She must have been burstin' to know if I'd seen the importance of that, but she didn't dare say any more. The law's a queer thing. There's a woman done a man to death—or done her best, anyway—and it won't touch her. And I dare say Mullins wasn't nearly so deliberate when he choked Mrs. Barton, but he'll swing right enough." He paused for further consideration. "Another odd thing is that, having done her bit in knotting a rope neck-tie for him, she'll probably spend the rest of her life in sackcloth and ashes prayin' for his soul."

It was on a morning of bright sunshine and blue skies studded with clouds like cotton-wool that Jack Barton heard the prison gate shut firmly behind him. The elation that he should presumably have felt at his unexpected freedom—for he had never dreamed of leaving the place except for the Old Bailey and the execution shed—did not exist. His face had a lost and vacant look. The streets were unfamiliar, the houses filled with people who had probably until a day or two ago considered him a murderer. The whole world had turned topsy-turvy, and although his innocence was now estab-lished he felt as though he had fallen out of a niche and been smashed to bits. The spectacular inner history of the Putney Cellar Case had thrilled the newspapers ; their special correspondents had roared like the engines of a dozen aeroplanes in action ; already Jack had received numbers of hysterical and semi-imbecile offers of marriage—in spite of the fact that for some weeks several thousands or millions of people had thought he probably had murdered his first wife and deceived his second. One of the Sunday papers had offered him a quite ridiculous sum for the story of his life with Beatrice. Standing on the pavement, shivering in spite of the sun, not sure in which direction to turn, he felt as though he had left himself behind in the prison, and that what remained was only a husk, futilely endued with a spark of life that made it possible to move and see and speak, but had no personality, no future, no hope. The chaplain, who had paid him a short visit before his release, had spoken about the blessedness of liberty restored, of peace and the days ahead. He had also added, more sternly, that Jack was fortunate in not being charged for what he had admittedly done—that is, broken the law by conniving at murder. A good citizen would have informed the police and chanced the consequences. The good man, fingering a little gold symbol attached to his watch-chain, spoke of the comfort of a blameless conscience. Jack, who was feeling disturbed and as ill as though he had been poisoned by his last prison meal, had not been able to give his full attention to what was being said, but so far as he could understand it, he was being assured that since he wasn't guilty of Beatrice's death, he really wouldn't in the least have minded hanging for it.

"Flaw in that argument," he had thought ; but he could not debate the point. He was beginning to wonder what on earth he would do with this life that had so mysteriously and suddenly been given back to him, like a piece of lost property from the appropriate office.

He had been standing on the kerb for some instants regardless of the governor's warning that it might be as well to get away while he could, before the press caught him, when the taxi drew up beside him. It had stolen upon him unawares, and as soon as he saw it he drew back, with an irresistible impulse to hammer on the prison door and ask for shelter.

The door of the taxi opened an inch or two and a soft voice said, " Jack ! "

He started, took a step away, then returned.

" Jack ! You don't want to get away from me."

He looked into that gentle, fearless face, saw how the past weeks had carved new lines round the eyes and mouth, and muttered, "You shouldn't have come. They shouldn't have let you."

" *I* shouldn't have come ! Do you think an army could have stopped me ? "

" I haven't anything now."

" You've got yourself."

His hands moved in a gesture of despair. " Oh, that ! "

" That's the only thing you've ever had that's mattered to me."

" A queer sort of self. I didn't treat you well, Jean . . ."

" You made me your wife. There isn't a queen on her throne who's got as much."

" It's no good," he said harshly. " I want to be by myself."

" I am yourself."

The words tore through the enveloping layer of apathy and despair. Here was something too true, too strong to be denied. He might feel broken, at the end of things, but this other self could never be defeated. He felt something stir in his heart, like the first faint prickings of spring in the winter mould. Jean's hand came out to touch him and hold him fast, drawing him back from the pit into which he had been peering. Jean's voice commanded him. He said her name once or twice, plunged blindly into the darkness of the taxi, and felt it moving, away from the prison and the fear and darkness he had known there, forward into the bright morning, forward towards liberty and hope and peace.

T H E   E N D

www.ingramcontent.com/pod-product-compliance
Ingram Content Group UK Ltd.
Pitfield, Milton Keynes, MK11 3LW, UK
UKHW040435280225
455666UK00003B/70